Praise

SATISFA

"Smart, funny, and exhilarating, *Satisfaction* is more than a rock 'n' roll-fueled road trip—it is a poignant look at our struggle for independence amidst the bonds of love and friendship."

—TIFFANY HAWK, author of *Love Me Anyway*

"A road trip into finding freedom, friendship, independence, and courage. Sometimes you *can* get what you want."

—JESSICA PALLINGTON WEST,
author of *What Would Keith Richards Do?*

"Reilly's *Satisfaction* deftly synthesizes the magic of the Stones with a modern coming-of-age tale that overflows with soul and leaves you shouting for more."

—ELISE MILLER, author of *Star Craving Mad*

"If you've ever wanted to leave it all behind to tour with the Stones but weren't the type, Andee Reilly's funny and charming debut novel will give you that Satisfaction and then some. Start it up!"

—ELIZABETH CRANE, author of *We Only Know So Much*

"A poignant story about two women's search for family, forgiveness ... and front-row seats."

—BETH KENDRICK, author of *New Uses for Old Boyfriends*

SATISFACTION

SATISFACTION

by
ANDEE REILLY

SparkPress, A BookSparks Imprint
A Division of SparkPoint Studio, LLC

Published by SparkPress, a BookSparks imprint,
A division of SparkPoint Studio, LLC
Tempe, Arizona, USA, 85281
www.gosparkpress.com

Published 2015
Printed in the United States of America
ISBN: 978-1-940716-64-0 (pbk)
ISBN: 978-1-940716-63-3 (e-bk)

Library of Congress Control Number: 2015938075

Cover design © Julie Metz, Ltd./metzdesign.com
Cover photo © Getty Images
Formatting by Stacey Aaronson

For anyone who has strapped on an air guitar, spent hours singing into a hairbrush, or worshiped the rock stars in posters hanging on their walls. Specifically, to the millions of Rolling Stones fans around the world. No fan base is as loyal and dedicated as you.

Catch your dreams before they slip away.

—Jagger / Richards, "Ruby Tuesday"

1

GINNY

Ginny braced herself. Adrenaline pulsed through her veins as the audience roared in anticipation and jumped to their feet. Keith Richards appeared, tousled hair pushed back by a skull-patterned bandana, his lit cigarette wedged safely underneath the strings of his guitar. The single spotlight focused on him alone until Ronnie Wood, with his skinny jeans and jet-black rooster tail, joined in. She recognized the distinctive guitar riff and the shaking maracas right away as they strummed the intro to "Jumpin' Jack Flash."

From behind Charlie Watts' drum set, Mick Jagger emerged. He sang one of rock's most famous openings, running to the front of the stage to shuffle, point, and dance. In his signature tight black trousers and a red muscle tee, Mick was in amazing shape. Veins popped up from his sinewy arms, and Ginny imagined running her fingers across the collection of thick purple rivers flowing down to his wrist.

He was smoking hot. Thin and cut, he kept right on

rocking the whole civilized world. Mick Jagger, iconic rock star—the world's most energetic, enigmatic man—captivated her. Ginny knew she wasn't the only one caught by his hypnotic allure. Twenty thousand hearts and minds belonged to him, if only for two hours.

The Rolling Stones were playing to a sold-out audience at the Staples Center in Los Angeles. Die-hard Stones fans wearing vintage concert T-shirts, women with the infamous tongue-and-lips logo tattooed across their exposed shoulders and lower backs, young couples, old couples, and parents with kids were all there to get a glimpse of the world's greatest rock 'n' roll band. Next to her, a man in a Mick Jagger mask spilled beer on her brand new sneakers, but she didn't care because she was totally into the concert.

In this audience, there weren't any fuddy-duddies waiting it out on their butts until the Stones played "Satisfaction." One song after another, they cheered, danced, and sang out loud. The guy in the Mick Jagger mask had pushed it up off his face to sing the words to every song. He was probably a bigger fan than Ginny, if such a thing were possible. She saw another man close his eyes and mouth the words to "Angie" as if he were remembering a recent, painful breakup.

Ginny had been able to score a great floor seat only eight rows back from the stage—one of the advantages of buying a single ticket. The best thing about her seat was that it was right next to the catwalk that would lead the Stones to the smaller Stage B, about a hundred yards from the main one. If she reached her hand out, she could touch the actual place where Mick would soon be strutting.

It felt surreal to Ginny to be at a concert by herself. She'd always had somebody attached to her side, making decisions for her. From her parents' house to her husband's, she'd never been on her own or free to make her own decisions. Furious with Ray for what he had done to her, she cursed the four wasted years she'd spent married to him.

Last night Ginny had sat in her car in the grocery store parking lot, trying to figure out what had happened. She'd just learned her husband Ray was sleeping with one of her coworkers. She once imagined that if someone ever cheated on her, she'd end up in a bar picking up the hottest guys around. She'd have to fight them off, proving to herself and to her man that she was desirable and he was plain stupid. Ginny had been looking for a place to drown her sorrows and get back at Ray. But she didn't know which bar to go to. At only twenty-two years old, she'd already missed out on that kind of fun. Instead she found herself parked alongside all the other boring housewives, craving chocolate.

The thought of a club or bar seemed like a good idea at first, but looking at the brightly lit market, she realized it had everything she needed: booze *and* chocolate. Domesticity might have kept her from the latest scene, but it had also given her wisdom.

At the concert, Ginny started to feel short of breath. She inhaled deeply, but as soon as she let it out, she needed more oxygen. Obsessing over her failed marriage was too much, but she couldn't help herself and tried to focus on something else.

Ray used to play guitar and write her beautiful love songs. He promised he was only going to work in construction until his recording contract came in. His band members, four guys from the Midwest with dreams of fame, were holed up in an

3

apartment in Hollywood at the corner of La Brea and Sunset. Before they were married, Ray slept on a makeshift bed in the living room of their shabby two-bedroom apartment. Musical instruments, magazines, and fast-food containers served as a barrier and offered some semblance of privacy. He and Ginny had sex only when the roommates were out. After, they would smoke weed and cruise the Sunset Strip, eating gyros and sneaking sips of the Miller Lite they smuggled in the pockets of their worn leather jackets. It didn't matter that Ray's sheets hadn't been washed in a while or that cockroaches scattered when she turned on the bathroom light, because the life of a burgeoning rock star was exciting.

They were young, beautiful, and happening, making the L.A. music scene. She pictured herself, the future Mrs. Ray Martin, being interviewed for an episode of *E! True Hollywood Story*. It was all part of the journey to the Big Time. Ray and his band were certain an A&R guy would offer them the lucrative recording contract they so deserved, but first they needed to figure out how to sell enough tickets to their own gigs to be able to play the right Hollywood clubs.

Back at the apartment, when Ginny would ask Ray to play "No Expectations," handing him a Rolling Stones playbook, he never grew suspicious. He sang about taking a journey by train or plane and the fate of love lost. She closed her eyes and imagined Mick uttering those words to her. If Ray knew what she was up to as she projected her fantasies onto him, he never let on. He picked up his guitar and played, singing to her, promising he'd forever be her one and only personal rock star. Now the guitar was in the garage, stacked somewhere beneath the Christmas stuff.

The crowd thundered their applause, and Ginny's attention returned to the stage as Mick wiped his brow and said something about slowing it down for a while. Keith strummed the guitar intro to "Waiting on a Friend," followed by the beautiful, melodic sound of a piano and Mick singing the opening sounds: *doo-doo-doo, doo-doo-doo, da-do.*

Ginny had heard the Stones were including this beloved song of theirs in some concerts on this tour, but she couldn't believe she was actually hearing it. From their critically acclaimed *Tattoo You,* the song was rarely played live.

She loved all their music, of course, but she'd always been drawn to that album. Ginny could recite why it was such an important one for the Stones. During the 1970s, some critics thought their music lost its relevance, but *Tattoo You* changed all that—according to her favorite music magazine review— and it was ranked as one of the top 100 albums of the 1980s. Memorizing lines from reviews to impress her friends, she had become a Stones aficionado. But on an emotional level, the music just plain moved and grooved her. Tonight, Ginny swayed along and raised her beer in a toast to Mick Jagger, rock 'n' roll god. Last night she had been listening to the same song when she made her final decision.

Once Ray admitted to the affair, he knew enough to stay the hell away. While Ginny was sipping (more like swigging) her third chocolate-raspberry martini, she packed her bags. She sat at the edge of her bed, trying to think clearly about what this journey would entail and scarfing down a handful of Hershey Kisses for good measure. She cursed herself for not buying giant chocolate bars instead as she spent too much time peeling away the wrapper for a tiny morsel.

She was tired of wasting time.

Ginny thought about the argument she'd had with Ray before she found out he was cheating on her. "Why didn't you tell me you wanted to go back to school?" he had asked, holding up the completed admission form he had found in her nightstand drawer.

Ginny shrugged her shoulders.

"Aren't you happy?" he asked.

"Sometimes," said Ginny. She knew she was supposed to want the life she had committed to; she was supposed to want marriage and children. Ginny faced the wall, willing herself miles away from him and yearning for the protection of an out-of-body experience.

She knew Ray would never have agreed to spend so much money on Stones tickets, but it felt good to buy them anyway. The escape they promised had been irresistible. Before she left home for the last time, Ginny removed a manila envelope from her underwear drawer and dumped the tickets on her bed. Tickets to see the Rolling Stones in places like Arizona, Oklahoma, Nevada, and Texas. She felt free, noting their singularity. These were not purchased in pairs.

2

BREE

There was that song again, the one about her, playing over the speaker system. Bree's face heated up to a bright shade of fuchsia, and she wondered if anyone saw her. But nobody was looking her way; they were way too preoccupied with their own dull lives. She was practically invisible as she served them.

To them, the song was just another one-hit wonder. How could they know that Billy Blade had written "Sarasota," this sappy tearjerker about a jilted guy and a heartless girl, about her? They didn't know their waitress was the pretender, the louse, the adulteress who said she'd follow him to the ends of the earth but hadn't. The woman accused of promises not kept, riddled with guilt as the singer repeated incessantly, "How far do I have to go for you to follow me?"

Bree spotted an old lady waving a spoon to get her attention. "My turkey sandwich has mayonnaise on it. I don't like mayonnaise."

The other girls hated waiting on the older customers, and she couldn't blame them. They were always fussy and usually tight with their tips. Bree didn't mind, though. She knew how to deal with them: just nod and do what they ask. Old people were far less complex than everyone else in her life. She took the plate back to the kitchen and dropped two pieces of white bread into the toaster.

She listened to the song, imagining that some women might be flattered to have something written about them played on the radio. The lyrics were dedicated to her, and she could have gloated about being the kind of seductress who dragged a man to his knees or bragged to her friends how she had inspired such heart-aching lines: "And I don't know what to do, / I'm still so much in love with you."

She hadn't sold her story to *People* magazine when Billy's band, Cutting Blades, had hit it big—and she could have. But it wasn't a song about how beautiful or charming or witty she was. It was about the lies she'd told. Her worst behavior arranged poetically and put to a melody. All her ugliness and vulnerability in verse, raw and recorded and played over and over again on radios across America.

Bree reassembled the sandwich and brought it back to the woman. "Here you go," she said, setting the plate the down. "Just the way you like it: no mayo."

"Thanks, dear," the old lady winked.

The transaction had been simple and straightforward, exactly how Bree liked life. It was people like Jerry, her full-time boss and part-time love interest, who complicated things. She should have known better than to get involved with anyone at work, especially somebody so needy. His twelve-step program was getting on her nerves, and asking her to an Al-Anon meeting had been the final straw.

"Bree, phone for you," Jerry called from behind the counter. He handed her the phone, and she noted the overly concerned look on his face. Currently working on Step Eight, he recited constantly, "List all persons we have harmed, and make amends to them all."

He's so much more fun when he's drunk.

"Mom?"

It was her daughter, Tori, on the other end.

Bree didn't have the time to take personal calls at work, and she certainly didn't feel like talking to her daughter.

"Hey there, Tori," Bree said, hoping her daughter didn't detect her uneasiness. "Can you call me later? At home, maybe?"

"I told you. I go by Victoria now."

"Sorry."

"Whatever. We need to talk."

"I've got five tables going right now. And the boss doesn't like us to talk on the phone during our shifts." Bree knew she couldn't expect her fifteen-year-old daughter to understand the choices her mother had been forced to make.

Jerry shook his head back and forth, probably indicating that he didn't mind a bit. She waved him away with her hands so he'd give her some privacy.

"I tried calling you at home, and I know you *never* answer your cell phone," said Victoria.

Bree imagined her daughter's face shifting in perpetual disappointment. This look was nothing new to her. She'd seen it when Tori was little and Bree forgot it was her turn to bring snacks to the Brownies meeting. And when they had a great apartment on the beach in Malibu, and some of Tori's friends

9

caught Bree sunbathing topless. And the next time she saw her daughter after missing one of many birthday parties.

She wouldn't mind Victoria's face so much if it the least bit resembled her own. But her daughter had inherited her father's thin lips, and Bree couldn't trust a person with no lips. Lips do everything. They're for kissing, for pursing together and whistling, for applying ruby-red lipstick, for blowing smoke rings, for telling secrets and lies.

"Grandpa called," Victoria said.

"And?" asked Bree. She inspected her tables, making sure nobody needed her.

"He says you won't call him back."

"I've been busy. Besides, he shouldn't be bothering you at school."

"Busy doing what?" asked Victoria. "Waitressing at that dump in Arizona?"

"It's honest work. It's what pays your expensive, private-school tuition."

"Dad's money pays my tuition."

"It's my money," said Bree, wondering when her daughter had become so nasty.

"A technicality." Bree didn't feel like getting into it now, but she had to defend herself. "I followed my heart. How can you blame someone for trying to fulfill her dreams?"

"When a woman becomes a mother, she loses that right," said Victoria.

Bree couldn't stand hearing Victoria echo her father's harsh judgments. "It's not that easy."

"Whatever," said Victoria. "Anyway, Nana's having one of her episodes again. She won't get out of bed."

Bree considered this. Two years had passed since she had last tried to endure the sweltering Florida summer. The wet heat that never fully evaporated; the sticky, humid kind that kinked her hair and left pools of sweat underneath her armpits and between her breasts. She vowed never to go back there. When Bree left Florida the first time seven years ago, she'd thought it had been for good.

She packed her car and took back both her life and her maiden name, Cooper. Her husband, Dimmit—everyone called him by his last name, including her—told her it was useless to fight it: both the heat and the custody battle that would eventually come. Both were formidable opponents. Whenever Bree adjusted the air conditioner below seventy-two degrees, he'd become irate, even going as far as threatening to take the A/C out of the house. It's not that he couldn't afford the bill, but somehow he had always been cold despite the blazing-hot temperatures. In protest, Bree fanned her face with both hands, like a crazy woman swatting at mosquitoes visible only to her. Summoning a breeze that would never come seemed more productive than trying to save her marriage.

"You're only making it worse. Just go with it. Embrace the heat," he said. "Let your perspiration cool you down. Our bodies are like cars, built with a natural radiation system called sweat."

His family lived in Palm Beach, and Dimmit had grown up in one of those mansions Bree and her parents used to drive by on Sunday afternoons, daydreaming about a life that seemed beyond their reach. So when Bree became pregnant and Dimmit proposed marriage, it didn't matter that he was fifteen years older or that she wasn't in love with him. She accepted.

After all, she convinced herself, *who couldn't learn to love a millionaire? How hard could it be?*

Dimmit could afford not to work, living off his hefty trust fund, but he loved cars. He owned a car lot where he dealt in foreign and exotic models. He was always trying to get Bree into some ridiculously expensive sports car. She winced at the idea of pulling into the elementary school lot alongside the other teachers' economy vehicles.

It had also been Dimmit's idea for his wife to become an elementary school teacher. Bree had wanted to teach high school English. She loved to read and write, but Dimmit said the older boys might get ideas having such a young, beautiful teacher introduce them to poetry about love, angst, and sexual frustration. Besides, he said, she wouldn't be able to handle the older kids. He thought it was ridiculous to imagine his wife trying to discipline teenagers when she couldn't even raise an infant properly.

After Tori was born, Bree had been paralyzed with depression and had terrifying thoughts about harming her child accidently. What if, overcome by fatigue, she dropped Tori? Would her daughter be better off without Bree around? She asked her doctor about postpartum depression, but he said a case of the baby blues was natural. She'd get over it. Bree couldn't help wondering if she had ever really recovered.

Overcompensating for her fear, Bree hovered over Tori. "What's wrong with picking up the baby when she cries?" Bree said, holding up her Dr. Spock book, defending herself against Dimmit's constant criticism. "It's okay to comfort her," she argued, even though she feared she didn't know what she was doing.

When Bree and Dimmit fought, Tori cried, her face growing puffy and flushed. The spittle dripped from her gaping little mouth and dried over her chin in a delicate layer of crust. He scolded Bree if she picked up the baby to ease her and said Tori would not know how to function in the real world; she'd always expect to be scooped up and rescued from harm's way. But wasn't her duty as Tori's mother to protect her little baby girl? It was ironic that her daughter still idolized her father. But it's easy to adore someone when they're dead. To Tori, Dimmit was the perfect father—tough but fair. But to Bree, he would always be the cold, inflexible man who used his money and influence to keep her child from her, cheating her out of motherhood.

"You still there?" asked Victoria.

"I can't leave right now," said Bree.

"I told Grandpa not to even bother. As usual, when people need you, you're not there."

Bree hung up the phone and went to bus the old lady's table. She had left a big tip, proving once again that elderly people were easy to please. Their expectations couldn't be any more clear-cut: they wanted efficient, friendly service. It was the people she loved who complicated things.

3

GINNY

The next morning, Ginny woke up in the downtown hotel. It was still dark outside, and she had at least an hour before she got up to drink coffee and flip on the television. She could put on HGTV or the *Today* show and not worry about Ray's running commentary on how stupid everyone and everything was.

She couldn't hold in her pee any longer and rushed to the toilet, hoping she had started her period. It wasn't like her to be so late. Because Ray made her feel like a freak, the only woman on the planet who lacked maternal instinct, she had stopped taking the pill to please him. He wanted children, and at one time, Ginny foolishly believed a baby might save their marriage.

Her husband and her mother, Virginia, agreed on just one issue: it was only a matter of time before Ginny's biological clock started ticking. While Ray pointed out hot pregnant celebrities on television, Virginia hired an interior designer to draw up plans for a nursery. Her grandchild would have the best of everything: a posh crib with hand-carved spindles and plush bedding; an antique armoire, the kind with ornate scrollwork. No tacky wallpaper with little pictures of jungle animals or cheap baby furniture scavenged from thrift stores or handed down from relatives who took pity because the parents were young and poor.

Ginny had already taken a pregnancy test, but she needed to see more physical evidence to confirm the negative result. Unfortunately, there was no blood. She could not stop thinking about what a baby could mean for her—the guarantee of a dead-end life with Ray.

Opening up the Rand McNally Road Atlas, Ginny enjoyed the feel of the paper map and traced her finger along the interstates, marking the cities where the Stones were playing. She flipped to the Southern California page and saw that Ray had highlighted a route leading all the way to the Mexican border. *Was this* his *getaway plan?* Ginny asked herself. Had he been planning to leave her all along?

Ginny wondered how long Ray and his new girlfriend had been sneaking around behind her back. Had Ray brought his new girlfriend over to meet his family? Did they like her better, even though Ginny had worked hard to swallow her unhappiness with Ray and try to get along with everybody, even when they'd criticized her? When she tried to dress up for one holiday dinner, the best Ray's mother had been able to offer was, "Well, that's an interesting style."

Just last week, Ray had been angry with Ginny for considering going back to college, as if he had any right to tell her what she could and could not do.

"I need you," he said. "Who's gonna take care of me if you're working all day and going to school at night? Besides," he added, "don't you think you oughta stick to more important things, like making me happy?"

At that moment, she wanted to smack Ray right across his self-assured face. Instead, she pushed her anger down until she couldn't feel anything anymore.

♪

GINNY CRAWLED BACK INTO BED AND WAITED FOR THE SUN to break. She thought about the college classes she'd like to take. Recently, when she went to see the school counselor, he told her she'd have to retake the general ed courses she had enrolled in a few years ago.

"I see you dropped out after only a month," said the counselor. "I'm afraid beauty school credits don't count."

Ginny was so embarrassed, she almost ran out of the admissions office. All the paths in her life seemed to be blocked off by orange construction signs reading "Road Closed Ahead."

She didn't want to take a math or an English class during her first semester back. Not until she felt more comfortable with the idea of surrounding herself with a bunch of eighteen-year-olds. (Even though she was only twenty-two, the counselor called her a "non-traditional student." *A nice way to say "old,"* she thought.) So she went for something less stressful, like a speech class. Once she had read that people would rather be abducted by aliens than speak in public. As an aesthetician, Ginny could carry on a conversation while slathering hot wax on a client's groin. The idea of speaking in front of a class was no problem.

It wasn't like she hated her job. Pampering loyal clients

gave her some satisfaction, but getting other women bikini-ready for trips to Hawaii while she was stuck at home floating on her blow-up raft in the pool didn't cut it anymore.

Before she dropped out of college, Ginny had given a few speeches. In a communications class, she'd talked about how Barbie could be a positive role model for little girls. As the first mass-produced doll that wasn't a baby, she enabled little girls to play with her without having to pretend to be Mommy. And Barbie could change careers with a change of wardrobe. She could be a doctor, a pilot, or a teacher. "Don't we want to give our daughters these options?" she'd argued.

Ginny tried not to blame her mother for the lack of choices in her own life. After all, when Ginny wanted to play softball, her mother drove her to tryouts. If Ginny had asked for a train set instead of a play kitchen for Christmas, Santa would have been sure to put it under the tree. It had been the subtle, unspoken actions that alerted Ginny to her limited potential. The way her parents had pushed Gerald, Ginny's brother, to take honors courses in high school when they were satisfied with her C average. They had encouraged Gerald intellectually and Ginny superficially. The most she could hope for was prom queen, rather than a high score on the SATs. If Ginny ever had a daughter, she'd be sure not to make the same mistakes.

Her professor said the Barbie speech was the first A-plus a student had earned in his entire career. Ginny was proud of herself, although looking back, she realized he probably just wanted to sleep with her. But she'd been innocent then, and she took men at their word.

College cost money, though, and she was currently out of a job. Ginny thought again of her swelling debt. It had been so easy to buy all those Rolling Stones tickets, just a mouse-click away. Had she been reckless and foolish to rack up huge credit-card debt, she wondered? Or had she been fulfilling her destiny?

Scrolling through her Stones playlist, Ginny stopped on "Not Fade Away." Written by Buddy Holly, it's an example of the Bo Diddley beat. The Stones' first United States single, it was released in 1964. But the first time Ginny heard the song, she hadn't known any of these facts. That kind of knowledge had come later, as she pored over books, articles, and documentaries about her favorite band in her quest to impress friends, gain recognition, and learn everything there was to know about Mick Jagger: the man who, when she was fourteen years old, changed her life forever.

Ginny and her family had just moved to Valencia, a Los Angeles suburb, and being the new kid at school sucked. For the first few weeks, she'd hidden in the library during lunch. She would have rather died than sit by herself, unwrapping an egg salad sandwich on wheat, a total loser. Then a girl named Cathy with braces, freckles, and a chest way too big for her skinny freshman body invited Ginny out to the field. The bad kids went to the field, that much she knew.

Past the spot where the kids played soccer, behind the net, six or seven kids sat cross-legged, smoking cigarettes. "Man, I'd love to smoke a bowl right now," said one of the guys. *The cutest one*, Ginny thought. He wore his blond hair longer than most of the other guys and parted in the middle. He had the whole 1970s surfer look going on, sporting a T-shirt with a red, white, and blue target and "The Who" written across the front. This whole group seemed to be a bunch of outcasts—kids born in the wrong era.

When Cathy introduced her new friend Ginny, the cute one wanted to know what kind of name Ginny was.

"It's short for Virginia," Ginny answered, hating her lame-ass name.

"What'd ya say your name was? Vagina?" A skinny, pimply kid asked loud enough that everyone heard.

Ginny felt her face burn with embarrassment.

"Shut up, douchebag." The cute one punched Skinny in the arm. "I'm Pete." He patted the patch of grass next to him. "Sit down."

When the conversation turned to music—which, Ginny learned later, it always did—she nearly blew it when she rattled off her favorites: Beyoncé, Mariah Carey, Gwen Stefani.

"Girl, you gotta listen to rock and roll: The Who, The Beatles, Led Zeppelin, and the Stones."

Ginny learned that each person in the gang had a signature band. Pete loved The Who, not only because he shared the same name as the lead guitarist, but also because they, "rocked harder than any other band ever has and ever will."

"If you want to hear something worthwhile," Skinny said to Ginny, "do yourself a favor and listen to *Houses of the Holy*. I mean, like, right now, dude."

"*Houses of the Holy?* Is that a band?" asked Ginny.

Skinny shook his head in disgust.

"Don't listen to him," said Pete. "Zeppelin's awesome and all, but The Who..."

"Shut up, both of you," said Cathy. "Let her find her own band. I dig Ozzy Osbourne. You can't have him. Someday, I'm gonna have his love child."

For each of these kids, the bands identified who they were, and once they found theirs, they were expected to become an *aficionado*—Pete emphasized his favorite word. Not only were they expected to own all their favorite band's albums, but they also had to be able to cite which song came from which album. Ginny would have to find her favorite if she was going to continue hanging out with her new friends.

♪

AT THE HOTEL, GINNY GOT OUT OF BED, PICKED UP HER clothes from the floor, and refolded them, packing them neatly into her suitcase. She didn't have much room to take extras on the road, but she wasn't about to leave behind her Rolling Stones lunch pail for Ray to rifle through. With the red tongue-and-lips logo emblazoned on both sides, it had been with her since high school. Inside she kept Stones-related mementos. She pulled out the ticket stub to her first Rolling Stones concert.

They had just announced a North American tour. When Ginny's father found out, he dragged out all his old Stones records and said he'd drive them. Instead, Ginny caught a ride with Pete's older brother. She could still remember that cold October night.

Ginny and her friends waited in the nosebleed section of Pasadena's Rose Bowl for the Rolling Stones to appear. The audience cheered when the lights dimmed and the strobe lights swept across the stadium. Onstage, a giant dragon-like creature hissed fire, and the fans went wild, screaming their allegiance. The stage lights pulsed to the beat of "Not Fade

Away," a song Ginny recognized from her dad's record collection.

Mick Jagger pranced onto the stage in a red crushed-velvet tailcoat, took a bow, and, through the song, directed the audience to give their love to him.

Ginny thought, *What is that? Who is that?*

Mick Jagger was the most beautiful, mesmerizing creature she had ever seen. Even though she could only see his projected image on the giant video screens next to the stage, at that moment she knew she had found her band. Mick peeled away his jacket to reveal a hard, tight body dressed in black, swaying to the music. Ginny didn't even notice the crowd. She was so immersed in Jagger, his uninhibited physicality oozing sexuality all over the place. He danced, he moved, he shook, he dominated the audience without the shame or awkwardness of boys her age. He commanded Ginny. She wanted him to take her right there in the stands, to straddle her on the cold plastic bleachers. For the first time in her life, she was turned on.

Even though that night she felt Mick would be her one and only man forever, she let Pete take her virginity in the backseat of his brother's car.

Being in the same room with Mick Jagger last night was enough for her to recapture the feeling she had when she first saw him strut onstage all those years ago. Before losing her innocence to Pete and her faith in Ray, before idealized men became real and disappointing, like life itself. She was going back to the beginning. Starting over.

4

BREE

Jerry ascended the stage of the local elementary school auditorium. Wearing a pair of dark blue jeans and a bolero tie, he probably imagined he appeared ruggedly handsome. Bree sat in the back row and fantasized about sliding out the side door. She saw her imaginary double standing up, gathering her purse and jacket, and escaping into the cold night and its accompanying freedom. The impulse was almost too overpowering, as she envisioned herself driving to Anywhere Else, USA.

But considering the Alcoholics Anonymous-sponsored poetry slam drew a crowd of only fifteen people or so, Bree realized she'd be missed and steadied herself for what was about to come. She knew it wasn't going to be pretty.

Removing a folded piece of paper from the front pocket of his gray plaid shirt, Jerry flattened it out on the podium and cleared his throat. "I'd like to dedicate this to Bree, who rocketed into my life like a shooting star."

Everybody stared at Bree. She nodded politely and tried to

smile, her lips sticking to her gums so her expression felt more like a grimace. Before the event, she had smoked a joint, just a little something to relax her through the festivities. Now she felt guilty, high as a kite surrounded by rows of metal folding chairs filled with people committed to sobriety. *If they only knew*, she thought, repressing an urge to burst out laughing.

She wondered about Jerry's simile. At first it didn't make any sense. Shooting stars appear only briefly to us as they descend into the earth's atmosphere and burn out. A short-lived moment, the bright flash slips away before the viewer even has time to think of a wish. If Jerry comprehended his comparison, he might be coming to terms with the idea that Bree would fizzle out as quickly as she'd arrived in his diner four months ago, looking for a job.

He never seemed insightful though. There were hints, of course, that Bree wouldn't be around for long. She had rented a sparsely furnished apartment on a month-to-month basis and kept one suitcase, packed with the essentials, in her car at all times. Jerry knew she'd barely commit to a four-pack of toilet paper, yet he continued to make plans for them and used phrases like, "we will be," "dating," "love," and "moving in together" to describe a shared future.

Jerry adjusted the microphone. Bree liked that he was tall. His good physique helped her to overlook his annoying habit of sticking his nose into her business. He was always telling Bree what to do. In fact, his favorite word was *should*, and he threw it in her face whenever he could, suggesting Bree *should* call her daughter more often. It was as if he believed that trying to master the almighty twelve steps gave him the moral authority to lecture her on motherhood.

"I wrote this sonnet with the help of a former teacher," he said, the paper shaking in his right hand.

Bree glanced down at the polished linoleum floor. The school auditorium was also where the kids ate lunch. She had seen a menu hanging on a bulletin board and recalled the tomato soup and grilled cheese sandwiches her elementary school had served on rainy days. A vague sense of homesickness settled in her stomach, but she wasn't sure where to connect that feeling. It was to a place, a home where she could put on a pair of sweats, tuck her feet underneath the sofa cushions to keep them warm, and read a book until she fell asleep. Tori's call the other day had stirred everything up. That sort of home life would never exist for Bree.

She could see that nobody had linked her to the "former teacher" comment. They couldn't blame her for the overly flowery, trite-ridden verse about to fill the auditorium. Last week, Jerry had asked her to help him write a sonnet. Instead she found a step-by-step guide on the Internet and wrote it on the back of a used order ticket from the diner.

Jerry wiped his brow with a red handkerchief he kept in his back pocket. He cleared his throat yet again and started to read.

"No more the object of my affection /A woman not so gentle with my heart/ That pleads for love, smashed it with rejection. /She went away, and now we're apart."

When Bree first met Jerry, she felt sorry for him because his girlfriend had just dumped him. They'd spent hours talking it through late into the night while she helped him figure out what had gone wrong. When the girlfriend skipped town, Jerry had to pay the landlord two months' rent, since he had cosigned the lease. Combined with the overdue utility bills, Jerry hadn't understood that he had been duped until Bree pointed out the reality of the situation.

It had been a relief for Bree to focus on someone else's failing relationships, so she welcomed Jerry's stories, his tears, and, at times, his relentless self-indulgence. Helping the neglected and misguided had become a hobby for Bree; picking up little pieces of broken hearts along the way and trying to put them back together to form an eclectic mosaic of mended souls. In each new place, Bree collected friendships that had lasted as long as a tank of gas.

In Santa Monica, there'd been Gaby, a single mother trying to raise her son alone while working two jobs. Bree had been happy to offer babysitting services. While in Malibu, she'd nursed a broken-hearted woman named Greer who had found her boyfriend in bed with another man. In both Portland and Seattle, it hadn't taken long before she was restoring self-esteem to women who had practically given up hope.

But the time always came for her to leave. If she stuck around too long, people asked questions about her past. Certain truths about Bree's character would be revealed, and judgment and disappointment would inevitably follow. These women and their budding friendships were the casualties Bree left behind.

Bree had wanted to believe Jerry was harmless in the beginning. Still pining for the one who got away, surely he wouldn't make a move on her, she had told herself. Except that two weeks after Bree started working for him, he was falling all over her. She should've known better than to get involved.

He was the worst kind of needy, moving from one girlfriend to the next, proposing marriage on the second date and drowning his ex with slobbering affection until she'd had no choice but to move to the next county just to get some air.

Sleeping with Jerry had been more an act of selfishness than charity. Bree had been trying to help him forget about his ex, and, feeling a little lonely herself, she'd spent the night at his house. The next morning, he was clearing out drawer space and handing her a spare key.

She didn't have much else going on, so Bree had decided to stay in Arizona for a few months and had welcomed his company while killing time and making plans.

A few lines later, Bree realized where Jerry's poem was heading. "But then, the other more fragrant and true /

A gardenia, grant by fate's gracious hand.

/ Simply a better fit, as if on cue / Descended upon this sad, broken man."

A guy next to Bree toasted her by raising a soda can wrapped in a neoprene cozy with "Keepin' It Real," printed on the side.

Bree nodded back at the man. She felt like a phony for allowing Jerry to continue wooing her even though she had no intention of staying. A better person might break the truth to him gently. She was all for "keepin it real," but sometimes that meant hurting people.

Before Tori called, Bree had imagined she would be moving on soon. Besides the disaster in Florida two years ago, she had lived exclusively on the West Coast and had believed going west was her destiny. Like all the great pioneers before her, she told herself she was seeking a better future. She had been running away for a long time, though, and hadn't found any great promise of fulfillment, spiritual or otherwise.

Bree regretted not responding to Tori's plea to come home, but it was for the best. There wasn't anything Bree could do to help. She'd only be a distraction. In the past, she had managed to destroy everybody who'd cared about her. In the years since she'd been gone, they'd dealt with her absence—thrived, in Tori's case. If sacrificing her reputation for the greater good was necessary, Bree was willing.

She hurt them because she loved them.

As Jerry continued with the sonnet, his voice grew louder, working up to the final couplet.

"Dear God, may I make a request of thee?

/ To bestow grace on Bree and me."

He refolded the poem and tucked it gently into his shirt pocket, perhaps so it could be close by. Bree imagined he saw tiny little lovebirds flapping around his pierced heart. Cupid had drawn his bow and struck.

Bree yearned for the open road.

5

GINNY

Fumbling for her keys, Ginny got into her Volvo station wagon. She hated the car. It was an old lady's car her parents bought for her after the accident. The dealer said it was the safest on the market. It had like a zillion airbags, and now it would be her fortress.

She drove through Los Angeles, which would take her to San Bernardino and then to Arizona. Later, if she had time, maybe she'd go to Santa Fe, New Mexico, to take a look at the southwestern art and turquoise jewelry. Ray didn't like to travel. Their last vacation, if you could call it that, was to Solvang, a little area north of Santa Barbara designed to resemble a Danish village. Ginny loved the town and buying up blue-and-white porcelain trinkets. They went wine tasting, and she'd thought they were actually having fun until Ray complained about the food and said he was bored and ready to go home.

No, he'd never take the route Ginny was on now. He'd go north, cut across the Mojave and past Edwards Air Force Base to avoid all the congestion. She considered going north at first because doing things his way had become so automatic, so unquestionably the way to go, that Ginny didn't know what *her* way would be. Perhaps she never had a way in the first place.

It was still early, and the traffic was light. Ginny sipped her sugar-free vanilla latte, congratulating herself for having the guts to leave her husband and quit her job. Even though she liked working with some of her clients, she knew there had to be more to life than squeezing zits and removing unwanted body hair. She had worked hard, building her business up so much that she barely had time to eat lunch on some days—but they still struggled to pay their bills, especially when Ray had to have the latest video game. He never understood Ginny's frustration.

It wasn't enough for Ginny. She longed for something more, but she couldn't even rate well on the "Intriguing Scale" of a *Cosmo* quiz she'd taken between clients at work. She scored woefully low, her responses landing her mostly in the Loyal and Organized category when she wanted more than anything to be Wild and Spontaneous.

"I want to be exciting. I want to be a High-Octane Hell-Raiser, not a Play-It-Safe Scaredy-Cat," she had tried to explain to Ray.

His response had been to ask her if she was on the rag, ready to chalk up his wife's dissatisfaction to raging hormones.

"You're an *aesthetician*." He emphasized the professionalism of the title. "That's more than a lot of people have. And besides, you said it was a great job 'cause you could make your own schedule. Be there for the kids when they got home from school."

"We don't have any kids," Ginny had said.

"But we're trying. Aren't we trying again?" Ray was always pleading with her. Once there was a time when she had wanted Ray's children. In the beginning, they were in love. So when Ginny had found out that she was pregnant, Ray asked her to marry him.

She dreaded breaking the news to her mother. Ginny knew her mother hated Ray, never forgetting to mention that he was fat, hairy—in all the wrong places—and a total burnout.

THE FIRST TIME GINNY BROUGHT RAY HOME TO MEET HER mother Virginia, he had been nervous, sitting in the formal living room as he sized up the pristine surroundings. Virginia's silver service set sparkled just so under the light inside the rich mahogany curio cabinet where it was displayed. Each piece that made up her impressive porcelain figurine collection had been dusted meticulously. Ray picked one up and rolled it around and around in his hand, like a rabbit's foot that might bring him luck. His palms must have been sweating, because he set it back down and wiped them on the ruffled pillow he was clutching in front of his crotch.

After he left, Virginia told Ginny that if Ray ever touched another one of her beloved figurines again, she'd "smash it over his big noggin."

Satisfied with just getting by, he'd never go anywhere in life, Virginia argued. Marrying an out-of-work musician and part-time construction worker was not what Virginia had in mind for her only daughter and namesake.

Four years ago, Ginny had every intention of driving to her mother's house to tell her she was going to be a grandmother, and, if the mood was right, ask her for the down payment on a house. Then the Stones' song "Tumbling Dice," a single from *Exile on Main Street*, came on the radio.

That was the first time she disappeared.

The rolling dice made her think of Las Vegas, a place that promised glamour and excitement, even a chance to start over if she wanted. Her full tank of gas beckoned her toward a certain freedom. She kept driving, wanting to see how long she could avoid the inevitable, knowing she couldn't disappear forever. Maybe she didn't want to. There was someone back home who wanted to marry her, but she could never see him again if she so chose. Trapped between her mother and her husband-to-be, she was always trying to soothe everyone else's hurt feelings. The insults and snide remarks from Ray to Virginia and hers back at him, had been too much for Ginny. It felt like she was always apologizing for loving two people who couldn't stand each other. With the blacktop in front of her, she had options. *Options*, what a beautiful word. The Stones blared through her car speakers, and she sang loudly, crooned for her life, her independence.

Everything would change forever. Could she keep driving beyond Las Vegas to who knows where? She was supposed to want this, *supposed* to want to get married, to have a family. She belted the song even louder, drowning out her thoughts.

For a few days, she stayed at the Excalibur, the cheapest hotel on the strip she could find. But after desperate pleas and promises from her mother and Ray that they would be nicer to one another, she drove back home and married Ray.

"They" were pregnant, Ray used to boast. He was excited, even embracing his disapproving mother-in-law by calling her with pregnancy reports, asking her if she wanted to be called Grammy or Grandma. *Life is going to work out after all,* Ginny thought. During the first trimester, Ray was sure the baby was a boy, and he bought a tiny football jersey and a foam ball to match. Said his kid would be the best running back in the history of football. Then suddenly, at week fifteen, Ray decided the baby was a girl—something his mother said about the way Ginny was carrying. He became protective, whispering against Ginny's belly, burying his face in the layers of maternity fabric. If anyone harmed a hair on her head, he'd have to answer to her father. They were happy.

But that was before the accident. Ginny, driving her little convertible, didn't see the car coming. There was a terrible blind spot, and she checked again and again before pulling out onto the busy highway. It seemed like the car came out of nowhere. There was the crunch of metal on the driver's side, then the spinning. She saw the center divider coming toward her, as she said later, in slow motion. It sounded like a cliché, but the whole thing happened so slowly. She closed her eyes as the car slammed against the cement wall.

When she woke up in the hospital, Ray said she'd lost the baby. "You," he said. No more "we" when it came to being *not* pregnant. She apologized, hoping her husband would say it wasn't her fault because accidents happen. He didn't.

♪

OUTSIDE OF LOS ANGELES, GINNY PULLED OVER TO THE SIDE of the road and dialed the last person on earth she'd imagined calling.

"Shannon, it's Ginny."

Ginny waited for Ray's girlfriend to say something, but there was only silence on the other end.

"Ginny Martin."

"I know."

"It's strange, I know. My calling you. And I'm not sure why I am, except I think you're the only one who can help."

The long pause on the other end made Ginny feel like an even bigger fool, and she considered hanging up. Phoning Shannon might have been a huge mistake. Did Ray tell her things about Ginny? Private, embarrassing things like how she wore control top underwear under her low-rise jeans to contain her muffin top because she was too vain to buy a bigger pair that actually fit her properly.

All along, Ray had been guilt-tripping Ginny into having sex while he was cheating on her with the manicurist at the salon where she worked. Ginny hadn't realized they even knew each other. At the salon party last Christmas, Ginny didn't feel well and went to lie down in the car for a few minutes. Ray wanted to leave, but she'd convinced him to stay and try to make friends. He didn't have any, she reminded him. Afterward he said the hairdressers were a bunch of weirdos, and he wondered how she could stand them.

He hadn't said anything about a manicurist.

When Ginny first found out about Shannon, it didn't make sense. Who would want *her* husband, she wondered?

The email chain between Shannon and Ray revealed everything. Apparently, Shannon threatened to come to Ginny's house to claim her man. She actually used those words. No longer was she the awkward manicurist hunched over the yellowing toenails of old ladies. She had become the other woman, and she was going to take care of her man. His marriage was a minor inconvenience.

Ray responded by telling her it was over, but Shannon wouldn't give up easily and called Ray an asshole. She said he had ruined her life and had promised he'd leave his wife.

As she read the emails Ray had left open on their shared computer, Ginny's hands started to tingle, and she felt a strange tightness in her chest. She stood up and wondered if she should take an aspirin in case she was having a heart attack. Then she realized she had been sitting on her hands, cutting off the circulation and possibly stopping the blood flow to the empty place in her chest where her heart used to be.

Ginny had managed to miss all the signs: the punching bag Ray hung up in the garage when he started his new workout regimen, the mini toothpaste and toothbrush kit she found in his truck.

"Don't you think it's time we told her?" That was Shannon's last email message to Ray.

The memory started to burn her eyes with tears, and she sniffed, hoping Shannon couldn't hear on the other end of the line.

"I love him, you know," said Shannon. "If that makes a difference."

"You don't know him." Ginny's throat tightened. She was humiliated. Even if she may have fallen out of love with Ray before the affair, the betrayal still stung.

"I know enough. I know you hate having sex with him. He says you're always turning him down."

Ginny repressed the urge to call her a home-wrecking

bitch. None of the other stylists at the salon could stand Shannon. She could be rude, but mostly she kept to herself. Then Ginny imagined Shannon sitting at her nail station, and all the women in the back room talking shit about her. At times, she was actually kind of sweet and vulnerable. Maybe Shannon was doing her a favor by trying to take Ray away. Ginny wasn't going to be the one stuck with him.

"He's all yours," said Ginny.

"What?"

"You won the big prize."

Shannon started to cry, not picking up on Ginny's sarcasm. "He broke up with me."

"Ray was never good at being alone," said Ginny. "So tell him I'm leaving for a while, and you're all he's got. And while you're at it, let everyone at the salon know I won't be coming back."

"I quit too. You don't think I know what they say about me?"

"Go back to work and tell them to mind their own business. And if they must know, say we're all just close friends."

"Are we . . . friends?"

"Yeah, sure."

"In another lifetime, huh?" asked Shannon.

"Maybe," said Ginny as she looked over at her passenger, an orchid, safely cradled in Ray's favorite cup holder.

Before Ginny left the house, she'd wanted to look around, perhaps for the last time. It wasn't a bad house. A little dated, but she'd miss it. She looked over at the windowsill, regarding the orchid she had babied for the past six months. Feeding it only room temperature distilled water, fertilizing it twice a month, and speaking to it in soft, loving whispers. The blooms were about to open. There were ten fat buds waiting to burst, and she would not be there to witness it, to welcome the delicate purple flowers into the world.

She had leaned over to apologize to the plant when she saw an aphid on one of the smallest buds. The little, white, mouth-sucking insect infuriated Ginny. Aphids were the worst. They were like men, like Ray, feeding on the most vulnerable, slowly extracting the life from their victims. And, like most men, they were attracted only to new growth, completely uninterested in the more mature leaves and flowers. Attaching itself to the smooth and delicate young bud, the predator would distort and mottle her flowers. She wouldn't allow it, and she squished the aphid between her fingers. The plant was coming with her, and she determined to save it along with herself.

"Oh, yeah," said Ginny. "And tell Ray I took the orchid."

6

GINNY

Sometime after dark, Ginny pulled into a Motel 6 parking lot almost two hundred miles north of Phoenix. It seemed like a logical place to spend her first night. Her father had taken the family there once on their way to the Grand Canyon. She considered going to see it again, but a side trip would take her too far off the path. Also, something about a big, gaping hole depressed her. A large void in the earth was only a reminder of the emptiness she felt and her insignificance in the universe. She had heard this realization actually cheered people up; their problems seemed small and temporary in comparison to this natural wonder that would remain long after they had passed on. But the idea made Ginny want to swallow a bottle of antidepressants.

She'd done the whole bit with her family, riding horseback around the edge, peering in, trying not to fall off the trail. They'd even tried hiking down when, a mile in, her mother had refused to go any farther, noting the hike up would be simply impossible. Exercising was overrated anyway, Virginia said, as she huffed and puffed her way back up the path.

Besides being in a familiar place, the area had a lot of chain motels. Ginny parked the car by the front door and went to the desk to get a room.

A middle-aged man came out from the back room. He wore a blue-collared shirt and tan slacks, and Ginny liked the friendly expression on his face. His appearance comforted her, like wearing a pair of fuzzy slippers. Craning his neck to see past Ginny and outside, he seemed to be checking out her car. "You need a single room?"

At first she assumed he was trying to see if she was going to sneak in a carload of freeloaders. But then he tilted his head to the side as if he were concerned. She imagined he was thinking she was a single woman without anyone to love and protect her.

"Just me. I'm on my way to visit someone," she said. *Not that it was any of his business,* she thought. *Why am I justifying anything at all to a complete stranger, and telling lies on top of it all?*

He slid the key over to her and said, "If you need anything, don't hesitate to call the front desk."

In the room, Ginny placed her orchid on the small table and dropped her suitcase on the bed. There wasn't any use in unpacking, since she'd get up early the next morning, have breakfast, and continue on her way. The room was standard-issue: a bed, a table, two chairs, and a desk. Exhausted, she collapsed next to her suitcase, but when she remembered the television special she'd seen about dirty hotel rooms with filthy bedspreads, she sat back up. Scientists had found all sorts of unmentionable debris, including E. coli, in hotel rooms across the country.

She wished she had a can of Lysol. The bed, the sink, and

the toilet could all use a good spraying. *What if the bed is crawling with bedbugs*, she wondered, lifting back the flowered bedcover to check it out. Ray used to make fun of her germ phobia, laughing as he wrapped himself up in the motel quilt. One of the rare times they actually went out of town, she caught him peeing in the sink. Even though the toilet was two feet away, he said it felt liberating. It was disgusting, thinking of some stranger spreading his dirty funk all over the room.

Ginny realized, though, that if she were going to be a true roadie, she'd have to get over it. She imagined she might have to sleep in her car or use a portable toilet—or, even worse, poop in the wilderness somewhere and bury it like a wild animal.

Finally checking her cell phone, she was surprised no one had called, not even her mother. Flipping through the TV channels proved pointless. Nothing was on that she hadn't already seen a million times. She picked up a tourist magazine, only to find its sticky cover repulsive.

Ginny opened her Rolling Stones lunch pail and fished out one of her favorite photographs: Keith Richards and Brian Jones sitting poolside at the Fort Harrison Hotel in Clearwater, Florida. They were young, probably no more than twenty-three. Both were shirtless, wearing blue swimming trunks, and mugging for the camera as they raised their martinis. They looked happy, and Ginny imagined they must have burst out laughing after the click of the camera. Brian was wearing dark glasses, but it was clear he was the handsomer of the two. Die-hard Jones fans would argue that Mick and Keith had no right to kick out Brian, the founder of the Rolling Stones, when his drinking and drug use had become problematic. Some even suggested that Mick had been jealous of Brian, vying for attention with the charismatic blond.

In 1969, at just twenty-seven years old, Brian Jones was found dead in his swimming pool. Today, there are hundreds of fan sites dedicated to him.

The photograph was taken while in Florida. There, the Stones played at Jack Russell Memorial Stadium, home of the Clearwater Bombers, the world-famous fast-pitch softball team. In 1965, the Beach Boys had performed there without incident, but only a few months later, when the Stones played to an audience of three thousand, they were able to get through only four songs before two hundred screaming kids rushed the stage. As they tried to push their way through the police barricade, a scuffle broke out. It was Clearwater's first riot and the last time a concert was ever performed at Jack Russell.

The legend went that one night at the Fort Harrison Hotel in Clearwater, Florida, Keith Richards woke up with a guitar riff and the phrase "can't get no satisfaction" in his head and recorded it. Sources say the tape contained the song's famous three-note guitar riff, followed by Richards snoring.

Ginny parted the stiff curtain and considered going over to the local dive across the street. Then she reconsidered, imagining the patrons who would frequent such a place. It was probably an intimidating mix of truck drivers, Hells Angels, and lonely, toothless hags. She remembered seeing a Mexican restaurant a few blocks away. She brushed her teeth and put on her lowest-cut blouse.

♪

SATISFACTION

SITTING AT A RESTAURANT BAR IN ARIZONA WAS THE LAST place Ginny ever imagined finding herself. On the ride over, she debated whether to get a table or to saunter in like she knew what she was doing and go right up to the bar. Her life had come to this—thinking about every mundane move. She felt paranoid, like her relationship status was a neon sign she wore around her neck, flashing between *wife* and *divorcée*.

Even her arms felt heavy and awkward dangling at her sides. But being a woman at a bar alone was a big deal to her. *Do I look like a lonely, desperate person waiting to be picked up?* She remembered her exposed cleavage and tugged her blouse up a bit.

A group of women sat at one of the tables nearby, celebrating a bachelorette party. They appeared to be about Ginny's age, and undoubtedly the bride-to-be was full of optimism and love, like Ginny had been once.

The bartender brought her a prickly pear cactus margarita and welcomed her to Arizona. At first Ginny tried to pretend she wasn't a tourist, but then she gave in and listened to the bartender tell her about the building. It was the oldest in the city, built in 1893 on the block that used to be known as Saloon Row.

In addition to the bachelorette party, there were a couple of old, crusty men, a group of young guys in baseball hats, and a few couples.

Ginny gulped her margarita, and a pain shot right between her eyes. She winced, rubbing the bridge of her nose.

"Ice headache," said someone from behind her.

The man attached to the voice was probably younger than Ginny. He looked too young—maybe eighteen, with a fake I.D. —but he was clean, and his brown hair was short and stylish.

Ginny was impressed a young guy would be so neatly groomed. Ray washed his hair with a bar of soap.

"It always happens to me when I drink something cold," said Ginny.

"Is this seat taken?" he asked while sitting down beside her. She saw him grinning at his friends at the end of the bar.

So this is what it feels like to be hit on in a bar. She was about to bombard him with questions about himself and general small talk, unsure about what she was supposed to do, but she decided to just play it cool. The Rolling Stones had written a song for occasions like this.

He said his name was Stephen, and he was a college kid out for the weekend.

"On your way to the Grand Canyon?" Stephen asked.

"Just passing through."

"Don't pass by too quickly."

Stephen slid her a shot of tequila that seemed to appear out of nowhere.

Smooth, thought Ginny. She wasn't sure how to respond. In her mind, she heard Mick singing "The Spider and the Fly," a song about a working-class woman picking up a younger guy at a bar.

She might have skulked away in shame until she remembered that in 1995, the Stones reworked the lyrics to reflect their own increasing maturity and changed the woman's age from thirty to fifty. *Better,* Ginny thought.

"You know," said Ginny, feeling relaxed and uninhibited, "I can think of more interesting things to do around here than go to the Grand Canyon."

They talked for a while, and Ginny started to feel

adventurous. She rested her hand on his leg, trying to imagine what it was like to be bold and sexy. He grabbed her hand. She could feel the strength of his grip and pulled away, embarrassed.

"How about another drink?" Stephen asked.

"I'm okay." Ginny felt lightheaded from the alcohol. He ignored her and ordered another shot of tequila.

"Watch this," he said as he licked the backside of her hand and sprinkled salt on it. He lifted her hand toward her mouth, and she didn't know what else to do but lick the salt and drink the tequila.

"You're good with your tongue." He leaned in and kissed her, moving his mouth gently down to the crook of her neck. Then he put his arm around her waist and tried to lead her out of the bar. Ginny was simultaneously stimulated and startled as she closed her eyes.

"Hey," he said. "Don't go to sleep on me."

"I'm just . . . resting my eyes."

"My dad used to say that." Ginny didn't want to hear about his father or know anything else about him except to see what more he had to offer that evening. She reached for her purse.

"Let's get out of here. I've got a room at the Motel 6."

♪

BACK IN THE HOTEL ROOM, STEPHEN UNBUTTONED HER blouse. He kissed her exposed shoulder. She pictured the scene in *Jerry Maguire* where Tom Cruise kisses Renée Zellweger's character for the first time, and she thought of how much she loved that movie.

Between the kissing and thoughts of romance that had been so absent from her life, she felt goose bumps running down her spine. Stephen helped her out of her blouse. Thankfully, she had been smart enough to wear her lacy, sexy bra tonight. He unbuttoned her jeans and led her to the bed. Ginny was surprised at his forwardness but liked it, aware that he was probably at his sexual peak and happy to reap the benefits. These might be Stephen's best years. Later he'd have his own wife to leave unsatisfied.

He stood over her, slowly pulling off her pants. She could hardly believe that she was being undressed. Ray insisted Ginny take all her clothes off first so he could slip it right in. No muss, no fuss, no foreplay, and certainly no chance of orgasm for her.

Stephen still had his clothes on, but Ginny could see his erection pressing against his jeans. She wanted to unleash it and maybe go down on him. She hardly knew herself; that was the last thing she'd wanted to do to Ray. But she had liked it when she and Ray used to have raw, lusty sex before they were married.

Ginny unclasped Stephen's belt and yanked his pants down to his knees. She maneuvered him onto the bed with her. He propped himself up on the pillows, smiling down at her. She gave him a naughty look. She liked the control.

But then he flipped her over unexpectedly, and the sudden motion sent the room spinning. Closing one eye to try to balance things, Ginny hoped the dizziness would stop soon. She focused on the table, only to see her faithful orchid glaring at her. Her stomach churned.

"I'll be right back," said Ginny. Stephen looked up from between her legs.

"You're kidding?"

"Be right . . ." she barely got the words out before she made it to the bathroom. The tile floor was cold and hard under her knees as she puked up a combo platter of tortilla chips, salsa, and tequila. She hated throwing up and sticking her head in the toilet, especially one in a cheap motel.

"You okay in there?" Stephen called from the bedroom.

"Yeah." She wished he'd go away. *The only way this could get more humiliating would be if he came in here and held my hair back while I threw up.*

Ginny waited in the bathroom, hoping to hear something that resembled him leaving—getting dressed, the door opening and shutting—but instead it was quiet. The sink was outside the bathroom, so if she wanted to brush her teeth, she'd have to do it with him there, lying naked in bed, hoping for something that wasn't going to happen anymore.

"Can I get you anything?" he said.

"No, no thanks. Maybe you should go."

"Come on back out here."

Opening the door, she poked her head into the room. He was still in the bed like she imagined.

"I'm sorry."

"Do you wanna try again?" he asked. *He's sweet in an odd way*, she thought.

"You actually want to do this?"

"Sure, why not?"

"'Cause I just puked my guts out. And that's right up there on the unsexiest-things-you-could-do-on-a-date list."

"Is this a date?"

Could this get any worse?

He didn't move, picking up the remote control instead. "Let's watch TV for a while. Maybe we can find some porn while your stomach settles."

"No, I'd rather not. I'm sorry. I feel really embarrassed, but can you please leave?" Ginny found her clothes piled on the floor and started to dress. Showing her sexy bra to a stranger wasn't fun anymore.

"Hey, I thought chicks like you were all hot for it."

"Just go." Ginny gestured to the door. She wasn't in the mood to figure out what he meant by that last comment.

Stephen put his clothes on and before leaving turned to Ginny. "Are you sure you don't want me to stay?" He grabbed her around the waist and pulled her close.

Ginny tried to wiggle out of his embrace, but he held her tight against his body. "You can't send me out there like this." He grabbed her hand and put it on his crotch.

"Let go of me," Ginny yelled.

Stephen tried to put his hand over her mouth to quiet her. "You're a dirty little tease."

"Get . . ." and before she could finish, Ginny puked again.

"You're disgusting. I'm outta here."

Stephen left, slamming the door behind him. Ginny hobbled over to the sink. She couldn't bear to look at herself in the mirror as she splashed her face with cool water to keep from crying.

7

BREE

Bree collapsed on the couch. Waiting tables was more demanding and just as physically exhausting as teaching a classroom full of kids. She kicked off her clogs, put up her feet, and contemplated her next move.

The one-bedroom apartment was functional and clean. But, most important, the landlord had only asked her to sign a month-to-month lease. Not that Bree hadn't walked out on long-term commitments before. A little thank-you note and a wad of cash usually staved off collection agencies hounding her with threats of small claims court and plunging credit scores.

Arizona was supposed to have been just a layover, a quick stop between the Pacific Northwest and wherever. The nagging feeling that she should go back to Florida to be near her family, her sick mother and her resentful daughter, weighed on her. Once she became a teenager, Tori criticized her mother constantly. Bree, tired of defending herself, avoided the fights because sooner or later, she was afraid she wouldn't be able to protect her daughter from the painful truth: all she knew how to do was run away.

Years ago, after Billy Blade left Florida and Bree behind, he hit it big in Hollywood. He asked her to follow him there, but she couldn't leave everything behind. She had a life in Florida that included a child and a marriage, even if it was an unhappy one. If putting more effort into making her husband happier would work, then she was willing to give it a try. Her relationship with Billy had been intense but brief, and Bree knew it was no use pining for a man she could never have. No more late-night partying with her friends, no more arguments with Dimmit. She'd be a good wife.

And it succeeded for a while. After school, Bree came straight home to clean the house, help Tori with her homework, and make dinner. Bree broke out her *Joy of Cooking*, lit candles, and wore lingerie to bed. Dimmit warmed up to her, and for a while they lived like two seemingly content but ultimately bored people. She stopped talking about her work because it annoyed Dimmit, and he stopped talking altogether.

One night Bree wanted to surprise him by making an incredibly complicated Greek dish for dinner. It took her most of the day: searching for the right ingredients, seasoning the white sauce to perfection, and assembling the layers of eggplant and meat sauce. She was trying to prove to him she was as sophisticated and exotic as any of the rich wives his friends had married.

Dimmit didn't show up until the next morning. He spent the entire night out without even calling to give her one of his typical lame excuses: One of his friends had thrown his car keys away as a prank, or he didn't want to come home late and wake Tori.

Bree was furious and flew at him when he came in the

door. She grabbed him by the shirt, shook him, and screamed, "Why?" It was odd she didn't want to know where he'd been or who he was with, but rather why he had reduced her entire life to a sham.

She recalled that he didn't even have the decency to make up a lie. In fact, he didn't say a word. She could smell the alcohol on him as he threw her arms off and pushed her to the floor. Bree curled up into a ball, afraid he might hit her if she moved. It wouldn't have been the first time.

"Get up," he yelled at her, "before Tori sees you like this."

"I hate you," she cried.

"Look at you," he said, a horrible sneer on his face. "Proof you can take the person out of the trailer park, but can't take the trailer park out of the person."

That afternoon, while Dimmit was at work and Tori at school, Bree was out of her mind with fear and anguish. With nowhere to turn, she packed her bags and booked a flight to Los Angeles. The decision was an impulsive one, but she naively believed that once she reunited with Billy Blade, he would help her fight for custody of her daughter. It had been a crazy idea hatched in a moment of desperation.

But there hadn't been any reunion with Billy.

After a year in California, she lucked into a studio apartment off Sixth Street in Santa Monica, just north of Wilshire Boulevard. A woman at the temp agency where Bree was employed was getting married and giving up her place. Technically Bree was subletting, so when the drains clogged or the lady upstairs left the bath water running and it started dripping through the ceiling, Bree couldn't call the management company directly. She felt like a squatter, sneaking around a poorly lit, three-hundred-square-foot place she'd never be able to call home. Not that it mattered. She had plans to move on, and the first step was getting her daughter back.

With all the fights, the talk of lawyers, closing of bank accounts, and canceling of Bree's credit cards, Dimmit refused to file for a divorce. He avoided the subject, called his wife horrible names if she mentioned it, and forbid his family from hiring a lawyer to clean up the mess. He wanted to avoid any more embarrassment than she had already caused them.

At first she didn't have the money or the nerve to pursue a divorce on her own. And Dimmit vowed to make Bree's life miserable if she crossed him.

One time Tori called in the middle of the night. When Bree picked up the phone, she heard breathing on the other end.

"Bob, is that you?" said Bree. A man in human resources at one of the companies she temped for had lifted her phone number from her personnel file and started calling late at night.

"Mommy?"

"Tori?"

"When are you coming home?"

"How would you feel about visiting California?" Bree asked, trying to put as much enthusiasm into the offer as she could manage. *Make it sound fun*, she told herself.

"Rusty too?"

Bree hoped Rusty was one of her stuffed animals, rather than the cocker spaniel Tori had been begging for just before Bree left.

"Of course." It'd be just like Dimmit to bribe his daughter.

"And afterward you'll come back with us?"

"No, honey. I live here now."

Tori started to cry. "I hate you," she said, accusing her mother of terrible things and stinging her with words she'd heard from her father: *abandonment, neglect, selfishness,* and *rejection.*

It took two years for Bree to convince Dimmit to allow Tori to visit her mother for a few weeks. When Tori was escorted off the ramp by a flight attendant into Los Angeles Airport, Bree couldn't believe how much her daughter had grown up. Her hair had been cut into a short, stylish bob, and even though she was only ten, Tori might as well have been eighteen. A set of headphones had replaced her favorite doll, Sally. A sweatshirt was tied around her waist, and she had a huge backpack slung over one shoulder.

Bree resisted the urge to tell her daughter to stand up straight and instead tried to hug her. Tori stood rigid, a look of indifference on her face, as if she were just another kid resigned to the fact that her parents were too screwed up and self-centered to make it work, and being shuttled from coast to coast was inevitable. Bree wondered where her daughter had learned to be so cynical.

She had come to the airport expecting some kind of reaction, so the one-word answers to her questions didn't surprise her.

"How are you?"

"Fine."

"How was the plane ride?"

"Good."

"Are you hungry?"

"Nope."

Unable to provide an excuse that made any sense to a child, Bree knew her long absence made her as credible as the tooth fairy, a silly fiction Tori stopped believing in when her mother forgot to leave a dollar after she lost a front tooth. Bree imagined that Tori saw her as a woman who was there one night, tucking her in and reading Curious George stories, and gone the next.

Undoubtedly, Dimmit had told Tori that Bree left them both to follow another man clear across the country. It would be like him to fill her daughter's head with stories of infidelity just to be spiteful. Of course, he wouldn't mention the fights, the philandering, the controlling, and the manipulation on his part. How could she explain to Tori that she had left her husband to escape an oppressive marriage, not motherhood?

During the drive from LAX through Venice Beach to Bree's apartment in Santa Monica, Tori remained quiet and withdrawn. It was only when she saw the groups of punks, homeless people, and tourists swarming to the beach that she defrosted. Sheltered by private schooling and privileged relatives and friends, Tori had probably never seen eccentrics like those outside her car window. When she read a "Meat Is Murder" sign held by an overweight bearded guy, she said she'd been a vegetarian for more than three months. It was the first full sentence she had spoken since her arrival.

When they got to the apartment, Tori hovered in the doorway. "You live here?" she asked, a look somewhere between curiosity and disgust on her face.

"It's temporary," said Bree, and for the first time, she saw it as an outsider might. There was a mattress on the floor, a set of TV stands, one television set that hardly received reception, a new DVD player purchased just for the occasion of her daughter's visit, and a tiny kitchen with a half-size refrigerator, a card table, and two chairs.

"Where am I gonna sleep?" Tori clung to her backpack.

"You can have the bed." Bree opened the closet and pulled out a sleeping bag. "I'll set up over here." She unfurled the sleeping bag and arranged it next to the bed. "It'll be fun. Like camping."

She had never gotten around to buying furniture for the apartment, and when Dimmit said Tori could come for a couple of weeks, Bree ditched the idea of furnishing the apartment all together. They'd be leaving soon anyway.

"No, Mom." Tori dropped her backpack to the floor next to the sleeping bag. "You'd better let me. You're too old to sleep on the floor."

The entire time she had been in California, Bree had squirreled away as much money as she could. During the day, she temped in various offices from Palos Verdes to Malibu, and at night she tended bar at a little dive along Wilshire. She was exhausted, but she had managed to save enough money to rent a small house and hire a lawyer.

After Tori reacted so badly to the idea of moving to the West Coast, Bree decided to take her back to Florida, where she wouldn't feel so displaced, and find a place in the Keys where they could both grow up. She hadn't made the best choices or been the best mother, and she was ready to admit her mistakes. But she had never once stopped loving her daughter.

Bree's savings, six thousand dollars, was peanuts, she

realized, especially when going up against the kind of lawyers Dimmit would hire—but it was enough to let Dimmit know she was serious. He couldn't continue to threaten her without repercussion. It might have taken a few years, but she had grown a backbone. She wasn't going to take it anymore.

During her time with Tori in Santa Monica, Bree didn't mind dipping into some of the cash she'd been saving to take her daughter wherever she wanted to go. They went to Hollywood and searched for celebrities, but they saw only Elvis impersonators and men dressed in gold clothing and makeup, pretending to be statues and posing for pictures with tourists. They talked about all sorts of grown-up things, like boys and kissing—subjects Bree knew Tori couldn't discuss with her father. The suspicions and distrust melted away.

When they went to Disneyland, Tori said, "This place doesn't compare to Disney World." Bree must have looked hurt, because Tori said she was having a great time anyway.

"Me too," said Bree, knowing Tori had given up purposefully hurting her mother. It had just been one of those honest comments children make, the kind that force you to stop and reconsider the kind of crap you've been deluding yourself with for so long.

The morning before Tori was supposed to fly home, they went to the Santa Monica Pier. Inside the Looff Hippodrome, a Byzantine Moorish–style building constructed in 1916, was a celebrated merry-go-round. Tori wandered around the carousel, examining each of the horses until she found hers.

"They're all hand-carved out of wood," said Bree.

Tori didn't appear to be impressed, and nor did she

probably care that there were fewer than one hundred carousels in the world with pure wooden horses.

"Nowadays they use fiberglass."

"I want to ride this one." Tori mounted a regal-looking black horse complete with golden and ruby-red armor and a blue saddle.

Bree swung her leg over the white one next to Tori's and waited for the ride to start. The music began, and they bobbed up and down opposite one another, so while Tori was on her way up, Bree was going down. They were never quite in sync, and it frustrated Bree.

Tori sat quietly. She didn't laugh or squeal like the other children, instead she closed her eyes.

"Are you dizzy?" Bree asked.

"I'm imagining." She tilted her head back. "Close yours."

At first, Bree was afraid. What if somebody snatched Tori from her horse, or she fell off, and Bree was drifting in never-never land, totally unaware and not in control of the situation? It would be another opportunity for Dimmit to rub the "irresponsible mother" accusation in her face.

Tori peeked at Bree. "Do it, Mom."

"Okay, bossy." Bree closed her eyes. "What do you see?"

"We're riding our horses along the beach. Daddy and I see them sometimes back home on Siesta Beach. My horse is called Thunder."

"I like that name."

"We're riding together."

"The two of us?" Bree hoped Dimmit wasn't included, but this wasn't her fantasy, so she tried not to interject too much.

"You're laughing so hard, you're almost peeing your pants."

"I am? What's so funny?"

"We're happy. People laugh when they're happy."

"I know," said Bree, wondering if she sounded defensive. How long had it been since she laughed out of pure joy?

"Now I'm cracking up because you look funny, laughing and bouncing up and down."

"What happens next?"

"It's getting dark," said Tori.

"And we go home," Bree said.

"Together?" asked Tori. The question nearly broke Bree's heart. What kind of life had she created that her daughter had to wonder whether she'd be going home with her mother? Mothers are supposed to raise their daughters, and Dimmit was doing his best to make sure that didn't happen. He was denying both of them a future.

"Together," Bree said, reaching out to hold her daughter's hand. The horses had synchronized, both of them on their way up.

They stayed on the merry-go-round until Tori had ridden just about every horse. When it was time for lunch, Tori wanted to eat at an outdoor café. She said she liked to people-watch while eating, something Bree also enjoyed. Even though they had been separated for a while, she couldn't believe how many traits she shared with her daughter.

Tori set down her slice of pizza and wiped the side of her mouth. She watched a woman trying to find places for all her shopping bags at the next table, and Bree could see that Tori was working up to something but took a sip of her soda instead.

"Why did you move to California?" she finally asked.

Bree had been waiting two weeks for this question and was thankful it hadn't come until she'd had time to prove she was a loving woman, capable of motherhood.

"It happened so fast," she said, knowing her daughter deserved more than a cop-out. "I always wanted you with me."

Bree's stomach knotted, and she pushed aside her unfinished ziti.

"But you could've come back. Daddy would've let you."

Tori reached for her hoodie and struggled to put it on.

Bree held up the sleeve so Tori could put on her jacket. "Daddy and I aren't getting back together, but that doesn't mean I don't want you to live with me."

"Here?"

"I've got another idea."

On their way back to the apartment, Bree explained the plan to Tori. Instead of flying into Orlando, where Dimmit would be waiting, they were booked on a flight to Miami. From there they'd rent a car, drive down to Key Largo, and check into a hotel for a few days until their rental house was ready for occupancy. They had grown so close over the past few weeks that Bree hoped Tori would be willing to give it a try.

Sometimes grown-ups had to make tough decisions, Bree explained, but in the end, it was for the best. Once they resolved their differences, and Mommy and Daddy were friendly again, Tori could visit her father on weekends and holidays.

No wonder her little girl had seemed so grown-up, Bree thought. Tori was being asked to understand a situation Bree could barely grasp herself.

She readied herself for the fight with Dimmit that was

sure to come. When they were still together, Dimmit was accused of all sorts of shady business practices, from false advertising to failure to pay off loans on trade-in vehicles to selling vehicles without possessing the legal titles. She once heard Dimmit on the phone clearly but calmly explaining that if these claims weren't dropped, he would find a way to make it so that not only would the accuser pay, but his children and their children's children would regret crossing him for the rest of their miserable lives.

Bree was no lawyer, but she knew the system favored mothers, and with a little savings behind her, she finally felt able to take him on. If she had to pay legal fees for the rest of her life, it was worth it to get her daughter back.

"I'm *so* full," Tori said outside of Bree's apartment, waiting for her mother to search for the key inside her big hobo-style purse.

"Since when can you finish a small pizza by yourself? When you were a baby, I could barely get you to eat a jar of peaches."

"You should've mashed a small pizza and put it in a jar. Then maybe I'd have eaten more."

"I doubt it. You were a fussy eater." Bree swung open the apartment door. "You better get packing." They only had a few hours until their flight. Along with the cash, Bree could fit everything else she cared about into the shoebox where she stashed her money.

"Mom?" Tori hesitated. "Where's my stuff?" She stepped inside the apartment and pointed to the chair where she had left her backpack.

At first, Bree didn't notice the missing DVD player or Tori's absent things. What caught her attention was the opened closet door, the bed pushed askew, and the clothes tossed around the apartment floor. Had they left it like that? She tried to replay the morning's events, and she remembered she and Tori had cleaned the apartment and folded her clothes in preparation for their departure.

The realization that somebody else had been in the apartment came slowly and painfully to Bree. Maybe it was the eternal optimist in her that made her want to believe someone couldn't be so low, but she couldn't deny what was right in front of her eyes.

"Go outside." Bree wanted Tori out of the apartment in case anyone was still there, and she escorted Tori to the doorstep outside.

"I'm scared," Tori cried.

"I'll be right back."

Bree went back inside and grabbed the cordless phone to dial 911. With the operator on the line, Bree searched the apartment. There were only a few possible hiding spots. She could see through the glass door that there wasn't anybody crouching in the shower, waiting like Norman Bates to stab her to death. She walked over to the closet and opened the door all the way. As she suspected, everything was gone, including the thief and all her money.

While they waited for the police, Bree broke the news to Tori. They wouldn't be going to Key Largo after all. Tori didn't understand. If her mother wanted to be with her, she cried, they could find a way. They didn't need money, she said, trying to convince her mother.

"You could come back home," Tori said. "Daddy still loves you."

"I can't," Bree said, gathering the few things of Tori's still left behind and putting them into a plastic bag. "As soon as the police get here, I'm taking you to the airport."

"Nooo," Tori wailed. "Not without you."

"I'll come for you soon. I promise," said Bree. She tried to remain focused and calm, but she wanted to cry too. She wanted to scream and howl and tell her kid how cruel and unfair life was, and she'd better get used to it.

"I don't believe you." Tori stopped crying and once again became the cold, uncaring girl Bree had picked up from the airport. "You're full of shit."

Bree went outside and waited for the cops. She wished she were all of those things she'd been called. A selfish liar wouldn't feel this kind of pain.

That evening, she dropped her daughter off at the airport and waved good-bye as Tori boarded a plane for Orlando to meet her father.

8

GINNY

Ginny's stomach was still in knots, aching with a strange combination of nausea and hunger. After last night, she vowed not to act so irresponsibly. A clear mind was what she needed on her pilgrimage. She also needed to save her money for hotel rooms, food, and maybe some cute outfits to wear to the concerts.

Relieved to find a diner just outside of town, Ginny needed to relax a bit, grab some lunch, and, if she worked up the nerve, write a letter to Ray. There were a few things she needed to say without his interruption, and texting or emailing seemed too wimpy. In her letter, she'd express both her anger and sorrow, tell him she was out finding herself and needed some time. She'd ask him to let her be alone for a while, to not call her. She'd contact him when she was ready.

A pretty waitress took Ginny's order and returned with a bowl of homemade chicken soup. Ginny inhaled the steam, thought of the facials she'd given to her clients, and felt, if only momentarily, a sense of healing. In an hour, Ginny had the ability to dissolve stress and turn a woman's day around.

Her only regret was that she couldn't transform herself.

She took out a pen and a pad of paper from her purse and started to write. *Dear Ray.* That's as far as she got before her eyes drifted out the window to the parking lot, then beyond to the mountains in the distance.

"Writer's block?" asked the waitress as she refilled Ginny's iced tea.

"Sort of." Ginny pushed the letter aside.

"When I was a teacher, I used to tell my students not to think too much. Just start writing. See what comes out. You can always edit later."

Ginny sized up the waitress. Her auburn hair seemed professionally dyed, which surprised Ginny, since she just assumed any woman who worked in a down-home diner like this one probably went through boxes of Spicy Cinnamon hair color from the local drugstore. She wore the same uniform as the other waitresses, but instead of white flats or plain tennis shoes, she had on a pair of baby-blue clogs. The hairdressers at the salon where Ginny had worked swore by them. Great for standing on your feet all day. They weren't cheap either, probably setting her back at least one hundred and fifty bucks.

Her nametag read *Bree.* "You were a teacher?" asked Ginny.

"Don't look so surprised."

"Oh, I didn't mean . . ." Ginny put her hand over her mouth as if she could stuff the words back in. It seemed that every day she was becoming more like her mother, passing judgment on people based on superficialities like appearance and types of employment. Virginia had deemed Ginny's neighborhood white trash based simply on some out-of-date exteriors.

"Don't worry about it," said Bree. "It was a million years ago. How's the soup? Can I get you anything else?"

"How far is it to Phoenix?" Ginny asked, glad Bree had changed the subject.

"About two and a half hours north on I-17."

Ginny sipped the tea and slid the letter back in front of her, waiting for Bree to go away.

"Give me a minute to finish out my tables, and I'll give you a list of some restaurants and shops you shouldn't miss."

"Not necessary. I'm only going for a day or two."

"That's a shame. It's a lot more interesting than this podunk town. I'm thinking of moving there someday. This place is getting old."

"I know what you mean," said Ginny. "Time to move on."

"Exactly." Bree sat down at the table. Despite her discomfort at this stranger taking a load off without being invited, Ginny noticed something in the way Bree agreed with such enthusiasm. Her entire demeanor changed; she perked up like a kid who'd just heard the school recess bell. Ginny had seen movies about this type of woman—the kind who can't settle down. When things get complicated, they're ready to pick up everything and take flight. Straight from the *Cosmo* quiz, a Wild and Spontaneous was sitting right in front of her.

"I could help you with your letter," said Bree.

"It's okay. I'm not in the mood anymore."

A man who also worked in the diner approached their table. He nodded politely to Ginny and said to Bree, "Before my frustration turns to self-loathing, I need to express my concern about you abandoning your tables."

"For Christ's sake, Jerry, just say what you mean."

"I wasn't going to interrupt, but you have a phone call. It's your daughter."

Bree hesitated for a moment. "Tell her I've gone home."

"I'll only lie for you this once. Soon you'll need to take responsibility for the decisions you make and the people you hurt."

"Yeah, I know. Thanks."

While Ginny's waitress and her boss debated whether certain tables were being neglected, Ginny felt a small cramp on her right side. She took a sip of her water. Maybe she was still dehydrated from last night's shenanigans. Suddenly she wished she could be left alone to get back to Ray's letter. Maybe he was the cause of her pain, sending his bad vibes all the way to Arizona. He'd probably made a little Ginny doll, and he and his stupid girlfriend were poking pins into it. No doubt she resembled a voodoo doll right now, her hair standing on end. In a hurry to leave the disaster site behind, she hadn't showered, and she could feel the flakes of last night's mascara on her cheeks like tiny little spider legs. Her clients would die if they knew she had broken the cardinal rule of skincare and gone to bed with a face full of makeup.

A sharp jab shot through her abdomen and Ginny doubled over, clutching at her stomach.

"Are you alright?" Bree asked.

"Fine, I just need to go to the bathroom."

"It's in the back." Ginny could feel them staring at her as she made her way past Bree and her boss toward the back of the restaurant. When she stood up, she could feel a warm moistness in her underwear. The cramps were getting worse, and the ache encircled her midsection, moving around her to settle into her lower back. The pain hunkered down, heavy and determined to stay awhile. She'd never been so happy to feel the familiar ache. When she made her way into the stall, her suspicions were confirmed.

She had finally started her period.

In the ten or so minutes Ginny was in the bathroom, thankfully nobody else came in. It was as if she were glued to the seat, too overwhelmed to move. She was no longer connected with Ray, and the conflicting emotions left her paralyzed for a moment. The possibility she might never be a mother made her a little sad. In a math class, she'd learned positive and negative numbers cancel each other out. Negative one plus positive one equaled zero. Ginny learned over on the toilet, hugging her calves to form the human equivalent.

"Hey, you okay in there?"

Ginny lifted her head to see blue clogs peeking in underneath the door. She must have been making noise, somewhere between sighing in relief and crying, because she hadn't heard Bree come into the bathroom.

"Aha," was all Ginny could utter.

"Your soup's getting cold."

"I'm bleeding."

"Okay." Bree paused.

Ginny tried to regain her composure, realizing she sounded like a twelve-year-old starting her period for the first time. "Would you mind getting me something from the machine? I'll slide a quarter to you."

"Not necessary." Bree walked over to the sanitary napkin dispenser near the sinks.

Ginny could hear some kind of jiggling. "The lock's been

broken on this since the Nixon administration." She handed a pad to Ginny underneath the door.

"Hope you don't mind, though. The only ones the boss is willing to pay for are as big and thick as a roll of paper towels. Real classics. I don't know where they get these blasted things. There's probably a giant warehouse stocked with restaurant supplies, and in between the jars of mustard and relish and rows of ice-cream-sundae glasses are boxes and boxes of sanitary napkins, circa 1972."

"Thanks," said Ginny, taking the pad from Bree's outstretched hand. It was a small act, passing the pad underneath the bathroom door, but the delicacy with which Bree handed it to her comforted Ginny. She started to weep.

"I know these aren't the kind with wings and all, but there's no point in crying about it," said Bree. The blue clogs walked away from the stall. "I'll send your soup back. Say it had a hair in it or something. Jerry'll gripe about it, of course. The scrooge."

The clogs were itching to leave. Ginny could see that and understood why, but she didn't want her to go yet.

"No," Ginny blurted out.

"No? You want something else instead?"

"Don't leave," said Ginny. "Give me a second. I'll be right out." Before she left the stall, she examined the contents of the toilet and thought about what could have been. After a brief moment, she flushed.

When Ginny opened the door, Bree placed the back of her hand on Ginny's forehead. "You're looking a little better. You were as white as a ghost out there." This delicate touch reminded Ginny of her mother, the loving, nurturing one she grew up with. The mother who used to let her play hooky from school, even though she knew Ginny wasn't sick. They'd eat bags of chocolate candy and watch soap operas together while Ginny yammered away about the boys at school.

With the daytime programs and the made-up stories about people Virginia had never met, Ginny wondered whether or not her mother had been capable of preparing her daughter for real life. Her mother had grown up poor, and she must have felt the need to hide her past in order to fit into the upper-middle class lifestyle her banker husband had provided for. Reality was shameful—a hidden scar that threatened exposure if it were scrutinized too closely. Ginny's perception of love, sex, and marriage had been founded on a Hollywood script that wasn't any good in the first place. She started to question how much responsibility she had in her failing marriage after all.

"A little clammy, but I don't think you have a fever." Bree made her way toward the bathroom door. "How about a cup of chamomile tea?"

"I don't normally make such a big deal about getting my period."

"It's fine." Bree started to leave.

"It's just, I thought I was pregnant, but I'm not." Ginny couldn't believe she was being so honest with someone she had only met.

"I'm sorry," Bree said, looking uncomfortable, shifting from one foot to the other.

"It's a good thing."

"That you're not pregnant?" asked Bree.

"It's complicated." Ginny washed her hands. "Anyway, too

much information. I'm making a fool of myself, as usual." She thought this woman was surely going to run as far away from her as possible. *I would, if some crazy woman like me were revealing everything in the women's bathroom.* "Diarrhea of the mouth" is what Ray used to call it. Nobody cares about all the mundane details of your life, he'd say.

"Are you all alone?" asked Bree.

Ginny nodded her head. "Yup."

"Maybe it's just as well." Bree put her hand on Ginny's shoulder. "Just means nobody to answer to. If you ask me, it's the *only* way." Bree fluffed her hair in the mirror. "Do you need a place to rest?"

"I better get going. I'm on my way to see a couple of Stones concerts." Ginny laughed. Saying it out loud sounded ridiculous, but it was also freeing. "I'm following the Rolling Stones on tour." She paused, waiting for Bree to react. When she didn't, Ginny continued, "Silly, huh?"

"Not at all," said Bree, and Ginny thought she saw a glimmer of "High-Octane-Hell-Raiser" attitude light up.

The bathroom door creaked open, and Bree's boss poked his head in. When he saw Ginny, he excused himself but continued into the room anyway, standing with his hands on hips like he was about to scold a naughty child. "I'd appreciate if you tended to your work and didn't leave the other girls to pick up your slack."

"You're right, Jerry," said Bree. "I'll be out in a second."

When Jerry closed the door, Ginny thought she heard Bree whisper something nasty under her breath.

"I have a better idea. Instead of giving you a list of things to do in Phoenix, I'll go with you. Want some company?"

Even though she and her orchid had a pretty good thing going, Ginny didn't hesitate. "Hell, yeah!"

9

GINNY

Ginny waited outside in the car while Bree finished her shift. To pass the time, she watched the diners come and go. On the way in, they stepped as lightly as empty vessels waiting to be filled with fried chicken and homemade pie. But as they exited this little restaurant in the middle of Arizona, sluggishness weighted down their stride, as if their stomachs had been filled with sandbags rather than comfort food.

A young couple chatted as they entered, and Ginny wondered if the conversation was genuine or simply a polite exchange, like when she asked people how they were without really caring to hear the answer. Was their interaction just a façade, a pretty wrapping to hide the unpleasant secrets residing within?

When she was a little girl, her mother used to point to people she didn't know and create an entire life for them. "You see that woman over there." She'd nod toward an attractive woman in her forties. "She's secretly saving up money so she can leave her husband." Or "That old guy—his name's Frank. He looks like a Frank, doesn't he? Anyway, he's afraid his young wife is going to leave him, so he's having an affair with his secretary just to get even."

The make-believe always seemed to involve deceit, the falsehoods people tell in order to hide their true feelings from their mates or from themselves.

Ginny felt like the biggest dupe of them all, bleeding out any future she and Ray could ever have together. She hadn't asked for any of it, yet she felt sick with guilt for believing their separation might be for the best. She and Ray could move on with their lives separately. And she couldn't help wondering if there was something wrong with her. Maybe now wasn't the right time for motherhood, but it didn't mean she wanted to give up the idea entirely. She'd left Ray because she wanted possibility, a chance to be something more, do something more.

She fished the Rolling Stones lunch pail out from under the front seat. The Mick Jagger and Keith Richards bobble-heads were the heaviest and largest items in the box. At seven and a half inches, the Mick doll stood with one hand on his hip while holding a tiny plastic microphone across his body with the other hand. Dressed in a red coat, a white button-down shirt, and black pants, he had a painted-on attitude that made him look more cross-eyed than cool. His lips were fleshy, and the longish, shaggy brown hair tried unsuccessfully to capture the essence of Mick Jagger.

The Keith doll looked like an orange Oompa Loompa, and his proportions were all wrong, even for a doll. Squat little legs poked out from beneath a cheesy leopard coat. He held his guitar up, vertical and geeky, instead of Keith's usual way of letting his axe hang from his body, low-slung and loose. His blank stare looked like a deer in the headlights, not like the hardcore rocker he actually was. Ginny imagined Keith would hate it.

The first thing most Rolling Stones biographies covered was the relationship between Keith Richards and Mick Jagger. They attended elementary school together but lost touch after Keith moved away. In 1962, while they were both in college—Mick at the London School of Economics and Keith at Sidcup Art College—they ran into each other at a train station in Dartford, England. Mick was holding Chuck Berry and Muddy Waters albums. After discovering their mutual love of American R&B, they formed a band, and the rest was history. The majority of the Stones' songs were penned by Jagger/ Richards, sometimes referred to as the Glimmer Twins, rock and roll's most famous duo.

Like any long-enduring relationship, theirs came with complications. Over the years they'd had their feuds, taking turns insulting each other through various media outlets. Ginny remembered reading an article about when Mick Jagger received his knighthood in 2003 that pretty much summed up their clash. "Jagger Knighted; Richard Rages." According to Richards, a respectable member of the Stones did not sell out and become part of the same establishment he'd spent his career rebelling against. The reporter had cited their 1967 album *Their Satanic Majesties Request,* reminding the public of their once bad-boy reputations.

The bobblehead dolls had been a present from Ray. Soon after they started dating, he'd been so excited to give them to Ginny that she'd barely walked inside his apartment before he yanked them from the bag, the receipt from one of the souvenir shops on Hollywood Boulevard floating to the floor. She couldn't help but wonder if his gift had been an unspoken confirmation that he'd understood the Stones were Ginny's first love, and he might never be able to compete with Jagger, whose stardom made men like Ray seem little and frightened.

"But *I've* got the girl," he had told her, holding her tightly "You're all mine."

Physically, she'd been his. But over time, her heart and mind, which had been left unchecked and starved, began searching for sustenance in small items contained in a lunch pail.

♪

A KNOCK ON THE CAR DOOR STARTLED GINNY, AND SHE couldn't believe she had missed the mop of red curls bouncing toward her. Bree's bright blue eyes peered in through the window. *She might be a little nutty,* Ginny thought, *almost too full of enthusiasm.* But she knew it wasn't fair to judge Bree that way, considering Ginny probably seemed more pathetic than any sane person should.

"Hey, you ready?" Bree popped a cigarette into her mouth. It was brown and expensive-looking, European or something.

"Sure." Ginny rolled down the car window. "Are you done?"

Bree shook her head. "Jerry thinks I'm on a break. We better hightail it out of here before he gives me one of his personal responsibility lectures again."

"He is sort of—"

"A jackass." Earlier Ginny had connected with Bree's

nurturing side, but the whole big-sister image seemed to be fading fast. Sure, they'd had a moment in the bathroom, but it hadn't meant anything more than mere coincidence—a woman lending a hand to another.

"Sorry." Bree exhaled smoke. "Sweet guy. Dumb as a rock, though. A woman can look past that for only so long, you know?"

Ginny knew.

Bree hopped into her bright-blue convertible bug, the tires squealing out of the driveway. The woman knew how to make an exit. Jerry would probably never see her again, and Ginny wasn't positive she would either. The little car whipped around so many corners, the station wagon could barely keep up. Ginny envisioned the two of them on the road in Bree's fun car, a car that belonged to *single* women, but it wouldn't be as comfortable as her wagon. Besides, where would Orchid sit? No, they'd take the bigger, safer car. This was Ginny's journey, and she needed to do the driving anyway. It was great to have a copilot along for the ride, but Ginny still needed to be in charge.

Even though she was in another state surrounded by an entirely different landscape, the similarities to home were striking. The tightly designed tract homes and green lawns sustained by constant watering reminded Ginny of Ray. The front yard happened to be his greatest source of pride, and he took it as a personal affront if the neighbors didn't keep theirs up. He was always confronting this neighbor or that one if they let their yards get too brown or full of weeds. Funny, Ray was a total slob—but when it came to his lawn, he was as neat and tidy as Martha Stewart.

That pretty much summed up her husband: always putting too much effort into the wrong places. When company was coming over and Ginny needed him to help her clean the house, he'd start reorganizing the garage or his closet. Instead of scouring the toilet, he'd open the tank to examine the valves. Rather than support his wife with love, he smothered her with neediness.

Bree's apartment was on the top floor of a three-story building. Ginny panted on the way up the stairs, the exhaustion taking hold of her.

"Take it easy," Bree said. "Maybe you should lie down for a bit."

"Maybe," Ginny agreed, finding herself captured once again by Bree's motherly nature. Ginny figured the apartment would be as full of character as Bree and her little car. But this was not the case. The first thing that struck Ginny was the blandness, the absolute lack of warmth. There were no personal objects displaying any kind of intimacy or individuality. It was clean and white, like the inside of a milk carton. Absent were the little accessories Ginny so adored and expected from someone like Bree. No colorful throw pillows to accent the sofa. No picture frames containing photos of frolicking family members looking into the lens to capture that perfect moment. No scented candles in pewter holders from a boutique import store. No pictures on the walls. No plants—real or fake. Nothing she couldn't throw into a car at a moment's notice and take off if she needed to.

Nothing she couldn't leave behind to start over someplace else, Ginny realized.

"Go ahead and grab something to drink from the fridge,"

Bree called out from the bedroom, where she was packing.

Ginny opened the refrigerator and found exactly five items. A bottle of soda water, a carton of orange juice, a loaf of bread, some stinky cheese, and a stack of envelopes.

"You keep mail in your refrigerator?" said Ginny. She didn't want to be nosy, but she had to ask. That was truly weird.

"It's so I won't forget to pay my bills."

She answered so matter-of-factly, Ginny almost felt stupid for asking. After pouring a glass of water in one of the two glasses she could find, she wandered over to the sofa. She passed something she had missed earlier: a picture frame. Bree and a teenage girl stared back at Ginny. Bree was smiling, but the girl wasn't. Her arms were crossed and she looked defiant and determined, it seemed to Ginny, not to display anything that could be misconstrued for happiness. They had the same eyes, though, and aside from the mother's enhanced shade of red, they had the same hair.

"Is this your daughter?" Ginny shouted through the half-closed door.

"That's Tori . . . I mean, *Victoria*." She exaggerated the first syllable. "Cute kid, but another pain in my butt. She's in boarding school. Got her whole life mapped out. Wants to be a lawyer. A chip off the old block." Bree stuck her head out and rolled her eyes. "Or not." She snickered and returned to her bedroom. "I despise lawyers."

Ginny sat down on the couch, sipping her bubbly water. *It must be nice to have a daughter*, she thought, even though Bree acted like hers was nothing more than an inconvenience. With Ray, she had just assumed she didn't want a child anymore and was over the idea of becoming a mother. But maybe she hadn't wanted to face the truth. She didn't want *Ray's* baby. Ginny changed positions, shifting the giant sanitary napkin.

But to hold a baby in her arms, *her* baby, might be sort of nice. Maybe there was something she could offer another human being. Some guidance or advice. She would tell her daughter not to underestimate her own value; she didn't have to settle for anyone or anything. *Who knows?* she thought. Her daughter could be a doctor, a professor, president of the United States.

She had once wanted to be something too, an artist or a teacher, but instead she'd gone to beauty school because it had seemed like the easier path. In high school, Ginny had taken the minimum required courses. Graduating was her goal, not getting into a major university. If her course load required more than a couple of hours of homework a night, she encouraged the school counselors to consult her records and consider removing her from difficult classes. She'd been tested for a learning disability in elementary school and had scored in the forty-ninth percentile for reading comprehension. The results had satisfied her parents, but when she'd asked her brother to explain, he hung his head and teased that it meant he had a dummy for a sister. Later she'd learned she'd been just one percentile from the norm, a definition that continued to haunt her.

Ginny had spent her days submerged in skincare products, rather than changing the world or shaping young minds. For now, though, she sat on a stranger's couch in Arizona without a husband or a child, waiting to make her next move.

"Ready." Bree emerged from the bedroom with a hatbox

and a faux-fur leopard coat slung over two rolling suitcases. "What's the sourpuss face about?" She crossed the room and stood in front of Ginny, reaching out to pull her up.

"Maybe this is a mistake," said Ginny. She ignored Bree's offer and stayed planted on the sofa.

"Which part? Leaving your husband? Following the Rolling Stones? Or . . . " She hesitated.

"No, I'm sorry. I didn't mean you." Ginny tried to assure her. "Even though we hardly know each other, I think you might be the best thing that's happened to me so far. I'm just wondering if I should do this."

"Or what? Go home with your tail between your legs! Are you kidding me? Honey, you're knee-deep in this already. You've committed, and I hate to bring it up, but there's nothing stopping you now."

That hurt, but Bree was right. It was Ray who chose to keep her down, to deny her every dream she'd ever had. And to top it all off, he'd cheated on *her*. She was knee-deep in this, alright, and there was only one thing to do: get a backbone.

"You're right." Ginny was tired of feeling sorry for herself.

"I know," said Bree, picking up the photo Ginny had placed on the coffee table. "I wish my own daughter would realize it once in a while."

Ginny wasn't sure how to respond. She didn't want to pry. "By the way, do you even *like* the Rolling Stones?"

"Who doesn't?" said Bree, brushing off the question, perhaps not realizing the sincerity with which it was asked and the importance of the answer.

"I mean, what's your favorite song, for instance?" *Please don't say "Satisfaction." That's the one people say when they don't know anything about the Rolling Stones,* Ginny thought. It's the song that gets every passive, listless concertgoer—the people who just happen to run into some free tickets or think they should see the Rolling Stones before the band stops touring altogether—off their lazy asses to hoot and holler and dance around while Mick sings about not getting any satisfaction.

"Let's see." Bree sat down at the kitchen table while she thought about it. "Gimme Shelter."

A respectable choice. Popular, usually included in greatest-hits collections, but rich with texture and complexity—an amazing song done live with the vocal accompaniment of Lisa Fischer.

Ginny thought about the Maysles brothers' documentary, *Gimme Shelter.* When she first became a Stones fan, she watched it every weekend—sometimes three or four times over a period of two days—and she even had the DVD in her Rolling Stones lunch pail. During sleepovers, her best friend, Cathy (the one who'd wanted Ozzy Osbourne's love child), fell asleep while Ginny examined footage of the Stones both on- and offstage. The filmmakers had followed the band during the final weeks of their 1969 U.S. tour, and Ginny watched it over and over again until she had memorized every scene.

Her favorite part was when Mick Jagger said to an audience, "I think I busted a button on my trousers. I hope they don't fall down. You don't want my trousers to fall down now, do you?" Wearing a stars-and-stripes top hat with his cape flung across his back, Mick let his long hair brush his shoulders. He looked like a hippie version of Uncle Sam as he flirted with the audience, taunting them with the possibility that he might unleash the danger that lurked beneath. They'd screamed and hollered, encouraging him to let his trousers fall.

Ginny had hugged her pillow and pressed rewind.

At the time, she'd been too young to realize the importance of the film or what its events meant as the 1960s came to a close. The Maysles had captured and documented a moment that would symbolize the end of the rock-festival era and the bitter conclusion of a movement meant to inspire hope in a country mired in the Vietnam War. *Gimme Shelter* culminated with the brutal murder of a young man during the Altamont Free Concert, a rock festival held in California in 1969 that was supposed to be the Woodstock of the west. During the Rolling Stones' set, Meredith Hunter was stabbed to death by a member of the Hells Angels, the notorious motorcycle gang hired to act as security guards. A festival that should have been about peace, free love, and good vibes— including Santana, Jefferson Airplane, and Crosby, Stills, Nash & Young—quickly degenerated into a night of chaos.

Four people had died, four people had been born, and the Rolling Stones were forever immortalized in the infamous concert of December 1969, known simply as "Altamont" by the millions of Stones fans around the world.

"Cool," said Ginny. "I love that song too."

"Whew," Bree said, wiping her brow in exaggeration. "I passed the test. I might be old, older than you at least, but believe it or not, I know a thing or two about music. You never know, I may have a few surprises of my own."

"You're not old."

"I'll never tell," said Bree.

"And I'll never ask."

"Good, then we can be friends."

"Okay, friend," said Ginny. "I think the first thing we need to do is make a plan."

"Plan?" Bree crinkled up her face like an unhappy teenager. "Oh no, I don't work that way. I end up wherever the road takes me."

"Not this time. You're along for the ride, remember?" asked Ginny.

Bree hesitated for a moment. She seemed stunned. "Hey, look who grew a set! Five minutes ago, you were ready to crawl home." Ginny had to laugh to herself. She was trying, and somehow Bree sensed it. They had a connection, after all; she was sure of it.

"I mean, I have a general idea of where we're going, but you should know I only have single tickets to the shows."

"No tickets for me!" Bree stood up from the table and flung her arms out in an extravagant show of defeat. "Forget it, then. I'm not going." Ginny couldn't help but notice how different they were. Bree was a petite woman, her puffy red hair and giant blue eyes too large for her body, a cartoon character whose flamboyance was magnetic. Everywhere she went, Ginny imagined, people were drawn to her. But Ginny was quiet and subtle. She tried to enter and exit rooms without much hoopla, and even though she wanted to be intriguing, she didn't want to make a fool of herself either.

But Bree was not a fool. She was fun and exciting and, best of all, *spontaneous.*

"Girlfriend, I haven't paid my way into a concert since . . . whoops." Bree covered her mouth as if to stop herself. "I'm giving away my age."

"I don't know. This is the Rolling Stones. Besides the tight security, the tickets go for at least three hundred bucks a pop."

"Please, I'm not saying we're going to break laws," said Bree. "I'm talking about finding creative ways to get good seats without paying a bloody fortune to the scalpers. Being *invited* in. That sort of thing."

Invited? She had no idea what Bree was talking about. "That's a relief." Ginny reached in her purse and dumped the tickets she had already purchased on the table. "I almost maxed out my credit card buying these."

Bree picked up the tickets, extending her arms as far as she could. Ginny figured Bree needed glasses but was too vain to admit it.

Ginny pulled out the schedule of tour dates, smoothing out the wrinkled pages. "I have tickets everywhere, but I was thinking we could fit in Santa Fe along the way. I've never been there, have you?"

"I've been everywhere."

Of course, you're a drifter, Ginny remembered. "This must sound boring to you, then."

"No way. Boring is what I've been doing for the last three months, listening to Jerry talk about us as if there were ever going to be an *us*. Poor guy. He tried. He asked me to marry him at least a dozen times."

"You said no?" asked Ginny.

"I've already lived that life. I'm all about experiencing new things, like seeing the Stones on tour!"

"Awesome," said Ginny. "I was just wondering one thing, though. You said there were 'creative ways' to get into concerts."

"You know, meeting the right people. That sort of thing."

"Oh." Ginny didn't get it until she remembered her old school friend, Cathy, telling her about women who offered special favors to security guards so they could get backstage to meet Ozzy Osbourne. "O-o-ohh, I see."

"It's not what you're thinking," said Bree. "Oh, sister, you've got a lot to learn."

10

GINNY

Bree drove Ginny's car to Phoenix while Ginny rested. Back in the apartment, her cramps had gotten pretty bad, the sharp jabs causing her to double over in pain. They stopped at a convenience store to pick up supplies: a bottle of ibuprofen, two packs of Always pads (with wings), a bag of Cool Ranch Doritos, and two bottles of fizzy water. Apparently Bree couldn't drink the flat kind.

As the fall sun was setting, they made their way through the cold desert. After wrapping herself in a soft blanket, Ginny leaned her head against the car window. The blankets and pillows had been Bree's idea. There was no way Ginny was camping out, but Bree had said they'd have to prepare for the worst. Hotels could be booked up if the Stones were in town. Ginny, of course, hadn't thought of this, and she was thankful to have an experienced traveler with her.

The desert terrain was scraggy and sparse in comparison to the brilliant orange-red sky. How she'd ended up smack-dab in the middle of nowhere perplexed Ginny. She hated the desert. Family vacations had always been to the beach or the mountains, not the barren and dry desert, where the temperature gauge had two settings: blazing hot or freezing cold. Nothing good ever came from the desert; old people went there to fade away and die. Six months ago, Ginny could never have imagined she'd be there, searching for solace with a complete stranger.

But it was quiet. A person could think here. In complete darkness, the stars blanketed the sky in clusters and globs. Ginny had never seen so many in her life. Back home, she'd be lucky to find Orion's belt. She peered through the front windshield to see the sky overhead and followed the lines of stars as they converged on the horizon. They seemed to be lighting the way, and for the first time in a long while, she felt calm and let out a big breath of air. The trip hadn't only been about running away from someone. It was supposed to be a pilgrimage; she was seeking the truth, and who knew whether she'd find it in Mick Jagger or the Stones or in the mysterious desert, a place she had never understood until now.

Ginny glanced over at Bree. She was wearing her glasses and listening to a talk radio show. When she noticed Ginny had woken from her nap, Bree lowered the volume.

"You missed a good one. This guy called in because he's worried his girlfriend might be *too* experimental for him. She becomes excited when he wears her lingerie."

"I'm not sure if I'd be into that," said Ginny.

"He likes it, but now it seems every time they do it, she insists he wear her panties and bra."

"But if he likes it?"

"Only sometimes. Once in a while, he'd like to have good old costume-free sex, he says. The problem, according to the doctor, is that this could be the beginning of years of deviant behavior."

"Like this could lead to other things—a gateway sexual act? What pot is to cocaine?"

"Exactly," said Bree. "Today, it's lingerie; tomorrow, who knows what?"

Ginny imagined Ray wearing her panties, his hairy belly hanging over a black G-string. "Hey, you gotta give them credit for being creative. Ray had zero imagination. Sex with him was like a chore, like doing the dishes or taking out the trash." The last time they did it, Ginny remembered, she'd looked up at Ray and thought that he was going through an awful lot of trouble for nothing.

"Men." Bree shook her head and seemed to be cataloging her experiences and subsequent disappointments. "It must have been good in the beginning?"

"I suppose it was," said Ginny. "But I'd only had two boyfriends before Ray. What did I know?" She didn't have much life experience.

Their sophomore year of high school, Pete and Ginny drifted apart. It seemed that their common bond of rock and roll was not enough to sustain a relationship. She started hanging with the more mainstream kids, the ones who ran for student body offices and thought smoking pot was for burnouts. These new friends had names like Hannah and Cameron and encouraged Ginny to try out for the cheerleading squad—which she did, but she didn't make it. They dragged her to the homecoming dance, and it was there that she was introduced to Danny, a gorgeous water polo player way out of her league.

All throughout freshman year, Ginny had watched Danny

at lunch as he hung out in the main quad with the rest of the in kids. She belonged to the out set, and her group of misfit friends wasn't helping her to achieve the kind of popularity she craved. Her only friend, Cathy, was flunking out; her parents had to send her to the alternative school where most of the other stoners wound up.

Surprisingly, Ginny's parents didn't object when she started dating Danny, a senior with a car and surging testosterone levels. She imagined her parents tried not to think about the latter.

Ginny was willing to do anything for Danny. When he asked her to wear her hair longer or her lipstick darker or her heels higher, she did. She loved him, ached for him. If he didn't call for days, Ginny physically hurt and couldn't go to school. Her parents didn't force her to go, either. Nobody noticed that her grades were dropping, and that she'd mope around the house or blare Fergie's "Big Girls Don't Cry," from her bedroom. She had given up the Stones back then—her new friends didn't approve. Her parents were too busy worrying about her older brother, who was failing high school and locking himself in his room, burning up his precious teen years in plumes of pot smoke.

Danny was drifting away from her, and she became desperate to win him back. She had to do something drastic, and throwing him a surprise birthday party was just the thing. With a couple hundred dollars saved up from doing extra chores around the house—helping her mom paint the living room and her dad clean out the garage—she could take Danny out to dinner, then bring him to her house for a huge party. Fortunately, her parents had agreed to stay upstairs while everyone was there.

The party was a complete surprise to Danny, and he seemed to be coming back around, telling everyone to thank his girlfriend for making it all happen. He never used that label, so when his friends busted out bottles of rum to mix with soda, and Danny asked Ginny to meet him in the bathroom and give him his real birthday present, she didn't say no.

When his ex-girlfriend, an uninvited guest, arrived Ginny didn't worry. She and Danny had cemented their relationship, making it official. And maybe it wasn't as romantic as it could have been, but it was passionate. Didn't he say he loved her? Lisa was two years older than Ginny. Sexy and confident, Lisa flirted shamelessly with Danny, tossing her hair around and rubbing up against his body whenever she could find the chance. As Danny and Lisa left the party together, Ginny finally realized she had been a trusting fool, used by the only boy she ever really loved.

She stood outside in the rain watching him leave, seeing herself beg Danny not to go. The moment felt unreal—she seemed to float outside of herself. The body preserves itself this way when the pain is too deep.

"You've only been with three guys!" shouted Bree, jerking her back to the present. "Child, you've been deprived."

"Tell me about it. It doesn't matter, though. I'm done with sex." Ginny pulled open the bag of tortilla chips, and for once didn't worry about the calories.

"I've said the same thing before, and it lasted for about two minutes. Besides, sex is good. Romance is even better. You just need to find the right man."

For some reason, it surprised Ginny that Bree was interested in love. She was so willing to dump Jerry at a moment's notice. "What about Jerry? He wasn't the right one?"

"Not my type. But believe it or not, that old windbag had a few moves left in him."

"No way!" Ginny was grossed out and could hear it in her own voice. She felt bad. "I mean, he was a good . . . " She tried to think of something quick, " . . . dancer?"

"How should I know?" said Bree. "I meant *lover.*"

Ginny took a swig of water. She didn't want to hear this.

"The guy knew how to use his tongue."

When she was mid-swallow, the carbonated water rushed back up through Ginny's nose. It burned, but she couldn't help laughing. The thought of weaselly Jerry being some kind of red-hot lover, the Casanova of Arizona, cracked Ginny up.

"What's so funny?" asked Bree. "I'm serious. Jerry's hot in his own way."

That was it. Ginny couldn't hold back even a little. She burst out laughing, irritating her already cramped stomach. Between giggles, she held her belly and moaned.

"I don't know why I agreed to travel with a crazy woman like you," said Bree.

If she hadn't started laughing herself, Ginny would have worried her new friend was serious.

Ginny calmed herself and fiddled with the radio dial, passing over "Hotel California," some easy listening, and a Mexican radio station before instantly recognizing Mick Jagger's voice singing "Sympathy for the Devil."

In unison, the women broke into song.

"Oooh, who—oooh, who!" They hooted the song's refrain as they drove on through the desert night.

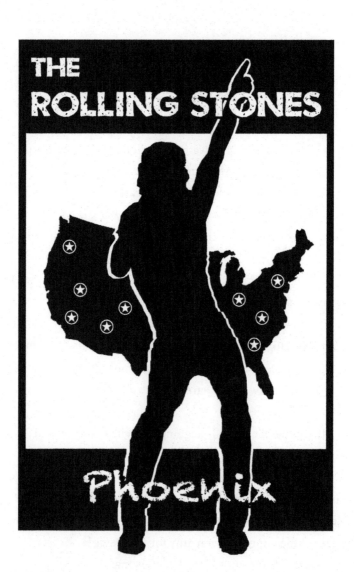

11

BREE

Bree worried she was becoming a lightweight. The cheap domestic beer hit a lot harder than she'd anticipated, and it was especially irritating the way the sun was bouncing off the cars parked in the lot of Sun Devil Stadium. The brightness blinded her, so she put on her shades, relaxed her way through the light-headedness, and settled down for a nice buzz.

For the past few days, Ginny had been driving Bree crazy with anticipation, but she tolerated it because she was enjoying her newfound freedom from Jerry. Maybe she was also looking forward to seeing Keith Richards in person. He was the kind of guy she could relate to. The dude had staying power.

She tried to remember the last time she had seen live entertainment without a date tagging along. Once she took her daughter to *The Little Mermaid on Ice*, and that was a disaster. Tori threw a tantrum because Bree had tried to explain her interpretation of the story, merely mentioning the significant fact that Ariel gives up her beautiful voice, essentially her identity, for a man. Instead of thanking her mother for the valuable lesson, Tori demanded to go home, accusing Bree of constantly ruining everything. Thinking back on it now, Bree realized that maybe her daughter hadn't been the precocious kid she wanted her to be—or that maybe she had been too harsh. The doctor had prescribed medication for the depression she couldn't shake since giving birth to Tori, but Dimmit wouldn't allow Bree to give in. He told her to buck up and rise above her weakness.

Bree craved mind-stimulating debate and companionship. Jerry was perfectly capable of holding his own in a conversation, but he hated confrontation and would quickly change his opinion to match hers. Even when she called him on it, he said she was right, killing off the debate before it had a chance to get interesting. She wanted a challenge, and looking over at her new young friend tearing off a piece of beef jerky with her teeth, Bree knew she'd found one.

"How can you eat that garbage?"

"No carbs," said Ginny, waving the stick of meat as if the absence of carbs might be visible to the naked eye.

"But the sodium. I hope your blood pressure's in check." Bree took a swig of beer. "That's a heart attack waiting to happen."

"But at least I won't need an extra-large coffin when they bury me."

She has a point.

Bree liked her new friend, and she decided right then and there to honor her commitment to another person and see this relationship through. Before she could move on, there were a few things she needed to teach Ginny. Bree wished someone had told her not to sell herself short. There are plenty of people ready to take advantage of young, smart women who have yet to realize their potential. They are grateful for only a fraction of what they deserve.

"I was a California girl once too," said Bree. "Did I tell you that already?" She hated people who recite the same stories over and over again.

"I think you mentioned something about Malibu."

Bree sighed. "I was tan and gorgeous back then."

"You're still gorgeous," said Ginny.

"You're just being nice." Bree scrunched and rearranged her curly hair.

"No, I mean it," said Ginny. "I hope when I'm your age . . ." She stopped, stuffing more jerky into her mouth.

"You can finish." Bree didn't want to be pitied. "I'm old. I know it."

"You're not old," said Ginny, blushing.

"Anyway," Bree continued. "I moved around a lot. Hollywood, Santa Monica, Malibu. I was a certified teacher and couldn't get a job parking cars."

"That sucks."

"Yeah, it did—until I finally met someone who helped me out."

"A man?"

♪

BEFORE BREE MET BILLY BLADE, HER HUSBAND, DIMMIT, had rarely come home before midnight, and she'd been stuck there caring for their young daughter. He "worked late," which was code for screwing around with his latest girlfriend. If Bree questioned him, Dimmit would respond by either making her seem paranoid, or, if she pressed, by accusing her of letting herself go.

Admittedly, in her depressed state, she'd become a frump, wearing the same clothes over and over again because she didn't have the time or energy to shop for herself. And, yes, she'd gained some weight. Nothing tremendous, but adding twenty pounds to a five-foot-two frame shows up in rolls and bulges even the baggiest of clothes couldn't hide.

One night, Sherry, the fifth-grade teacher, asked Bree to come out with her for a couple of drinks and to listen to some music. A band was playing at a local club, and Sherry was all hot and bothered over the drummer. Married, with two kids at home, she wanted somebody around to make sure she didn't do anything stupid. Bree refused to be the morality police but was honored to be asked. Sherry was one of those women with a huge personality, the kind who always paid compliments and made you feel like the most interesting person in the room.

People were attracted to Sherry. Everybody wanted to be her friend and be flattered by her. But she could also be cruel. Her admirers had no idea that as soon as their backs were turned, the insults would fly. She'd compliment a woman on her hair to her face, then mock her fat ass as soon as she walked away. Caught up in it, Bree had shared in the compliments and reveled in the backstabbing. For once, she had belonged to the cool girls' club.

One night a week became three and four. Bree left Tori at home with a babysitter. At first Dimmit didn't mind Bree's going out a few nights a week. At least it got her off his back, he'd said. She lost weight and started to become less frumpy, or so she thought. Right when she started to get her self-esteem back, Dimmit decided it was time to end her friendship with Sherry.

But by then, it was too late. Bree had already fallen for the lead singer of Cutting Blades, the band she and Sherry had been going to see. When Billy Blade walked out onstage, she felt like a teenager again. Her stomach fluttered, and she gushed like a groupie. While Dimmit was a large, imposing man, Billy was thin, delicate, and artistic. They'd hooked up almost immediately, and Bree hadn't been able to help but feel a little vindicated about sticking it to Dimmit. After Billy's sets, he'd take her somewhere private and play music for her. She told him that she was married and had a daughter, but he didn't ask for the details. They never discussed the real world, anyway. He sang to her, she read him the poetry she secretly wrote, and they made love wherever they could.

One night, a few months into the relationship with Billy, Bree and Sherry showed up at the club to find that the band had canceled their performances indefinitely. There was an urgent message for Bree to call Billy. When she did, he asked her if she loved him.

"You know I do," she said. "What's going on? Why aren't you playing tonight?"

"I'm leaving for Hollywood. Right now. Come with me."

"It's not that easy," Bree said. "I have a kid."

"It is that easy. Will you follow me or not?"

"To the ends of the earth," Bree said, believing it at the time.

That night, Billy left for Hollywood. Bree didn't see him again until months later, when she watched his music video on television for the first time. "Sarasota" was a huge hit, and the song and video were played over and over again. Billy stared in the camera and sang:

"You said that you would follow me to the ends of the earth/ Now how far do I have to go for you to follow me?" Bree had known the question was for her, immortalizing her worst memory.

When she finally arrived in Los Angeles, ready to pursue her relationship with Billy, she didn't know how to contact him. He had become famous. She tried calling his agent but found it pointless—they transferred her from one person to the next until she gave up. Someone told her musicians hung out on Sunset Boulevard and grocery shopped at Rock 'n' Roll Ralphs. Bree felt like an idiot, hovering over the produce on the off-chance Billy Blade would come walking through the automatic doors, shopping cart in hand.

Finally, she found out his band would be at an awards ceremony in Beverly Hills. She put on her lucky red boots and stood out in front with the rest of the groupies, waving albums and pens and waiting for an autograph, and, if they were lucky, the chance to meet one of the band members. Bree sucked it up, checked her ego, and, when Billy emerged from the limo, pushed her way to the front.

She called his name and got close enough to hear him ask, "Do I know you?" But he didn't wait for an answer—he went back to the car to help a beautiful blonde actress to her feet.

That was the last time she'd seen Billy Blade in person.

♪

"NO, NOT A MAN." BREE TORE OFF A PIECE OF GINNY'S BEEF jerky. "A nice older woman hired me to work at a stationery store she managed. She even let me move in with her until I could save enough money to find a place. Besides, when's the last time a man did anything for us?"

12

GINNY

Phoenix, Arizona: Sun Devil Stadium

On the way into the stadium, Bree walked over to a guy selling tickets. She laughed and flirted, touching the man on his arm, then his chest. Ginny couldn't make out what they were saying, but she could see the man lean in and whisper something.

"Oh, you're naughty," said Bree, walking away with a shit-eating grin on her face.

"Look what I got." Bree handed Ginny two ground-level tickets. "They're still too far back from the stage, but once we're on the field, it's no problemo."

"How much do I owe you?" Ginny asked, fishing in her purse for the little cash she had. Anything over a couple of hundred would put a major dent in her budget. She already had a ticket to the concert, but Bree scoffed at anything less than a floor seat.

The Phoenix ticket was the first concert ticket outside of California that Ginny had purchased. She had a terrible seat because she waited until the last minute to buy it. She clearly remembered the moment she hit the Buy Now button, because it had been a breaking point for her.

Anticipating her mother's arrival at dinner that Sunday night, Ginny thought that it would take just one more time, one more argument between her husband and her mother, and she'd break. As usual, Virginia and Ray got into it, arguing over Virginia's dog, Benz.

Virginia insisted Benz sit at the table and pulled a bar stool up so the dog's head was about even with Ray's. And when Ginny uncovered the casserole dish, Virginia said, "Oh, lasagna? Benz can't eat that."

Ginny tried to kick Ray under the table so he wouldn't engage her mother. He ignored her. "Why don't I run to the store and get it some real dog food?"

"No, no, I don't think so." Virginia shook her head furiously, as if Ray were suggesting they feed the dog cyanide. "I don't trust those Chinese. They're a cheap, cheap people. Don't you remember when they poisoned the pet-food supply?"

Ginny cringed at her mother's racist remarks.

Ray seemed to be enjoying the conversation. "Why would the Chinese want to kill Benz?"

"Oh, my dear." Virginia opened her thermal lunch container and pulled out a bag of bite-size chicken pieces. She hand-fed her dog one morsel at a time. "They're jealous. They don't understand our ways.

"For God's sake, they eat dog over there," Virginia continued. "Can you imagine that kind of savageness?"

"I don't know," Ray said. "Dog might be tasty."

Virginia gathered up Benz and left the table.

After the dishes had been hand-washed—Ray was too cheap to pay for dishwasher repairs—Ginny went on a spending spree. The Arizona concert was the first in a long line of many to come.

Ginny could hardly believe that she was in another state, following the Rolling Stones on tour. This moment had lived only in her dreams, and she considered snapping a photo and sending it to Ray and his new girlfriend. Imagining the two lovebirds gallivanting through *her* house made her sick to her stomach.

"Don't worry about the money." Bree quickened her pace toward the entrance.

Even though Sun Devil Stadium was far less intimate than some of the smaller tour venues, it was open to the outdoors, and the crisp fall evening was perfect for a concert under the stars. It was the kind of romantic setting Ginny had wanted to experience with Ray, but that moment never came. Or, if it did, it wound up as a fight because Ray was hungry or uncomfortable or bored. At first Ginny's disappointments ended in tears, then later a wave of strange, inexplicable numbness.

"Let me pay you back," said Ginny. She hated the idea of owing anybody anything.

With Ray out of work most of the time, she'd often borrowed money from her mother to pay the bills. Virginia had deposited a couple of hundred bucks a month in Ginny's account. Ginny never told Ray where the extra money came from, and he never asked. Her mother, on the other hand, asked all the time if Ray knew what a bum he was.

"They were free," said Bree. "The guy asked me if I needed tickets, and when I said yes, handed them to me and told us to have a good time."

"Are you kidding?" Ginny couldn't believe how her luck was turning around. The only things she'd ever gotten gratis were soda refills at the local fast-food joint.

"C'mon, let's pick up the pace." Bree kept looking behind her as if to see whether they were being followed.

"So the guy just *gave* them to you?"

"That's right." Bree started to jog.

Ginny ran after her. Once they made it inside the stadium, she stopped to catch her breath.

"You're full of it. Now how much do I owe you?"

"I'm telling you, nothing!"

Ginny suspected Bree might be lying. Her lip curled up like she was doing an Elvis impersonation.

"Then why are we running away from him?"

"Well." Bree scrunched and rearranged her hair. "I might have told him you had a debilitating disease and your dying wish was to see the Stones in concert."

"What?" said Ginny. "You just stole that guy's tickets."

"I did not!" Bree put her hands on her hips, as if she were genuinely insulted Ginny would suggest such a thing. "I implied the Make-A-Wish Foundation might reimburse him."

Ginny was speechless, considering what she should do. She couldn't exactly return the ticket to a guy who must have known he was being duped. *There has to be some degree of personal responsibility*, Ginny justified to herself.

"So now I'm dying?"

"Of course not. Anyway, scalping tickets is illegal," said Bree. "He should know better."

Once they were on the ground level, Bree insisted they try out different seats, moving forward row by row until the rightful owners showed up and kicked the two women out. Ginny was totally embarrassed, apologizing right and left. She was not a line cutter, let alone a seat stealer.

Bree, however, argued with anyone who tried to claim his rightful seat. She denied any wrongdoing and said the error was his. If he threatened to call security, Bree would look at her own ticket and finally say, "Oh, you're right. How silly of me. My mistake."

A mere twenty rows from the stage, they finally found two unclaimed seats. When a guard approached, Bree rambled something about accidently flushing the ticket stubs down the toilet, but not before she moved a little closer to him and asked how it felt to be in such a powerful position. Ginny couldn't believe how easily he fell for it, even offering to move them up if anything became available.

This time, the Stones opened with "Start Me Up." Another track from *Tattoo You*, it was the first Rolling Stones song sold to advertisers. It was rumored Microsoft had paid $14 million for the rights.

"I love this song," said Bree, singing along with Mick.

"Do you have to go to the bathroom?" Ginny had to pee but recalled the long lines she'd seen outside the women's restroom. Holding it in was way too uncomfortable, though. She could hardly concentrate and felt like she was going to wet her pants.

"Nope," said Bree, taking another sip from her giant beer.

Is she a camel or what? Ginny thought.

"I gotta go."

Bree finished her beer and handed the cup to Ginny. "Use this."

"You mean right here?" asked Ginny, noting the thousands of people surrounding her.

"Nobody's watching *you*," said Bree. "All eyes are on them." She gestured to the stage. "I'll block."

Ginny realized that in a way, she was all alone in her little world, a small being in the midst of many. The realization freed her. Nobody was there to scrutinize or judge her. She couldn't believe she was doing it, but she dropped her pants and squatted over a twenty-ounce paper cup.

The release was just what she needed.

♪

WHILE THE STONES WERE PLAYING "PAINT IT, BLACK," a 1966 song from Brian Jones' era, Ginny saw a flicker of light out of the corner of her eye. Bree was lighting a joint that dangled from her glossy lips. She closed her eyes and sucked until the cherry tip flamed brightly.

"They're going to kick us out!" Ginny waved the smoke away, trying to clear the air so nobody would smell it. "What about all the people around us?"

"Where do you think I got this?" Bree passed the joint to Ginny.

"No, thanks," said Ginny.

"Go ahead," said Bree. "Take a hit. You might like it."

"I better not."

"Give me one good reason."

"I don't know," said Ginny. "I might freak out or something." She remembered obsessing over her breathing patterns the last time she got high.

"You won't. Besides, if you do, I'll take care of you."

"Oh, that's a big relief. Anyway, I know better. It's *illegal.*" Ginny couldn't help using Bree's same words about the ticket scalper against her.

"I don't like to think of it in those terms." Bree's gaze drifted off as she attempted to get philosophical. "You see that big, beautiful sky up there?"

The stage lights illuminated the smoke as it wafted across the sky. A myriad of moving colors dissipated into the atmosphere.

"This is the Wild West. Normal rules don't apply here. You call it drugs," Bree gestured toward the joint, "I call it sacred medicine."

"You need medicine, alright."

"C'mon. Loosen up."

"It'll probably kill me," said Ginny.

"Are you kidding?" said Bree. "It'll cure you."

Ginny took the joint and inhaled. She held in the smoke briefly and exhaled, repressing the urge to cough. After a few moments, she said, "I don't feel anything."

"You will," said Bree. "Just relax."

Ginny tried to let go of her tension, and after a few minutes, she felt something she hadn't in a while. Contentment.

"I should have done this a long time ago," she said, bringing the sacred medicine back up to her lips for another hit. Ginny turned her attention to the stage when she heard the familiar opening beat of a cowbell. The Stones started playing "Honky Tonk Woman."

Mick Jagger climbed into a cherry picker and hovered

above the crowd. He looked as big as the Empire State Building. Ginny was practically lying on her back, fully reclined, as he was floating above her. She closed her eyes not only to get her bearings, but also to imprint the moment in her memory.

Mick's voice sang out from the cosmos. She imagined kissing him, feeling his soft, full lips against hers. For a moment, time and space stood still. He was on top of her now. Ginny and Mick would be locked forever in a virtual climax, their bodies connected through time and space.

Ginny leaned into Bree and whispered, "Damn, that was some good shit."

13

GINNY

A few days later, they were on their way to Santa Fe. Bree insisted they stay by the Plaza, the best spot in town. After shopping and perusing nearby galleries, they'd clink their margarita glasses together and polish it all off, according to Bree, by eating blue corn enchiladas and mole. Usually Ginny preferred a combo platter with safe choices like chicken tacos or rice and beans, but she was determined to try new things on this trip.

As they pulled up to the hotel's circular driveway, Ginny didn't worry much when the valets came to retrieve her car or when the heavy wooden doors leading into the lobby seemed to open on their own, as if the two women were about to meet the Great and Powerful Oz. What got her—what made fear shoot from her scalp down to her stomach and out to her pocketbook—was the rich-looking old-style furniture, the luxurious upholstery, the paintings on the walls, and the vases of fresh flowers adorning every available surface. This was not the modest hotel she had in mind.

They hadn't discussed money, but when Bree picked this

particular hotel because it was "within our budget," Ginny wasn't sure how to ask what that meant. Considering Bree had just quit her job, Ginny figured their situations, or "budgets," were about equal. Flying by the seat of her pants, Ginny was maxing out her one credit card while Bree peeled off cash from a wad that would surely expire.

Ginny resisted the urge to kick off her flats and run her feet across the Mexican pavers that covered the floor. She wanted to lie down and press her cheek against the cool red clay. It had been a long day of driving.

"Beautiful," said Bree when she walked into the lobby. "I hope this place is okay with you?"

"Sure," said Ginny, spying the murals of conquistadores and their pretty dancing señoritas. She knew Santa Fe was a popular travel destination, an authentic Spanish settlement unlike her native Valencia, California, which was named after a city in Spain known for its sweet orange trees. In the eighth grade, she had given a report on the subject, citing an article from the 1960s about a development that advertised homes situated on rolling foothills. They couldn't build enough one- and two-level homes designed around the master plan of paseos, she explained in her presentation to the class. She quoted the article just to hear herself say "paseo-strolling" aloud. Were there any underground walkways in Santa Fe to explore, she wondered?

"As long as it's not too expensive," added Ginny.

Bree shook her head and shrugged her shoulders at the same time, which struck Ginny as an obviously evasive response. Thanks to Ray, she was well-versed in reading the body language of bullshitters.

A woman cradling a small dog in her arms stood in front of them, waiting to check in. Ginny mentally jotted down the name of the hotel so she could tell her mother about it later. Virginia refused to travel unless her dog came along. Benz seemed to have replaced the grandchild that eluded her.

The dog cocked his head sideways and started barking at Bree.

"Oh, that's nice," said Bree and barked back.

Ginny repressed the urge to laugh, but the woman in line pretended she didn't hear them. Instead of responding, she stiffened her posture, and Ginny recognized the insulted look on her face. It was the same disapproving but hurt look her mother wore whenever Ray and Benz had their strained interactions.

"He's cute," said Ginny. Bree shifted impatiently, waiting for their turn at the front desk.

"Don't you like dogs?" Ginny asked her, worried she had another Ray on her hands.

"Dogs, I like. It's their owners I can't stand."

Owner. Ginny's mother would have cringed to hear Bree dismiss their relationship that way. Benz was Virginia's baby. She carried him around as if he were a helpless newborn. Ginny used to threaten to buy her mother a Baby Bjorn so she could tote the dog around like all the other suburban mommies.

Ginny approached the pooch, reaching out her hand toward its head. "Hi, little one."

The woman pulled away before Ginny had a chance to scratch it behind the ears. "You don't have to pretend."

"Excuse me?" asked Ginny.

"I heard your friend. Barking at poor little Zoey. She gets

nervous around strangers." The woman started to get worked up, shaking her finger at Bree and Ginny. "This is a pet-friendly hotel. If you don't like it, they're other places for people like you."

"People like us?" Bree asked. Ginny could've sworn she saw a smile creep across Bree's face.

"Pet . . . " the woman stammered, apparently looking for exactly the right word. " . . . haters," she finally eked out as she carted little Zoey to check in at the front desk. Bree shook her head. "Told you. *Owners*," she said.

"Should we go somewhere else?" Overhearing the expensive rack rate quoted to the woman and her dog gave Ginny a bad vibe, and she wanted to leave. "I saw an economy hotel just outside town."

"No." Bree picked up her bags and approached the front desk. "I'll make sure to ask for a room far away from dogs, babies, and any combination thereof. And don't worry about the money."

Easier said than done, thought Ginny, picking up a brochure for the Georgia O'Keeffe Museum. A place Ray would have hated, which was why she'd make sure to hit it first thing in the morning.

They were offered a suite at a much lower rate than what the dog and her companion were paying. Ginny wasn't sure why they were getting such a good deal, except she noticed the hot guy working at the front desk smiling at them as the two women made their way to the elevator.

"What was that about?" asked Ginny.

"Nothing." Bree waved. "I may have promised we'd meet up with him later."

"What!" Ginny cried.

"Don't get squeamish on me now. Welcome to the game."

Before she could decline the invitation, the elevator arrived and a woman who must have been eight months pregnant emerged. Her husband—Ginny assumed they were married—waved his wife out of the car, protecting her in case the doors closed unexpectedly. Ginny recalled the elevator scene in *Jerry McGuire* where the deaf couple signed the famous line "You complete me." *What was it about elevators,* Ginny wondered, *that inspired romance?* They always made her feel awkward, everybody stuffed inside like size-eight thighs squeezed into a pair of size-four skinny jeans.

She imagined her mother making up a story about the couple, usually one that included unnecessary drama and despair. *The unborn baby was fathered by the man's twin brother, who recently died in a tragic car accident.* For once, Ginny might like to tell Virginia that people *can* live happily ever after.

When Bree opened the door to their room, all Ginny wanted to do was sink into the fluffy white bed. She was exhausted, but she couldn't allow herself to fall asleep so early. They were building momentum and still had lots of Stones shows to see.

"I'm going for a walk," said Ginny, her suitcase barely touching the floor.

"Now?" Bree was in the bathroom, inspecting the shower. "Let me clean up, and I'll come with you."

"It's okay." Ginny wanted to be alone. "I need some air. Take a shower, and when I get back, we'll grab dinner."

"You and your plans." Bree had already turned on the faucet, allowing the steam to seep into the room. "Hey, while you're out, see if you can't muster up a couple of interesting dinner companions."

"Yeah, sure thing," Ginny mumbled as she slid out the door.

♪

GALLERIES LINED THE STREETS OF THE HISTORIC PLAZA, and Ginny admired the many desert landscapes that captured the quiet beauty of the environment. Some lucky tourist would get to take one home, a reminder of her time spent here. She stopped in front of a painting of a pueblo village. Underneath it read "Taos, New Mexico," and for a moment, she considered another side trip. *Maybe next time*, she told herself. The Stones would not wait for many detours.

At the back of one gallery hung a large nude. A plumpish sort of woman—*zaftig*, she liked that word best—was lying on her side with her back to the viewer. Only her profile was visible, and there was almost no background. Surrounded by an aura of pale blue, the woman looked like she was levitating on a field of paint. It was minimal in style, but Ginny was drawn to the simple beauty of it.

Next to it was a smaller painting by the same artist, more detailed than the previous piece. A woman and a young girl—a mother and daughter, perhaps—were pictured holding hands in a green field of grass. Like the nude's, their faces were away from the viewer, but the close relationship between the subjects was intimated through the tone and lyricism of the piece.

Ginny suddenly felt lonely, missing her eccentric but loving mother as she admired the artist's ability to capture the quiet bond of unconditional love between a woman and her child.

Strolling past the shops, Ginny wished she could finally put her disastrous marriage behind her. She still hadn't contacted Ray, but it was too confusing sorting out all her feelings. *How does one come to terms with loss and gain all at the same time?* Her heart ached, her head throbbed, and part of her wanted to go home to her mother, crawl into her childhood bed, and allow herself be taken care of. But then she imagined her mother's told-you-so about Ray. It just wasn't possible. A home with her mother or with Ray didn't exist anymore. Bree, the road, and the Stones were her life right now, and she had to make it work.

Where there should have been rage sat a dull emptiness, still and stagnant. Ray had pushed her to the point of numbness. Just in time, Ginny thought of the song "Emotional Rescue." The disco-inspired hit from the Stones album of the same name cued up on the soundtrack of her life that had been following her since the beginning of her journey. She whispered the lyrics, waiting for her savior, the knight in shining armor Mick promises to be in the song.

As always, the answer was right in front of her. It was, and had always been . . . the Rolling Stones.

The streets were empty except for a tourist or two. Ginny figured everybody was out to dinner. While she enjoyed the peace, it seemed eerily quiet. She shivered, wrapping her arms tighter around her body. She had been in such a hurry to get out of the room that she had forgotten a jacket. It was probably time to head back anyway, she figured, and walked toward the hotel.

She took long, fast strides. It felt good to move her legs. The cold air rushed in through her nose, and she blew it back out through her mouth, a technique she'd learned in the only yoga class she had ever taken. One of the girls at the salon had said Ginny needed to expel her negative energy and invited Ginny to accompany her to a class. Stopping in the middle of the sidewalk, Ginny closed her eyes and did one of those *namaste* things. Somehow it seemed appropriate right now— she'd try anything if it would bring her tranquility. As she was about to bring her palms together, she heard a high-pitched scream.

Ginny opened her eyes and realized she was completely alone. She peered down an alley toward the sound, hoping against hope that somebody would come to the rescue.

She imagined a helpless child or elderly person hurt and needing an ambulance. Many people would turn and walk away, figuring it wasn't their problem, but Ginny remembered the time when she and Ray had a fight at the mall. He abandoned her there, and a stranger gave her money for a cab ride home. Ginny reached for her phone to call 911, then remembered she had left it in her car underneath the front seat.

The screaming tapered into a low moan. Despite her fear, Ginny ventured deeper into the alley.

The sound was getting closer, and she slowed her pace. She didn't want to startle anyone, especially somebody who was already hurt. As she got closer, two cats darted from behind a dumpster, running off to continue whatever it was she'd interrupted.

Ginny's heart was beating a million miles a minute, and

her legs buckled. *Stupid cats.* She put her head in her hands and laughed, deciding to keep this incident to herself. Bree thought Ginny was uptight as it was.

The alley was dark and creepy. She hadn't noticed before, when she was so intent on following the noise like Alice down the rabbit hole, but this passageway smelled like urine and wouldn't lead to any magical place. Ginny heard people whispering behind her. Two men were approaching. Walking out as quickly as she could without running—Ray always accused her of being paranoid—she tripped over the curb.

She collapsed to her knees and her purse flew onto the street, its contents scattering every which way. *Damn cheap purse.* The zipper had broken as soon as she brought it home. It had been on sale, and the store refused to take it back. She'd really wanted the designer handbag she'd seen at the department store. Its soft, buttery leather and silky lining had beckoned her, but with Ray out of work half the time, the purchase couldn't be justified, and she'd been stuck with an ill-functioning pleather knock-off.

She got to her feet and stuffed her wallet back into the purse. Brushing the dirt from her clothes, she was more than ready to head back to the hotel. Everything was in check, she assumed, until a golden tube caught her eye. Her lipstick had skidded into the middle of the street. She should just leave it there, her instincts told her as she heard the men getting closer. But that lipstick was thirty bucks a tube and her favorite color. *It'll only take a sec to run out there and pick it up*, she thought, and besides, maybe Ray had been right about Ginny. She was paranoid, always fearful of the worst possible scenario.

Big fat mistake.

When Ginny stepped back onto the sidewalk, the men were there waiting for her. She stood still, not knowing what to do. *How can I be so stupid?* One of them brushed up against her. They stood directly between Ginny and the safety of her hotel. She could see the lights off in the distance and considered barreling through the men. Her only other option would be to turn and walk the other way, but then she'd be going further into the city and into the unknown.

Ginny knew nobody was going to save her. Alone in the middle of a nightmare, she was surrounded by men who were about to probably rape and kill her. She was going to die in the middle of Santa Fe, New Mexico. She'd never get to see the rest of the Rolling Stones concerts or go backstage and meet Mick Jagger.

All the self-defense moves Ginny had ever seen on TV seemed useless right now. *If the bad guy gets you in a stranglehold, slide down and away from his grip*, she remembered hearing on a recent talk show. But what should she do when they were standing right in front of her? *Never let them take you from Place A. Move from Place A to Place B, and you're dead* ran through her head like a survival mantra.

She could kick them where it hurts and bolt. Both the men were short, coming up to Ginny's shoulders. They were strangely little but mean-looking. One reminded her of a Mexican hombre from one of those old spaghetti westerns her father used to watch, and the other was a scrawny, skinny, fidgety white guy.

Ginny started to cross the street.

"Hey, where you going?" They followed her.

"I've got to go," said Ginny. "My husband's back at the hotel. It's our anniversary, and he's waiting for me. I needed to make a reservation for dinner." She couldn't stop lying even though it made no sense, and she saw from their blank stares that they couldn't care less.

"We scare you or something?" asked the hombre.

"No," said Ginny, as if she was protecting their feelings, an old habit she reverted to even with potential killers.

They moved in closer to crowd her. "We just want to talk to you. Man, you're a good-looker," said the white one, running his hand through Ginny's hair.

She could smell the nicotine on his fingers and the reek of dirty clothes.

"My husband's going to come looking for me," said Ginny, swallowing hard.

"What d'ya think?" asked one to the other. "I think she's lying."

"Liar," said the hombre.

"You're not married."

"I am," cried Ginny. "And if I'm not back soon, he'll call the police."

He grabbed her left hand, showing it to her. "No wedding ring."

"My husband's like that. He worries."

These creeps were going to ruin it for her. Steal everything, rob her of her dreams, maybe even her life. Ginny swung her purse, smacking the hombre on his head, and kicked him in the balls. The white guy laughed at his friend getting beaten up, and before his good humor ran out, a large group of tourists walked around the corner. They seemed to be drunk, hollering and hooting. Ginny, never happier to see a group of obnoxious strangers in her life, screamed to get their attention and spooked the two attackers away.

But not before they grabbed Ginny's purse and ran off with everything she owned.

14

BREE

The only song clearly transmitting through the cheap clock radio was one where a woman griped about her crappy life. Bree would have preferred something a little more upbeat, less sappy and depressing, but it was better than nothing. Better than silence, than being alone with her thoughts. She had become one of those people—the kind who needed noise to drown out the persistent buzzing of her mind. A clear-cut case for the headshrinker, just like a friend she used to tease because he refused to sleep unless the TV was on, infomercials blabbering all night long.

She had become someone who needed distractions. But she could not afford to care about what sort of person she was and preferred listening to a stranger croon about an abstract pain rather than think about how she'd let another person down in her own life.

The shower felt good, and she remembered the many times she'd had to wash away the smell of food that always lingered in her hair and skin far longer than it should have. Waitressing was hard work, schlepping hot dishes to and fro, her fingers burning because Jerry left the plates under the heat lamp too long. Clearing the tables, she learned early on to avoid the chewed-up bits of food spat back out because they were fatty, gristly, mushy, pinkish, grayish, or just plain mysterious in origin. As disgusting as the nasty, regurgitated morsels scattered around the edges of the plate or hidden under crumpled napkins had been, it wasn't the worst part of the job. It was the routine she couldn't stand.

Same customers. Same TV show. Same boyfriend. Same orgasm.

Next time she'd try something else: maybe an outdoor job at a park, or she could hawk peanuts at baseball games or collect payment for parking. Making change and meeting new people might be nice. Maybe working at a fancy hotel would be fun. The possibilities made Bree giddy, and she hummed along to the tune as she towel-dried her hair and waited for Ginny to return.

Wrapping herself in a robe she'd brought along, Bree remembered when she accidentally took it from a day spa one afternoon after a massage. Stealing it hadn't been her intention, but by the time she got home, it was too late. What could she do? That was back when she and Jerry first started dating. At dinner she'd laughed about it, telling him how it had conveniently found its way into her bag.

He lectured her about honesty and had advised her to return it first thing in the morning. The guy had zero sense of humor. He hadn't called yet, but that didn't surprise her. Knowing Jerry, he'd probably phoned his sponsor first, who then had the good sense to tell Jerry to chill out and allow his anger to subside before saying something he'd regret.

He is so predictable.

When she was angry, she let it out. Repression wasn't her style anymore, but on the flipside, she didn't hold grudges. "Get it out and move on" was her motto. Wanting to get it over with, she dialed Jerry's number. It went straight to voicemail, but before she could leave a message, the call-waiting signal beeped.

"Did you just call?" Jerry asked, out of breath.

"I was about to leave a message," said Bree, angry with herself for answering without checking the number first. She would have preferred the recorded version of Jerry.

"Where are you?" Jerry cried. "I was about to call the police."

"Without calling me first? A bit extreme, don't you think?" asked Bree.

"What am I supposed to think? You've been gone for days!"

"Maybe I needed a vacation." Bree paced around the room. Her path was limited between two beds, a table, an armoire, and three chairs.

"I thought to myself, *What kind of person abandons her customers? Maybe she's sick.* So I went to your apartment."

"What?" Now Bree was angry. How could she spend three straight months with a man who, in the end, didn't have the slightest idea who she was? "Are you stalking me?"

"I was worried."

"That's sweet of you, Jer . . ." Bree knew he hated the nickname, but she continued. "A friend needed my help."

"A man?" The question hovered in the air.

Bree hadn't considered the possibility Jerry might think

she'd run off with another man, and she allowed the awkward silence to continue a moment longer.

"I need a break."

"From us?" His voice was shaky, unsure of itself. She could hear a rustling sound on the other end, as if Jerry were fidgeting like usual. He liked to doodle on a pad of paper near the phone, drawing clouds and lightning bolts.

"From everything." Bree dug through her suitcase, searching for a favorite sweater.

"I understand the concept of space, Bree. I do. You might think I'm just a simpleton, but if you consider coming back to me, I was thinking you could move in with me. I know you're not into marriage or commitment." She imagined Jerry air-quoting the last word. "But maybe it's about time we settle down."

Is there a nice way of saying "not in a million years"? "Maybe," said Bree.

"It'll be terrific," he said, sounding an awful lot like a cheerleader. *Give me a T-E-R-R-I-F-I-C!*

"Love you?" he said, more like a question than a declaration.

Is he asking my permission? "See you soon."

She hung up before he had a chance to press the love idea any further.

Before fully submerging into that guilty feeling that had become as familiar to her as an old pair of flannel pajamas, she heard a recognizable song coming from the radio. Bree cranked it up loud enough that her singing blended seamlessly with the band's. "Don't Get Me Wrong," she belted, remembering how much she loved the Pretenders.

Jerry would be better off without her anyway, she told herself. Just as she was about to settle down with the idea, somebody pounded at the door.

She didn't answer. In her experience, unexpected guests spelled trouble. A disappointed lover wanting answers, a nosy neighbor asking questions, Mormons seeking wayward souls—the list of undesirables went on.

The knocking became frantic and unceasing.

"Hurry up! Let me in," said Ginny on the other side.

"Where's your key?" Bree asked, unlatching the lock. Ginny pushed her way past Bree, scurried to the window, and closed the curtain. She collapsed into one of the beds, burying her face beneath a pillow.

"You're scaring me," said Bree. "What's going on?" She sat on the bed's edge, nudging Ginny so she'd turn around.

"I, I can't talk about it," said Ginny, bursting into tears. If this were two years ago, if the woman in front of her was just a teenager and they were anywhere but Santa Fe, Bree still wouldn't know what to do. She had failed her own daughter—how was she supposed to help a total stranger?

Ginny seemed so helpless, and it was becoming more and more obvious to Bree that she didn't appreciate her own worth. Bree would give anything to be Ginny's age again, and even though she seemed foolish in many ways, Bree still liked this sad young woman sprawled out in front of her.

The last time Bree found herself in this position, perched over a sobbing girl, trying in vain to pry out information, it had been with Tori. Bree had finally gotten custody and had rented a house in Florida so they could be together.

She came home from a date around midnight to find her

daughter lying in bed, still in the dress she had been wearing for the school's winter formal.

"Where were you?" accused her daughter. "I needed you."

When Bree asked what happened, her daughter clammed up and refused to answer. She only glared at Bree. It was the beginning of the same cold look her daughter would come to perfect. She learned later that Tori and her date, an older boy, had had a fight—about what, Bree never found out. What Tori was sure to tell her, however, was that she'd been accepted into St. Andrew's, a private boarding school near her paternal grandparents and far away from the likes of her mother.

The dance had been a total disaster, which was no fault of Bree's. She had done everything to make her daughter's night special. When they shopped for a dress, Bree hadn't pushed the adorable electric blue one or the red suede number she saw hanging in the junior's section. Tori wanted to have the dour black dress more appropriate for a funeral than a winter formal. Bree wanted to please her daughter and bought her the dress anyway, even suggesting a sexy pair of rhinestone-studded heels to go with. Tori declined and opted for the pair of plain black ballerina flats.

Bree tried to play the part of the perfect, doting mother the night of the dance. Tori, her friends, and their dates had posed for pictures as Bree snapped away. They agreed to wait for the limousine at Bree's house because she was the cool mother. The one who didn't hassle them, who didn't search their purses for little bottles of booze, didn't question the boys when they disappeared for a while and returned with their eyes glazed over. She'd even given Tori money and told her to stay out as late as she wanted. "Lots of exciting things happen on these special nights," she told her daughter. Tori gladly accepted the cash but rolled her eyes at her mother's "inappropriateness," a word she'd use later against Bree.

"I wish my mom was like yours," one of Tori's friends had said.

"You don't know her," Tori had replied, unaware her mother was in the next room and could overhear every word. Bree had tried to swallow her hurt feelings and sent them off before getting ready for her own date.

Back at the hotel, Ginny rolled over, wiping her eyes. She tried to catch her breath in one of those stuttering, syncopated inhalations.

"I can't help if you don't tell me about it." Bree rubbed Ginny's shoulders.

"My purse, my money."

"Wait, what?" Bree stood up and moved their stuff around, lifting up clothes, searching under coats and pillows. "It's got to be here."

"No." Ginny blubbered into the pillow. "It was stolen. I was mugged."

Mugged. It took Bree a while to process the word, to comprehend its meaning and full effect. Like the time her apartment had been broken into in Santa Monica.

She saw Ginny shaking. "Look at me," Bree said, forcing Ginny to sit up. "Are you hurt?"

"I thought they were going to rape me, but I kept repeating to myself, *Don't let them take me from Place A to Place B.*"

"I saw that on TV too," said Bree. "But we should call the police."

"No." Ginny grabbed Bree's wrists and held them. "It doesn't matter. It's over."

"What do you mean, it doesn't matter? Of course it does." Bree released herself from Ginny's grip.

"Those creeps are long gone, and I'm not about to spend the entire night in a police station looking through books or whatever, trying to identify people I could barely see in the dark anyway."

"But the police can help," said Bree. "I dated this cop once, and he said the single worst thing a woman can do is not to report a crime. It perpetuates violence against women."

Ginny went into the bathroom and splashed cold water on her face. "I'm not interested in standing up for the entire female gender." Ginny dried her face with a hand towel and threw it to the floor. "It's over."

"What's over?" asked Bree, hanging the towel back up. "You keep saying that, but I don't know what it means."

"It means I'm broke. Busted. I have no money. The best I can do is ask my mother to wire me enough so I can go home."

"You can't do this," said Bree. "Fine, you're not going to call the police. You're going to let bad guys roam around Santa Fe in search of unsuspecting victims. I get it."

"I'm so tired." Ginny collapsed into one of the uncomfortable-looking desk chairs. "I can't . . . "

"You can," said Bree, sitting across from her. "If you don't call the police, that's your choice, but canceling this trip, this adventure, is not. I'm involved now." Bree thought about Jerry, her old job and bland apartment. "We have to move on."

"I appreciate what you're trying to do," said Ginny. "But I can't afford it anymore. I couldn't afford it before, but at least I had a credit card. That was something. Now I've got nothing."

"You can get a replacement card."

"Sure. Should I have it sent care of the Rolling Stones? We don't have any real address, remember?"

"What if I fronted you the money? You can pay me back later."

"No, I couldn't." Ginny shifted in her chair. "I'll take you home tomorrow morning, and when I get back, I'll send you the money for our room tonight."

"I've got the money," Bree blurted, knowing she couldn't reveal the information in any other way. "I have lots of money."

Ginny examined her, and Bree couldn't be sure what Ginny was thinking, but it probably had something to do with her recent job as a waitress.

"And you worked at the dumpy diner for kicks, right?"

"Kind of," said Bree. Now she was the uncomfortable one. Her financial status was a major detail she never revealed, even in her most serious relationships—the ones that lasted over six months.

"Even if that's the case, I can't take your money."

"Not *taking*," Bree reminded her. "Borrowing. You'll pay me back someday."

"This was my trip, my *fantasy*, as it turns out. I probably should have never gotten you involved in the first place." Ginny paused and seemed almost embarrassed. "It's just that you were a Wild and Spontaneous."

"A what?" Bree was amused. She'd been called a lot of things in her life, but that was the most flattering.

"Never mind," said Ginny. "The point is, I dragged you

into this mess, and now you're supposed to pay for it? I don't think so."

"I've got the money. It's just sitting there, collecting dividends or interest or whatever it does." Bree waved her hand in the air like it was all beyond her. In reality, she knew exactly where her money was invested and how much it was earning.

"I can't," said Ginny. "I wouldn't feel comfortable."

"Having the freedom to follow the Stones on the road is the opportunity of a lifetime. You can't let something as insignificant as money stop you."

"Easy for you to say."

"It is easy for me to say, because I was broke once too. I missed out on so much, and it wasn't the lack of money that stopped me." Bree thought about the time she had finally gotten ahold of Billy Blade's personal number and called him. She wanted to tell him that she was ready to follow him to the ends of the earth, just as she'd promised. When he answered, she hung up. "It was fear. I can't tell you how much regret I have."

Ginny hung her head. "I guess I know a little something about regret."

"You know the song 'Sarasota'?" Bree figured she'd have to lay it all out if she was going to convince Ginny to take a chance.

"'You said you'd follow me to the ends of the earth,'" Ginny whispered the lyrics. "'Now how far do I have to go for you to follow me?' I love that song. It's a classic."

"A classic? Am I that old?"

"Of course not!" said Ginny. "But I don't see what this has to do with anything."

"It's my song."

"Oh, like 'Angie' is *my* song?"

"What I mean to say is that it was written about me." Bree could tell Ginny wasn't buying it. This was the precise reason why she never told anyone about Billy Blade. "I met Billy in Sarasota, Florida. Before he was famous."

"No way! You and Billy Blade? For real?"

"Yup. That's the story."

"What happened? Why aren't you together? He was so gorgeous!"

"I guess he wasn't into excessive baggage like a woman with a crazy, jealous husband and a kid."

"So is that why you have so much money? I mean, do you get royalties for the song or something?"

"If only it were that glamorous," said Bree.

"I totally get it if you don't want to talk about it."

"My husband came from money. He was loaded. I didn't want any of it. I only asked for custody of my daughter." Bree paused and laughed a bit. "When he said 'over my dead body,' I guess he meant it."

"He died?"

"He was always throwing fits, trying to control me with his bad temper." She tried not to think about him anymore, but late at night, when she couldn't sleep, his memory haunted her and made her reach for the bottle of antacid she kept bedside. "While he was at work one afternoon, I guess you could say a miracle happened."

"He dropped dead," Ginny said. "It's like karma."

"Except my daughter blames me. She thinks her father died of heartache rather than a heart attack." Bree scrunched her hair again, a nervous habit she'd given up trying to shake. "Maybe I did kill him. Anyway, aren't you dying to see the Stones?" Bree dangled them in front of Ginny.

"Well," said Ginny.

"C'mon. Let's get all of this negativity behind us. Inhale," Ginny took a deep breath in. "Exhale and surrender." She blew out. "That's the spirit," said Bree. "You in?"

"I guess so," Ginny said. "But I'm paying you back. Every cent."

15

GINNY

Albuquerque, New Mexico: University Stadium

Ginny watched the Rolling Stones from the fifty-yard line. Relegated to viewing the concert on giant video screens beside and behind the stage, she felt too far from the action. The first time she saw the Stones in concert, this kind of seat had been good enough, but now it seemed more urgent that Ginny be nearer. She hated feeling removed from the band she had left her whole life behind to pursue, and she wanted to be close up so she could feed off their energy and get juiced up for the rest of the journey. Bree had been able to land a better location for herself and begged Ginny to accept the companion ticket. Refusing to indebt herself more to Bree unless it was absolutely necessary, she settled for her less than spectacular situation.

There was a huge difference in the types of fans farther from the stage. Mostly they sat through the songs, and someone behind her had the nerve to complain about Ginny blocking his view because she refused to sit down too. Some of them had even talked their way through songs like "You Got

Me Rocking," a fast rocker they probably hadn't recognized from *Voodoo Lounge*. When Keith took the microphone to sing "Happy" and "You Got the Silver," some of the so-called fans treated it like an intermission and went to the bathroom.

Trying to forget about the indifferent and uncommitted types, Ginny listened to the music. When an encore was imminent, everybody lit up their cell phones, including the bores sitting nearby. Mick came out in a fresh green silk shirt and sang "Brown Sugar."

The audience was up and dancing, even the annoying guy behind her. Ginny figured she wouldn't see Bree until after the concert, so she was shocked to see her working her way through the crowd. She was tiny enough to fit between them without anybody blowing a fuse, and she settled in the minuscule space between Ginny and her neighbor.

"You totally missed it," she said. "I was third row center. And . . . " She paused for effect. "I met Mick Jagger!"

Ginny's stomach twisted. "What do you mean, *met* him? How?" *That is totally unfair*, Ginny thought. It was bad enough that celebrities, regardless of their patronage or loyalty to the Stones, had complete access—but now Bree?

"Well, I didn't *meet* him, meet him. I sort of waved from the audience, but I swear he looked right at me. Don't worry," Bree assured her. "I've got a plan."

"I thought you hated making plans."

"Don't give me any lip right now," said Bree. "I know how we can get backstage." Ginny envisioned herself standing around with a bunch of groupies while they waited for their shot at Mick Jagger. She wasn't sure how she'd get his attention or what she might do with it, but she was willing to give it a try. Even though the music was what she had come for, she was still dying to meet Mick Jagger, the man who had practically shaped her whole life.

Once they made it off the field and outside the stadium, Ginny could hear "Jumpin' Jack Flash." Tonight, instead of opening with it like they had done in L.A., they closed the show with one of their most widely recognized songs, one that had been played on every tour since its release in 1968.

She wasn't sure what their mission was, since she'd heard during the fireworks that the Stones exit in separate town cars —in any color but white, and with tinted windows—dispersing as quickly as possible. Other backstage demands, she'd read, included a pool table, an executive toilet for band members' use only, and two smartly dressed hostesses with waitstaff experience.

"We'd better hurry up," said Ginny. Their only chance might be to intercept Mick on his way out. Next time, they'd have to get backstage *before* the concert. That's where the action was.

Bree grabbed Ginny's hand and picked up the pace. "Then c'mon, slow poke."

"Are you sure you know what you're doing?" Ginny followed Bree.

"This ain't my first rodeo, darlin'," Bree said in a phony Texas accent.

The music echoed across the near-empty parking lot. A few fans trickled out from the stadium in order to avoid the traffic. Bree and Ginny were running as fast as they could around the outside of the stadium in search of a mystical door that would lead them to the Stones.

"My ears are ringing," Ginny said, picturing all the over-fifty fans with cotton stuffed in their ears for protection. *I'm not about to become one of those.*

Bree stopped and leaned over, holding her side. "Wait. I'm dying here."

"How is that possible? Look at you. You're in great shape."

"Oh yeah, ever hear of the skinny obese?"

Ginny was a little out of breath herself. "We've gotta get to the gym more often."

"If I want to get all sweaty and out of breath, I'll have sex."

"Whatever works," said Ginny. Bree had a smart-ass answer for everything, and sometimes Ginny felt like she was still twelve years old, getting teased by her older brother.

"Look," said Bree. She pointed over to a group of people standing outside a door.

The chance had come. She couldn't believe that in a few minutes, she might be occupying the same airspace as Mick Jagger. The anticipation was overwhelming. What was he like in person? Would he be perfect, just like she'd imagined?

As soon as the song ended, the fireworks show began. Ginny knew they were running out of time.

"Do you smell something?" asked Bree. Ginny hoped she hadn't accidently let a little gas slip while running.

"It's not me." Bree lifted up her feet and checked the bottom of her shoes.

Ginny rotated her sneakers, only to find a stinky brown smudge. "Oh, shit!"

"Literally," said Bree. "You can't go in there like that."

"Oh, you don't think so?"

Bree laughed and ran behind a parked car. "I'm serious."

Ginny dragged her foot along the pavement. "Help me," she said.

"I'm not getting near you, smelly girl."

Ginny wanted to cry. "Mick Jagger's probably right on the other side of that door, and I smell like dog crap."

"We don't even know if it's from a dog," said Bree. "I'd say, from the looks of it, that's human."

"Very funny," said Ginny, partly worried Bree was right. There wasn't a dog to be seen for miles.

"Follow me." Bree came out from behind the car and moved a little closer to the group of people. There were about fifty of them, mostly women, standing around a closed door.

They stopped behind a small brick wall and squatted to keep out of sight. Ginny scraped her foot clean on the pavement, but the scent lingered. From the new purse Bree had insisted on buying Ginny, she pulled out a sample perfume vial she had also picked up in Santa Fe and dumped it on her shoes.

"Shhhh." Bree waved her hand at Ginny.

"What? I didn't say anything."

"But they can smell you."

Ginny raised her head up to take a look.

"They're all dressed up too. I'm not ready for this." In her meeting-Mick-Jagger fantasies, she was always wearing a killer new outfit, at her ideal weight, and never smelled like excrement.

A gorgeous young woman, size zero with boobs out to there, knocked on the door. When it opened, the rest of the crowd stood on their tippy toes to peek inside. A large man allowed the woman to pass through.

"I think there's a special code," said Ginny. "Did you hear it? Three knocks, then pause, then knock two more times."

"Don't be ridiculous." Bree stood up and marched to the door. "Just act like you know what you're doing."

"What do you mean?" Ginny ran after her.

"Do what I do. Flirt a little, and we're in like Flynn." Ginny was thinking she'd have to leave the flirting part to Bree when her phone rang.

"Not now," said Bree. She gave Ginny the stink eye. "We need some element of surprise."

"It's probably Ray again." He had started calling a few days ago, leaving long messages about turning over a new leaf and making other promises she knew he wouldn't keep. Ginny turned the ringer off, but she couldn't help wondering what Bree had meant by "element of surprise."

"You're going to have to deal with him sooner or later," said Bree. Ginny knew she couldn't put off the inevitable any longer. "But it's gotta be later."

The door opened again and Bree pushed her way to the front of the crowd, pulling Ginny with her. She would have rather lingered in the background and was embarrassed by Bree's assertiveness. Another key ingredient of the meet-her-favorite-celebrity fantasy was that she didn't have to beg for contact. Somehow the celebrity always found his way to her—at a party, or introduced by a mutual friend, or she was inexplicably famous too and at the Grammys or Academy Awards or VMAs—and she was actually cool enough to be in their presence.

"Hi there," Bree said to the bodyguard. "My friend and I would sure like to get inside."

"I can't let you in unless you have a pass." The man waved in another beautiful young woman.

"That girl didn't have one," said Ginny. She could feel her face flush like it used to when she was the second-to-last kid picked for the kickball team. Athlete she was not, but those tweens the bouncer was letting in didn't hold a candle to Ginny's sheer devotion.

"She's a friend," he said.

"Aren't we friends?" Bree must have seen that Ginny was ticked off and moved closer to the bouncer, blocking Ginny out while she picked up his hand, flipped it over and ran her finger along his palm. "You've got a long, exciting life ahead of you," she said. "You're cute too. I like a man with a clean-shaven head."

The other women leaned in to listen. Up close, Ginny could see that some of them were old enough to be her mother.

"Yeah, we're all friends," they yelled. Apparently they weren't going to let Bree get away with whatever she was trying to pull.

"Let us in," another one said.

"If they go, we go," someone else shouted. A mini riot was about to break out, and the man seemed a little scared. He probably wasn't sure how he'd handle a bunch of ticked-off middle-aged women.

"I tell you what," said the doorman. "I'll let these two in." He gestured toward Bree and Ginny. "And maybe they'll come back for the rest of you." Bree winked at Ginny, and the bouncer stepped aside. *Hallelujah.* Ginny would have cried out loud had she not been telling herself over and over again to play it cool. Her mouth went dry instead.

"Step aside," someone shouted from the crowd as they started to rush the door. "Wait," another one yelled. "They're leaving. The Stones are leaving!" Everybody went silent. As stealthily as sharks, four gray town cars glided past them, through the parking lot, and onto the highway. Then they disappeared into the dark night.

16

GINNY

Ginny closed the hotel room door, gripping the handle so it wouldn't slam shut. The empty pizza box and bottle of wine were still in the hallway, and she pushed them to the side, careful not to wake her roommate.

Trying to come to terms with her failed marriage, she was having a hard time sleeping and wondered if she shared some of the blame, as Ray had suggested the day Ginny found out about the affair. She couldn't be responsible for his actions, but she felt like a loser anyway, the same one percent off from the norm that she'd always been.

It had been a long time since Ginny had a sleepover with a girlfriend. Her high-school friends had gone away to college, and the rest of her relationships with women faded after she got married. Now she had no friends, period. This fact had hit home a few months ago, when she'd been thinking about her upcoming birthday party but had scrapped the idea when she envisioned the attendees: Ray, her mother, and Benz, wearing party hats and gathered around a cake with twenty-three candles ablaze. *Hell, no!*

With the morning paper, Ginny headed to the dining room. At least she wouldn't owe Bree for the free breakfast. Besides Bree's restlessness and occasional mumbling, another thing that kept Ginny awake the night before was anxiety about her lack of funds. Still uncomfortable about letting Bree pay for everything, Ginny snagged a stack of hotel stationary pads to keep track of her expenses. She'd pay back everything. She was determined not to depend on other people for the rest of her life. The trip was about seeking freedom, but once again, she found herself in debt.

All alone at eight in the morning, Ginny sat at a small table overlooking a garden. The sun was shining, but Ginny knew it was cold outside. She had been fooled enough times by the desert climate to realize that although the sky was clear and bright, it could be bone-chillingly cold on a fall morning. Yet it was serene, and she had time to think about their next move.

She pulled the concert schedule from her pocket and smoothed down the tattered corners. In a few days, the Rolling Stones would be in Oklahoma City. If they left soon, they'd make it with ease. These plans comforted her. She valued having something to look forward to.

After reading her daily Aquarius horoscope (*You are practical, realistic and stable in your feelings*), Ginny located her second-favorite part of the paper, the entertainment section. There was an advertisement for the latest Rolling Stones concert film. She knew it was a sign she was doing the right thing, even if she had to live on borrowed money. She hadn't seen the movie yet because she had wanted to go to a theater in downtown Los Angeles with Ray. Fat chance he would've agreed to that.

She thought about making her own Stones movie. If she were filming their concert, what would she do? Someone who understands the Stones, who really gets it, knows a Rolling Stones concert is where polish meets soul. As professional as the Stones were, as slick as their performances might be, and as many times as Mick sang the same line or Keith played that same riff, it felt like they were doing it for the first time. Mick was always jumping around, doing his funny little chicken walk with his hands on his hips, posing with all his attitude, like he was the one who put the *raucous* in *rock and roll.* Keith, meanwhile, closed his eyes and threw his head back and laughed, as if he were hitting the most perfect note of his entire career.

The filmmaker who could capture that complexity and contradiction, thought Ginny, would succeed. The Stones were still raw and could still rock. Maybe they could do it blindfolded, but every time they played "Brown Sugar" or "Sympathy for the Devil," and as many times as the fans had heard them do it, the show still felt fresh and magical.

♪

"ARE YOU SURE YOU WANT TO LEAVE?" ASKED BREE, buckling herself into the passenger seat. "We didn't get to shop or go out to dinner. What a drag!"

"I'm sorry," said Ginny. Why did it seem like she was always apologizing? "There's a movie theater in Oklahoma City, and since we have some time before the next concert, I figured we could see the latest Stones documentary."

"It's all Stones, all the time." Bree yawned. "Get me to the nearest Starbucks."

"The movie is supposed to be awesome. Everybody's talking about it."

"Like who?"

"Like everybody," said Ginny. She turned the ignition and reached underneath her seat.

"Got it." Her license and registration were bundled together neatly with a rubber band alongside her cell phone. After the robbery in Santa Fe, they were the only three things she could call her own. "Ray always bugged me about not keeping this stuff in my purse. Who's the irresponsible one now, jackass?"

"That's good," said Bree. "I can't do *all* the driving. Besides, someone needs to give Orchid a little attention." She clutched the plant to her chest. More buds had opened, and another was on its way. "I still don't know why you want to go to the movies when seeing them live is so much better."

"It's supposed to be incredible."

"Says who? The *I-don't-have-a-life* fans on the Internet?"

Ginny let the statement hover for a moment as she hazarded how to handle it. It was a loaded question, perhaps even a thinly veiled insult.

The Volvo eased onto the highway. Ginny tried not to sound too concerned, too needy, but she had to know. "Do you think I have no life?"

"You're with me, aren't you?"

"Yeah," said Ginny.

"Then yes, you don't have a life." Bree folded the pillow she had lifted from the hotel, wedging it between her and the window, and closed her eyes. "But I'm not going to any damn movie."

♪

ALL GINNY HAD TO DO WAS STAY ON INTERSTATE 40 TO Oklahoma City. An easy drive, she figured. What she hadn't planned for were the stretches and stretches of land and highway. She wasn't used to being out on the road, the only car for miles around. Growing up near a major metropolis had left her unprepared for the desolation of open territory. Miles and miles of dirt, rocks, and hills stretched out before them. The dry terrain reminded Ginny of driving to Las Vegas times a thousand. The landscape seemed to continue forever without a soul in sight. She grabbed the straw from her soda and chewed on it to stay awake.

Bree wasn't much help, slumped down in her seat the whole way through Albuquerque. Even though Bree failed to understand direction, had the map turned the wrong way most of the time, and was generally a lousy copilot, Ginny envied her. In her pink cropped jacket and matching scarf and bright red hair, she was a shiny piece of cinnamon candy. A Hot Tamale that burned Ginny's mouth, but she had found herself addicted despite the pain, chewing and swallowing until she emptied the box.

Wearing blue jeans and a plain white T-shirt, Ginny examined her own look. If she were a type of candy, she'd be a Milk Dud. Chewy, sweet, and loved by all, Ginny was dependable. Just as the *Cosmo* quiz had pegged her from the beginning.

When they approached Amarillo, the traffic started to pick up, and the onslaught of cars freaked Ginny out. She found herself in the fast lane going fifty miles an hour. A line of cars formed behind her, and she cranked her steering wheel to the right, cutting off a car in the next lane. Then she was riding the tail of the car in front of her.

She was out of whack, but before she could get it together, she saw flashing lights in her rearview mirror. "Shit, a cop."

"What'd ya expect? He probably thinks you're drunk."

"What do I do?" Ginny put on her turn signal, unsure of whether she should exit the freeway or pull over to the side.

"Whatever you do, don't let him give you a ticket."

Ginny eased the car to the side of the road. "I guess I was kind of driving like an idiot."

"Maybe you were." Bree became quiet and serious, as if it were a matter of life or death. "Maybe you weren't." Ginny didn't understand Bree's coded language.

"What I'm saying is," said Bree, "don't admit to anything. I told you about the police officer I dated, right?" She straightened up in her seat. "Anyway, when the cop asks you if you know why he pulled you over, say no. Otherwise, your admission is as good as a confession."

"Should I cry?" Ginny glanced in her side mirror to see the police officer getting out of his car.

"Hell, no," said Bree. "Crying's for amateurs."

"What, then?"

"Flirt with him."

"But he's a cop," said Ginny.

"He's still a man, isn't he?" Bree fluffed her hair and checked her makeup in the rearview mirror. "He's coming. Now don't be so uptight. Relax. Smile—laugh, even. And if you can, touch him."

"Touch him?" *What do I have to touch to get out of this ticket?*

The cop was at her window. "Do you know why I pulled you over?"

Ginny forced a smile and said, "Why, no, officer, I have no idea." She batted her eyes several times. It seemed to work in the movies.

"You were driving kind of erratically back there." She threw her head back, opened her mouth wide, and gave the best flirtatious movie laugh she could. "Did I break the law or something?"

The cop didn't seem to find anything amusing about the situation. "License and registration, please."

Ginny handed the cop her identification, knowing it was the crucial moment. She had to touch him. The arm, the hand, where should her wandering fingers go? If she casually brushed him below the belt when handing him her information, would it kill her? No, she couldn't do it, she finally decided. *Just like a Milk Dud,* a little voice said inside her head.

Bree would do it, she told herself as she attempted to feel up a middle-aged police officer.

"Ma'am." The cop stepped back from the car and Ginny's naughty hand. "Please step out of the vehicle."

♪

GINNY PASSED THE SOBRIETY TEST WITH FLYING COLORS and, after a long and extremely embarrassing lecture on sexual harassment and bribing a police officer, got back into the car, traffic ticket in hand.

"What was that?" asked Bree.

"You said to touch him. You didn't say where."

"I meant on the hand or the arm! Are you crazy?"

"I'm with you, aren't I?" asked Ginny.

"What's that supposed to mean?"

"Yes, I am crazy."

"Maybe so," said Bree. "But I would have gotten out of the ticket."

17

BREE

I'll pull up next to their car, and you point toward the exit," Bree said as she tried to get around the pickup truck in front of them and next to the two guys she was following. "Let them know we're getting off the freeway."

"I don't think so." Ginny shook her head back and forth, completely unwilling to cooperate. "They're holding a reservation for us at the hotel."

Bree continued to follow the car anyway, so Ginny put on a baseball cap and shades like she was a movie star hiding out from the paparazzi.

"I think it's a great idea. I'm bored." Bree blurted out the words without caring whether Ginny would feel rejected by them. She was so sensitive, a hurt little puppy, terrified if Bree even hinted at disapproval. She'd have to figure out a way to teach Ginny not to care so much about what other people thought, if such a lesson could be taught. Maybe self-consciousness faded on its own with time, one benefit of getting older.

"I'll take the driver," Bree said, turning on the car blinker. "I think he's the more *mature* of the two."

"Take them both," said Ginny. She put her feet on the dashboard.

Somewhere between New Mexico and Oklahoma City, Bree decided Ginny needed to loosen up and have some fun. She was taking the whole Stones mission a little too seriously, mapping out every step of their trip from Oklahoma across the rest of North America. Relying on anybody for happiness, including Mick Jagger, would only lead to disappointment. Bree was ready to implement her tough-love strategy.

While driving, Bree searched for attractive men they could flirt with. There were lots of guys out there for both of them, and she couldn't wait to put the memory of Jerry behind her. He had been especially clingy, and she wasn't shaking the guilt easily.

"I'm done with guys," said Ginny. "I don't even want to tell you what happened to me in Arizona."

"Arizona?" Bree hadn't considered Ginny had done any-thing more than drive straight through from Los Angeles.

"I had too much to drink one night," said Ginny. "The night before I met you."

"I thought you looked hung over."

"This guy I met at a bar kept ordering tequila shots, and the next thing I know, I invited him to my room."

"You?" asked Bree. "Little Miss Uptight?" It had become clear that Ginny had absolutely no experience with men aside from her husband. She couldn't believe they were talking about the same woman who had just tried to get out of a traffic violation by pawing a highway patrol man. He should've arrested her for assault instead of letting her go with a ticket.

"I threw up on him."

"I'll bet you left quite an impression," said Bree. What could she expect from a woman whose sum sexual experience included two high school boyfriends and one louse of a husband? Ray sounded like a real winner, the kind of man she abhorred. An ignorant buffoon too insecure to let his wife blossom into the woman she thought Ginny could be. After the groping incident with the police officer, Bree had taken over the wheel. They were just a few hours outside of Oklahoma City when Bree spotted two men trying to get Ginny's attention. Clueless as usual, Ginny picked her cuticles and didn't notice the car trying to stay neck and neck with them. When they finally honked to get Ginny's attention, she pulled the visor down and moved it in front of her window to block them out, chatting on about nothing important—the weather and the landscape or something equally monotonous.

Bree was trying to get Ginny to open up, but Ginny kept avoiding serious subjects, like the fact that she was running from her husband and hadn't called anyone to let them know she was safe. Not that Bree was one to criticize. She didn't need the past dragging her down either.

"Anyway, if you're so bored," said Ginny, her voice wavering between an offended whimper and genuine anger, "I can drop you at the airport."

It was the first time she had seemed to really annoy Ginny, and although Bree was no stranger to provoking anger, she tried to backpedal. "You know what I mean." She tried to punch Ginny in the arm, but she moved out of the way. "I could use the distraction."

"I'm not hooking up with total strangers."

"It might be fun," Bree said, trying to entice Ginny. Bree

felt like she was riding alongside her teenage daughter, who was always judging and sighing at her ridiculous attempts to lift the girl's constant sour mood.

"It might be disgusting. We don't even know what they look like up close. Even worse, it could be dangerous."

"There they are," said Bree, stepping on the gas pedal to catch up. "Flash them or something."

Ginny crossed her arms over her chest. "You flash them."

"I'm driving. Besides, we don't want to scare them away."

"That's exactly what I'd like to do. They're probably creeps."

"It's two guys with Oregon plates. How dangerous can they be?"

"Plenty. Ever hear stories about serial killers? They're all mild-mannered and charming until they're decapitating bodies."

"I have pepper spray in my purse," said Bree. "But I'm sure they're harmless. Look at them. They're a couple of hippies."

"A lot of good pepper spray will do us when we're locked in a dank basement, gasping for air."

Bree pulled up next to the car and waved. "What did I tell you? They look nice, kind of cute in an outdoorsy way." The guys laughed, waving back.

"I never understood the whole flashing thing anyway," said Ginny, giving a superficial smile to the guys. "I mean, what do I get out of it?"

"A sense of power, I suppose."

"Yeah, well, it's stupid. I don't want that kind of attention."

"Don't take it for granted." It's easy to dismiss what comes so freely, thought Bree. Men used to practically twist their heads off to get a look at her as she passed by. She could go to any store or restaurant and never have to ask for help. The men would magically appear in front of her, always at her service. Now, in her thirties, she felt as though the attention paid to her was spotty, that her magnetism faded in and out like a weak cell-phone signal. Sometimes she felt practically invisible.

"I want a man to like me for who I am, not how I look." Ginny took off her hat and went into full primp mode, brushing her hair and applying lip gloss.

"You're a hypocrite," said Bree. The guys' car started to merge over to the exit lane. Bree saw them look back to see if they were being followed.

"Look who's talking," said Ginny.

"What's that supposed to mean?" Bree catalogued the time she and Ginny had spent together, searching for any inconsistencies. Hadn't she always been up front? Wasn't she the model of doing and saying exactly what she meant?

"Never mind," said Ginny.

"You claim you want a man to like you regardless of your looks, but only a minute ago you said you didn't want to hook up with those guys because they might be too ugly."

"It doesn't matter anyway. Say goodbye to your distraction." Ginny waved the exiting car away.

Bree cranked the Volvo to the right and followed them off the freeway. She was no hypocrite. She had said she was looking for some fun, and damn it, she was going to get it.

"We don't have time," Ginny yelled.

"Don't be so uptight."

"I hate that you think I'm uptight."

"Then don't be."

Ginny threw up her arms. "If those two dudes get any sick ideas, I'm gonna pepper-spray the bunch of you."

"Including me?" said Bree, laughing. Nobody was going to get her goat. For the last decade, she had become a survivor, and that entailed a certain amount of concealment. The last time she'd expressed sadness and vulnerability, the world had taken a big dump all over her. She wouldn't let that happen again.

"*Especially* you," said Ginny.

The men pulled into a truck stop, and Bree followed them, making sure to stay a few cars back. She parked strategically in the lot in front of the market so they could watch the guys fill up on gas without being spotted. Ginny wasn't the only one afraid of unpleasant surprises. Bree wasn't about to make nice with a creeper.

"I hope you're happy." Ginny crossed her arms and legs, practically tucking her body inside of itself. "And I'm not uptight."

"You're so uptight, you couldn't stick a tenpenny nail up your—"

"Is that necessary?" Ginny interrupted, and Bree thought she saw tears forming in her eyes.

"I don't understand," Ginny continued. "Weren't we having a good time? Just the three of us?" She clutched Orchid.

"It's still just us," said Bree. How could she explain that her guidance wasn't an act of betrayal? Bree just wanted to nudge Ginny along the path to her own sense of fulfillment. It seemed as if Ginny, like so many women Bree had met along the way, had been brainwashed to believe that only so much was possible and that women were meant to accommodate the desires of others, taking nothing for themselves. Bree's own mother had forfeited her dream of going to New York to become an actress in order to support her husband's career.

She wanted to grab these self-sacrificing women by the shoulders and shake them. *Your time on the planet is limited,* she wanted to say. *Have fun, follow your dreams, and experience a meaningful life.*

"I'm only trying to help," Bree said.

"This is helping?" Ginny yelled. "Stalking two guys?"

"Not stalking." Bree couldn't stand Ginny's loaded language.

"Let's say they're hot. Then what? Are we going to mess around in the bathroom? Hey, better yet, I hear these places have showers. Maybe we can do it in there."

"You're completely misunderstanding me. It's for your own good."

"I think it's pretty twisted. No wonder your daughter—"

"You toss and turn every night in bed." She cut Ginny off, unable to bear what she might say next. It wasn't as if she could know what had happened between Bree and Tori, but she had obviously been speculating for a while. Bree thought about what she might have revealed so far, and she was furious a verdict might have been reached without her testimony.

She didn't feel the need to explain everything, like the fact that Dimmit hadn't changed his will before he died, so Bree had inherited the house, his business, and his hefty trust fund. Right up until the end, he must have thought she was coming back to him. She had sold everything, haunted by the memory of her previous life, and had moved back to Florida, renting a house to share with Tori. By then it had been too late to win her daughter's love back. Tori believed all the lies her father had told her about Bree: she was unreliable, more interested in chasing men and avoiding responsibility than providing a stable home for her daughter. Tori left for boarding school, arguing that she needed to attend the prestigious St. Andrew's in order to get into a good university. But Bree knew the truth. She had failed as a mother.

Now she tried to take a nurturing tone with Ginny. "You have the weight of the whole world on your shoulders. You need to get some closure. Time to move on."

"I *just* left my husband. Sorry if I'm too slow forgetting about people and leaving them behind. You seem to be good at it. I guess you can teach me a few things about abandonment."

Bree felt a heavy pounding in her chest and panicked. Unlatching the seat belt, she threw it off. The metal buckle hit the window and made a clanging sound. They both jumped. The door was locked, and she searched for the button to release her from the confinement. She needed space.

She closed the car door behind her, leaving Ginny inside. The keys were still in the ignition, and Bree heard the unmistakable sound of the door locks clicking shut. Ginny smirked and pointed toward the guys they had been chasing.

They seemed to be looking around for someone, but when they apparently didn't see them, they opened their back doors. Two small children emerged, rubbing their eyes as if they had been sleeping while their fathers flirted with two strange women.

Married men were the worst offenders. She'd seen it a million times, committed men lulling women into friendships as genuine as their hairpieces. Once the unsuspecting victim felt comfortable, like she could be herself, out came the jerk with some lame pickup line. One time a married man had told her he was never going to leave his wife, but he'd love to *pursue* a relationship with her anyway, as if his honesty could earn him an all-access pass into her bedroom.

She wasn't surprised, but she imagined Ginny was particularly insulted because of her own recent breakup.

Ginny laughed at Bree, locked out of the car and banished like a criminal. Bree recalled the time she'd smacked Tori right across the face when she'd mouthed off in the middle of a department store in front of the cosmetics lady. They had both been embarrassed and hadn't spoken for weeks afterward.

Bree saw something familiar in Ginny's eyes. She'd been hurt too. Unhappy about her friend's condemnation, she was taking sweet revenge. For a moment, Bree could almost hear her daughter calling out to her, telling her mother to stop the teasing. It took a moment for her to catch her breath.

The only thing she could do was play it off, be the pretender she'd been accused of being her whole life. People believed Bree was callous out of selfishness. *It was ironic*, Bree thought. She'd only ever wanted to protect everybody else.

She shrugged her shoulders and laughed. Knocking on the window, she said to Ginny, "I'm going to the store. Want anything?"

♪

IN THE TRUCK STOP'S CONVENIENCE STORE, BREE'S EYES adjusted from the sun to the fluorescent lights. The store was packed with a variety of road warriors, from the northern snowbirds making their way to the desert to the truckers waiting for a shower or grabbing a hot cup of coffee. Rows and rows of candy and potato chips lined the aisles, and Bree searched for something to snack on. Not that she was hungry. Still reeling from Ginny's verbal punch in the stomach, Bree felt more like taking an antacid than eating.

After grabbing a couple of bottles of water, she located the fresh-produce section. Her selections included a withered orange, a bunch of green bananas, a fruit cup that included several maraschino cherries, or a red apple. She examined the apple. It wouldn't have been her first choice—she preferred Gala and Fuji apples and found the dark red ones on the mealy side—but it was free of dents and bruises, so she dropped it into her basket.

Behind her was a display of beef jerky taking up the entire end cap to one of the aisles. Ginny would be in hog heaven. Plastic bins were stacked on top of one another. Bree wasn't sure what to buy, dried beef that had been peppered or soaked in teriyaki or jalapeno sauce. Some were sold as thin strips, others as fat, beefy sticks. After debating for what seemed like an absurdly long time, she filled a brown paper bag with turkey jerky.

On the way to the register, she walked through an aisle that could only be categorized as miscellaneous. The shelves were lined with fleece blankets, coffee mugs with the truck stop's logo, cup holders, ankle wallets, and snow globes. On the bottom row, just below the hanging wind chimes, Bree spotted a collection of garden stakes, small enough for plants like Orchid. With all the new buds opening, she had been drooping a bit; a green metal plant stake with a seashell on the top that read "This Is Where I Bloom" was just what she needed.

Bree was in line to pay when she felt somebody bump into the back of her knees. They buckled, and she was about to turn around to slug the person when she saw Ginny smiling at her.

"Hey," she said.

"Hey, yourself."

"Guess what I did," said Ginny. "I walked right up to those jerks and asked if they were looking for a little action."

"In front of their brats?"

"Damn straight."

"Ha! Good for you." Bree couldn't have been more proud. Maybe she shouldn't hang up her mentor cap after all. "What did they do?"

"Acted like I was crazy or something. Told their kids to get in the car and drove away, practically mowing down a little old lady crossing the street."

Bree was about show Ginny the turkey jerky when "You Can't Always Get What You Want" came on the radio.

"Shhh," Ginny said, looking up to the ceiling, as if she were searching for the source. "This song's from *Let It Bleed*. Did you know the original cover art was designed by a friend of Keith Richards, and it recently sold at auction for fifty thousand dollars?"

"I had no idea," said Bree, trying hard not to reveal her indifference. There'd been enough tension for one day. "Let's take off."

"Fine by me," said Ginny. "But I'm driving now."

THE
ROLLING STONES

Oklahoma City

18

GINNY

The lounge at the Oklahoma City hotel was more Ginny's style than the stuffy resort back in Santa Fe. The lobby was bright and funky; the blonde furniture, upholstered in primary colors, reminded her of the upbeat modern motif she had suggested to Ray when she'd been thinking of redecorating. He said as long as he didn't have to pay for it, he didn't care what "mo-fuckin'-tif" she wanted.

Ginny plopped onto a red sofa and picked up a purple throw pillow, hugging it tightly.

"Want a margarita?" Bree asked from her yellow velvety armchair. She picked up the bar menu. "With chips and guacamole?"

At the mere mention of the drink, Ginny smelled the tequila and broke out into a sweat, remembering what a fool she'd made of herself with Stephen back in Arizona. *All that boozing and sex with a stranger!* She was ashamed to admit it, but she had always wanted to experience a little irresponsible fun, envious of her friends who went off to college and emailed Ginny about their nights of debauchery. Even though

Ginny didn't quite follow through with Stephen, she had outranked her friends. She was the worst kind of sinner, a married woman picking up a stranger at a bar.

"Hey, where'd you go?" asked Bree, snapping her fingers in front of Ginny's face.

"I'm fine." Ginny plastered on a phony smile. "Just not in the mood for a margarita."

"It's a free country. Pick your own." She handed Ginny the menu.

The logical part of Ginny realized she needed to get over the waves of guilt that kept creeping up on her. It wasn't like she owed Ray anything, but she couldn't help feeling like sooner or later, she'd have to deal with him. Earlier that afternoon, Ginny had talked to Virginia, who said Ray was falling apart. He called her almost every night, inviting himself over for dinner and peppering her with questions about Ginny's whereabouts. Virginia said she could only lie for so long and admitted feeling sorry for the "old deadbeat."

Ginny wanted to be like Bree. Smiling and happy, she seemed perfectly comfortable sitting in a strange hotel bar awaiting her next adventure. Tired of being the buzzkill and swearing off fun—and men—for all time, Ginny hoped tonight would be a new beginning. A favorite teacher from her brief time in community college liked quoting new-age gurus. "The point of power is in the present moment," Ginny remembered him saying. She was ready to release the past.

"I don't know," said Ginny, reading the menu.

"What do ya feel like?" asked Bree.

Ginny hesitated. It was all too expensive. The amount she owed Bree was adding up. "Champagne?"

"Hey, champagne." Bree's eyes wandered off as if she were remembering an evening filled with the bubbly and, undoubtedly, a man to go with it. "That's a great idea." Bree got the waitress's attention and pointed out a bottle. "And bring four glasses."

Ginny didn't need to ask about the extra glasses. "Always be prepared."

"There's my little scout." Bree winked. Ginny scanned the room and saw nothing but a bunch of balding, overweight men and recoiled at the idea of toasting with any one of them.

After showing Bree the bottle, the waitress uncorked it and filled the glasses. Bree lifted hers. "Cheers."

"To new beginnings."

"To the Rolling Stones," said Bree.

"To Mick Jagger," Ginny added, taking a sip. Bree smirked but didn't drink to Ginny's final toast. *I've gone too far again. Toasting to the Stones was good enough, but drinking to Mick Jagger was too much*, thought Ginny. Insecurity crept over her again. She was trying to come up with a way to break the awkward silence, when a man approached, large in both height and girth.

"Let me guess." He pointed to Ginny's Stones T-shirt. "You're here for the actuary convention." Ginny was confused. *What on earth is an actuary?*

"Amway?" he continued. Bree laughed, pouring him a glass of *their* champagne. "Only one more guess before I give away your glass of champagne to that guy over there." She pointed to an old guy in a plaid dress shirt.

He closed his eyes and buried his head into his hands. "I've got it! Rolling Stones groupies."

Groupies? Ginny hated the word. Her love for Mick went deeper than sexual fantasies. The Rolling Stones and their music represented all that was right in her world, and she didn't appreciate people belittling her enthusiasm.

"Is that your final answer?" said Bree.

"Final answer," he said, placing his hands together and closing his eyes like he was praying for the big win.

Bree handed him his championship glass of champagne.

He plopped down next to Ginny on the sofa. The cushion sank, trying to accommodate his largeness, and Ginny found herself holding onto the arm so she wouldn't slide any closer to him than she had to. She wanted to yell out *no deal, no deal,* but that was a different game show entirely.

"I'm Rocky," he said.

"What a fabulous name," said Bree, changing the pitch of her voice so it was sort of high—flirtatious and helpless-sounding all at the same time. "I'm Bree." She offered her hand, and he kissed it. "And this is Ginny."

Ginny nodded hello. Rocky was getting on her nerves, intruding on their girl time. But she didn't want to be obviously impolite, something her mother would do if she found a person undesirable.

"So, what do you do?" asked Ginny, trying to fake interest. Ray once told her it was a rude question to ask—probably because he was always out of work.

"I make people laugh."

Was he kidding? Ginny wanted Rocky to go away, while Bree seemed to be taken in by him.

"I know what you mean," said Bree. "People are laughing at me *all* the time."

"At least I try to." Rocky stretched his arm out so his hand brushed Ginny's sleeve, a total high school move, she thought.

"I was on cable last month." Rocky seemed to be waiting for a moment of recognition. There wasn't one, and Ginny felt sorry for him. He'd picked the wrong pair to try to impress—Ginny couldn't afford the premium channels, and Bree would never commit to anything that required a contract.

"Ohhhh," said Bree. "You're a comedian. I love that!"

Rocky pulled his arm away from Ginny. He had clearly found his audience, and she was relieved to be free of his attention.

"I'm on tour right now. I'm a huge Stones fan, so I try to coordinate with their schedule."

"See," Bree leaned over and poked Ginny's arm. "You're not the only one."

One what? wondered Ginny. *Fanatic, weirdo, loser?* Her insecurities were relentless tonight.

"She's right," said Rocky. "You see that guy over there?" He pointed to a skinny old man wearing a tie-dye shirt. "That's Jonny. He goes on every tour to every state. The guy doesn't miss a gig."

"That's some serious dedication," said Bree.

"If you start a conversation with him, it'll only be minutes before he whips out old pictures of himself. He used to look exactly like Ronnie Wood."

"I don't see any resemblance," said Ginny. In her opinion, he looked like a scarecrow, skinny and disheveled. "And is he wearing a wig?"

"It's not easy getting old. Not that I would know," said Bree, clearly fishing for a compliment.

"What? You?" said Rocky. "I thought you two were sisters."

Bree beamed at his praise. Rocky had said the right thing, and they seemed to be getting pretty cozy, finishing off Ginny's celebratory champagne. "Is he rich?" asked Ginny. Her little notepad, tabulating the costs of their adventure, was filling up.

"Nah. Let's just say if you need something a little stronger than champagne, Jonny's your guy."

"I'll keep it in mind," said Bree.

"Is that right?" asked Ginny.

"Just in case," said Bree. "I like to keep my options open." Ginny could tell Bree was buzzed by the way her eyes got shiny. Rocky was probably stupid enough to think she was getting all starry-eyed over him. He patted the empty space between Ginny and him, and Bree squeezed herself in. Rocky whispered something to her, and they laughed hysterically. To Ginny, Rocky didn't seem funny. In fact, for a comedian, he was rather serious and dull.

A lone attractive man had taken a seat next to Jonny. *Poor guy*, Ginny thought, and within seconds, out came Jonny's wallet, the pics tumbling down, a pathetic showcase of what once was.

The new guy must have caught Ginny checking him out, because he widened his eyes at her as if to say, "Save me from this crazy person."

It didn't take long for Bree to catch on, and she called the waitress back over. "Here," she said, filling up the last empty champagne glass. "Take this over to the gentleman sitting at the bar."

"Wait a minute." Ginny tried to stop the conspiracy.

"He's dying over there, and he's cute," said Bree. She was right about that. He looked like a model, but one of those slightly older guys, the kind she'd seen in weekly circulars. Men who wore sweaters draped around their shoulders and had their shirts tucked in all yuppie-like. That's what Ray used to say when she slid the newspaper inserts in front of him, hoping he'd take the hint. The guy at the bar looked like Harrison Ford, slightly past the *Indiana Jones* era, and he was on his way over.

"Thank you for this," he said, raising the glass to them, "and for rescuing me. Interesting guy, but..." He sat down. "I think he might be wearing a wig."

"I think so too," said Ginny, and she giggled in the most ridiculous way. She couldn't help but feel like a nerdy freshman girl sitting next to the hot high school quarterback.

"Craig Mitchum." He shook Bree's and Rocky's hands.

Ginny's palms were sweating, and she wiped one off before offering her hand. *Be cool*, she told herself. She was flustered, without a cohesive thought in her head.

"Are you here to see the Stones too?" *What a moron! Could I think of a less interesting thing to say?*

"No, I'm doing consulting work for the hotel."

"Oh yeah?" asked Bree, managing to pull herself from the private little world of Rocky the Comedian.

"It's boring stuff."

"Sounds fascinating," said Ginny. *Great, way to blow it,* she thought. *As soon as a guy thinks a woman's interested, he's as good as gone.*

"I travel around the country to different hotels and train

managers, customer service employees, that sort of thing. Basically, I help companies figure out how to make people happy."

"Hey," said Bree, poking Rocky in the ribs. "That's what you do. Travel around and make people happy."

"Oh, yeah?" asked Craig.

"He's a comedian," said Ginny.

"Wait a minute," said Craig. "Were you on TV last month? I thought you looked familiar."

"Finally!" Rocky flashed a cheesy, show-biz smile, and Ginny imagined that his headshot captured the same look. Bree stood up and grabbed Rocky's hand. "Let's check out the pool."

"But it's dark out," said Ginny.

"Exactly." Bree winked.

Ginny panicked. "Wait." She wasn't ready to fly solo yet. "I don't have a key to the room," she stammered.

"Check your back pocket. I saw you put it there. See ya," said Bree as she galloped out of the bar, Rocky chasing close behind.

"So," Ginny sat back down. "Where are you going next?" *A reasonable way to start a conversation*, she thought.

"I've got some time off. Maybe I'll go home for a while."

"Where's home?" she asked, wondering what the difference was between sounding interested and prying. She crossed her arms over her chest, then uncrossed them, remembering an article she read about body language. She didn't want to send the message that she was closed for business.

"I have a little house on the beach in South Carolina. I try to get back there at least once every few months."

Brain, don't fail me now, thought Ginny. *Don't let my mouth say something stupid.* "I guess your job keeps you on the road a lot."

"It does. But what about you?" He moved closer to her. "Are you here for the Rolling Stones concert tomorrow night?"

"Yeah." She sounded like a dorky kid, and she was probably blushing.

"Do you live in Oklahoma?"

"Just passing through." Ginny had been afraid this was going to come up. How could she explain her situation without sounding like a flake?

Craig seemed intrigued, and for the first time Ginny noticed the cleft in his chin.

"It's kind of stupid." She was melting, becoming putty in his hands.

"Pretty and stupid. My favorite combination."

"Pretty?" Ginny asked, trying not to dwell on the fact that he may have just called her stupid.

"The most beautiful woman in the room."

"If this were any other room, I'd be flattered."

"I suppose some Stones fans aren't what they used to be," he said.

"Bree and I are going to see as many Rolling Stones shows as we can."

"That's not stupid."

"You don't think so?"

"You're following your dreams. You can't beat that."

"No, you can't," said Ginny.

"Hey," Craig lit up like he'd just had the most amazing idea. "Would it be okay if I stuck around and checked out the concert with you?"

Ginny thought about it. It seemed like kismet or karma or whatever people called it. When she'd opened her mind to new possibilities, a *real* man had entered her life.

"Are you kidding?" she said. "I'd love it."

"But I don't have a ticket." Craig shrugged, as if that might kill the deal.

"Don't worry. With Bree around, there's always a way."

♪

GINNY ROLLED INTO THE HOTEL ROOM AROUND MIDNIGHT, expecting to find Bree wide awake and asking for details, but she wasn't there. Her bed remained untouched, and her bag was still mostly packed. *Is that her habit?* Ginny wondered. Leaving her suitcases full because she'd never know when she'd need to hit the road at a moment's notice.

She clicked on the TV. A reporter was standing outside a hospital:

"Rolling Stones fans are gathered outside of this hospital in Miami where Keith Richards is reported to be undergoing treatment for a brain injury. While in the Bahamas on a short hiatus between shows, Richards fell from a coconut tree. Witnesses claim to have seen Richards climb halfway up the tree before losing his grip. After the fall, he brushed himself off and then proceeded to ride a Jet Ski, where a second accident occurred. We are waiting for confirmation, but I wouldn't be surprised if the Rolling Stones are forced to cancel the rest of their North American tour."

19

GINNY

Her world came crashing down. Not only was Keith Richards's health in jeopardy, but the tour was probably canceled as well. The Stones might never go on the road again, and where would that leave her? Suddenly Ginny felt foolish—putting her entire fate in the hands of a rock and roll band was ridiculous, but she knew her purpose was more than being a traveling devotee. This had been a mission of healing and self-discovery, but once again, her journey had been derailed. She secretly feared the sad truth was there wasn't going to be anything to discover.

Sitting in her car in the hotel parking lot, Ginny needed somewhere quiet and familiar to think. She tried to call Bree, but typically, her friend didn't pick up. The woman used her phone more like a clock than an actual communication device. Besides, Bree was probably having too much fun with Rocky to be bothered.

Without the Rolling Stones, Ginny had nothing; the mission was kaput. She eased back the seat, pumped up the lumbar support, and breathed in the scent of the piña colada air freshener dangling from the rearview mirror. All the spaces in the parking lot had filled up since they checked in. How many of the cars belonged to disappointed Stones fans who would have to pack up their bags and head on home?

Maybe her destiny was to be nothing more than a dull married woman stuck in a Southern California 1970s tri-level house with air-conditioning, a pool in the backyard, and a plaque outside that read "Welcome to Our Home." But she could learn to live with the uneventfulness of her life. It was Ray's constant need to keep her from developing as a person that she was trying to break free of. He discouraged her from going back to school, was hardly interested in current events, and generally had nothing to say except to inform her when they were out of groceries. Sometimes, though, Ray could be smarter than he let on. Perhaps he realized Ginny had grown beyond him a long time ago.

In some twisted way, Ray's affair with Shannon might have been his way of taking back control. Ginny had once read a book advising her to shower her man with compliments. Men cheated not because another woman was more attractive, but because of the way the other woman made him feel. *What bullshit!* Ginny thought. What about the way he had made her feel? Didn't that count for anything?

Ginny looked around the backseat of the car only to notice Ray's junk: fast-food wrappers, half-eaten fries wedged between the seat, and dirty, sweat-stained socks strewn on the floor. She thought about her options.

She could go back home to him, her husband, her *man*, her future, while he sat on the couch in his dirty tube socks and too-tight jeans, watching TV and guarding the remote control like a belching, gaseous dragon. Observing her primate husband sprawled out, newspaper strewn around him like the lining for an animal's cage, she could try to remain fulfilled. Undoubtedly he'd be wearing his favorite pair of jeans he had bought probably a decade or so ago. They would be unbuttoned, his belly flopping over the waistband like a tube of dough waiting to be flattened out and baked.

Or, better yet, Ginny could move back in with her mother and participate twice a month in the Painted Ladies Club, a group of five older women who gathered to take art lessons from Pierre Bordeaux, a man who had answered Virginia's newspaper ad seeking a private instructor. He spoke with a French accent and wore a bandana tied around his neck, just like Picasso. *A total phony.* Ginny's mother said his real name was Marlon Lipkowski, but she had promised to keep his secret because she was also considering signing her paintings under a French pseudonym, something like Claudette or Genevieve.

Her mother had grand plans to be the premier dog portrait painter to the stars. She spent hours on the Internet researching celebrities and their pets. Sketches of Oprah Winfrey's, Paris Hilton's, and Ozzy and Sharon Osbourne's dogs hung in her studio, and many paintings of her dog, Benz, posing in various outfits, decorated her walls. Surely she would be a smash, she had told everyone, bragging about the fact that practically everybody had flipped over her work. She even landed a commission to paint Mrs. Highsmith's little Yorkshire terrier wearing a top hat.

Her father had been the anchor her mother needed, and Ginny missed him. He'd been steady and logical, and he'd accepted his wife for the eccentric artist she was. Encouraging Ginny's mom to learn and explore, he'd welcomed travel and taken her all over Europe—which, he argued, was the cradle of all great art. When the cancer overtook him, and they knew death was near, he told Ginny that her mother had been his first and only real love. Ginny realized she might never love her own husband in the same way, especially after what he had done to her.

She pulled a piece of fabric from the Rolling Stones lunch pail and inhaled. It still smelled like the laundry detergent her mother used, and she thought of her father and his clean undershirts and socks that Ginny had helped her mother fold.

Every night for a year, she wore the tie-dyed T-shirt purchased at her first Rolling Stones concert. When she and Pete approached the concession stand, it glowed, standing out from the rest of the plain concert shirts. Bright oranges, yellows, and reds mixed together in a psychedelic combination of colors. Even the giant tongue-and-lips logo on the front was a spiral of blues and greens.

Ginny had to have the shirt, and she didn't care that it came only in extra-large. It hung like a dress on her, and after failed attempts at belting it or tucking it in, she decided it would become her nightshirt. Snuggling in one hundred percent cotton, she dreamed of rock-and-rollers. When the shirt became holey and unwearable, she cut out the logo, folded it up, and put it into her lunch pail.

When Ginny's father saw the tie-dyed T-shirt for the first time, he wanted to teach his daughter all about psychedelic music and made her listen to the seventeen-minute version of Iron Butterfly's "In-A-Gadda-Da-Vida." It wasn't until a few months later, while listening to the Stones' "She's a Rainbow" and "2000 Light Years From Home" that Ginny heard the Stones' version of psychedelic music.

In 1967, Keith Richards' house in Sussex was raided, and both Mick and Keith were arrested. It was a salacious event, and the newspapers played up the fact that during the bust, Mick's girlfriend, Marianne Faithfull, wore only a fur rug that she let slip every now and again.

While they waited for their trial, Mick and Keith went to Morocco—the winter vacation spot for swinging Londoners. (Near the end of the movie *Almost Famous*, one of Ginny's favorites, Kate Hudson's character, a famous groupie named Penny Lane, buys a ticket to Morocco.) Morocco was to the Stones what India was to the Beatles. During the Stones' trip to Morocco in 1967, Anita Pallenberg left Brian Jones and hooked up with Keith Richards—the beginning of their tumultuous thirteen-year marriage.

The Stones explored Tangier and its colorful bazaars filled with snake charmers and fortune tellers, and they traded in their slick mod look for flowing shirts and silver bracelets. They were transformed there. Ginny would have given anything to be on the plane to Morocco with Penny Lane.

A knot formed in her stomach. Ginny's choices were limited, and the most dismal prospect of all was she would be home for her five-year high school reunion next summer. The night she found out about Ray and Shannon, Ginny ran into Sandy Spellman at the grocery store. A former snotty cheerleader, Sandy had packed on at least fifty pounds after graduating. She peered inside Ginny's cart, noting the vodka, raspberry-chocolate martini mixer, and bag of chocolate.

"Must be that time of the month," she said, then had started going on and on about the upcoming reunion, naming all of the attendees, making sure to emphasize the popular kids. "Oh, but you wouldn't know them," she was sure to add. "And there's going to be a taco bar and a DJ!"

Sandy had spoken with such zeal that the stock boy stopped to ask her if she had found everything she'd needed.

Ginny imagined herself alone and unpopular, chowing on a bunch of tacos and talking to people she hadn't seen in years and never even liked in the first place.

She rested her head on the steering wheel and started to cry.

20

BREE

ree woke up wedged into the loveseat. Her face was
pressed against the back cushion, and it took her a
moment to figure out where she was. She sat up and
scanned the unfamiliar surroundings before remembering she
had fallen asleep in Rocky's hotel room. He was passed out in
the side chair, his legs resting comfortably on the ottoman.
Even though his head was thrown back and his mouth hung
wide open, he wasn't a bad-looking man. A gentle giant, he
was snuggling the blanket tossed around his shoulders.

During the evening, there had been a few moments of
laughter. Rocky's sense of humor was just the kind she
appreciated, dry and self-deprecating. But as soon as the booze
wore off, Bree found herself once again comparing a man to
Billy Blade.

The first time she and Billy met for a secret date, it was a
warm spring Saturday afternoon. She had only seen him
perform a few times when he invited her to his house in
Bradenton, just north of Sarasota, Florida. It was in the seedy
side of town, near the Tropicana plant, but it was the only

place where Billy could stay true to his art, he said. He didn't want to take a mind-numbing nine-to-five job, slaving for the man and his military-industrial complex. So he and five guys rented a house, paying less than two hundred dollars each. The roommates weren't home when Bree arrived. Billy unscrewed the top of a jug of cheap wine and poured two hefty glasses full of chardonnay.

"What do you want from me?" he asked.

Bree was startled by his candor. She had never met a man so up-front. Dimmit was the type of guy who'd flirt shamelessly with the secretary while swearing up and down there wasn't anything wrong with his marriage.

"To hang out, I guess," she stammered.

"I can do that." Billy lit up a joint and passed it to Bree. "But I have to warn you. I already have plenty of friends."

They smoked and drank wine, Bree feeling freer by the minute. Billy got out his guitar and started playing something he'd written recently.

He was strumming his guitar and laughing like he was engaged in a private dialogue between himself and his instrument. Bree watched, fascinated that someone could be so passionate about his art. She admired the communication. Why, she wondered, had she settled for someone as cruel as Dimmit? With all his money, he'd never be as rich a man as Billy.

"Here," Billy said, handing Bree a harmonica. "Play along."

"I can't." She wanted to tuck the thing under her thigh and hide it away forever. "I have no musical ability whatsoever."

"Sure you do," Billy said. "Close your eyes and listen to the music. When you're ready, start playing."

She closed her eyes and put the instrument to her mouth. At first, she pressed her lips on the left-hand side and blew. The high-pitched shriek startled her, and she dropped the harmonica on her lap, the cold metal burning her thighs.

"It's okay," said Billy. "Try again."

Instead of concentrating on Billy's guitar playing, she shut her eyes and thought about her life. She had married a man whose lying and cheating had become too much to bear, had a child she loved but feared she didn't know how to mother, and worked at a job she had begun to hate. The repression was as stifling as Florida's humidity. Nobody cared about her or wanted to hear the music she could make if given a chance. She wanted out.

Billy stopped playing. "That was amazing," he said.

"What?" Bree opened her eyes.

"You're a natural."

"But I wasn't even playing." Bree wiped the spit from her mouth. "Was I?"

For a long time after they broke up and Billy went to Hollywood, she kept track of him, following the success of Cutting Blades, buying their albums, and singing their songs, "Sarasota," being the only exception. It was still too painful to belt out unflattering lyrics about herself. Could she ever get used to that? Their first single reached number one on the Billboard Hot 100, and the album went platinum many times over. They were at the height of their success when Bree moved to California. Nominated for a Grammy for best new artist, Billy was probably on top of the world, unaware it would all soon come crashing down.

Cutting Blades's next release didn't produce the hits the

band needed to solidify their reputation. The critics panned it, which sent the band into disarray. At least that's what she read in a magazine article. The guitarist struggled with a heroin addiction and committed suicide. He had been Billy's best friend, and Bree knew the guilt must have been too much. Billy disappeared, and although Bree continued to worry about him, she convinced herself she had to move on.

Then the band tried to reunite with a replacement guitarist. She tuned into entertainment television shows, waiting for interviews and news about their upcoming tour. Everything was on track for a big summer extravaganza, complete with other one-hit wonders, but apparently the musicians couldn't get along, and the reunion tour was canceled.

Bree picked up her shoes off the hotel room floor and walked quietly past Rocky. Worried he'd want to finish what they started earlier, she didn't want to wake him. They had fooled around a bit, but she hadn't been into it. Bree shut the door to Rocky's hotel room, disillusioned once again.

21

GINNY

Ginny woke up exhausted, having watched the news until dawn, waiting for more information about Keith's condition. When she finally crashed, she had a terrible nightmare. Somewhere on an island, she was sitting on a white-sand beach. Craig had brought her a blended cocktail—the kind with an umbrella and a slice of pineapple on the side. Just as she was about to take a sip, Ray and her mother had emerged from the water like scaly aquatic creatures. Snorkels were stuck to their faces, and their fin-like feet kicked sand all over Ginny as they tried to drag her back into the ocean.

She continued waking up from one nightmare after another. The worst was when Craig had actually morphed into Ray, the two of them the same man. She hadn't been able to escape. Her fitful nights were becoming unbearable.

Bree returned earlier in the morning and alone, much to Ginny's relief. The last thing she needed was Rocky crashing in their room, and she wasn't about to sleep in the bathtub or vacate the premises like a college girl being kicked out by her roommate. Not that she knew what that was like. Ginny used to listen politely to her friends tell their college horror stories while she finished up cosmetology school.

The hotel room was quiet now, the sun peeking through the heavy blinds. Planet Earth was still rotating and life continued, even though for her, it was practically over. What had he been thinking? Keith had ruined everything.

Maybe the reporters had it wrong, Ginny prayed. Hope still lingered somewhere in the back of her mind. It was only speculation that the tour would be canceled. What did the people on TV know anyway? Weren't they always over-dramatizing everything?

She threw on a sweatshirt over her oversize holey T-shirt and pajama pants and slid her feet into a pair of fuzzy slippers. Turning on the TV wasn't an option because she didn't want to wake Bree, and she wasn't getting any Internet connection on her phone. Ginny grabbed the key card and headed to the elevator.

She pushed the call button frantically, but it was taking way too long. Instead she found the stairwell and ran down six flights, a flushed, frazzled mess. Under normal circumstances, she wouldn't have cared less about how she looked—until she spotted Craig sitting at the front of the restaurant in full view.

In order to get to the television set in the lobby, she had to cross Craig's path, but she'd rather die than let him see her like this. She didn't want to show a potential love interest her unkempt self until she was able to work a little magic on him. Creating mystery was key, at least according to the latest fashion magazines. Articles like "Thirty Ways to Bewitch Your Man: The Truth Revealed!" advised her against ex-posing pimples, bad breath, and greasy hair until well after *I love yous* had been exchanged. And even then she'd be risking it.

There was a pillar to hide behind, and Ginny darted over to it. Once Craig had his head turned, she could run by and find out what was going on. A massive crowd of people, clamoring to check out of the hotel, presented another obstacle. She recognized most of them from the bar the night before and listened closely to see if she could hear anything. The fans were fleeing the premises for a good reason, it turned out. It wasn't another nightmare, as Ginny had hoped—it was real. The Oklahoma concert had been canceled.

Craig continued to eat his breakfast, oblivious, holding up a newspaper. Last night she had been so paranoid about being scrutinized, she could barely work up the nerve to check him out fully. He seemed so smart, so grown-up, actually *reading* the articles. Ray got all his information from VH1's *Behind the Music.*

Clean and put together, but not in an uptight way, Craig looked like his breath was fresh and his hair smelled like peppermint and rosemary. If she happened to fall into his arms, she'd find that his skin was soft, but not in a girly way. No, he was all man, especially the way he would hold her firmly in his arms and kiss her passionately before . . .

Ginny was way into her daydream when Craig spotted her and waved her over. *Shit!* She patted down her hair, remembering she hadn't brushed it in at least twelve hours. Her pajama pants had a big pizza sauce stain on the right leg, and she wasn't even wearing a bra. She could pretend she didn't see him. *Just keep going,* she told herself.

"Hey, Ginny," he called. "Over here."

Or not. She shuffled over in her dirty slippers, reminding herself not to breathe on him.

"Where are you going all dressed up?" He scanned her from head to toe.

She could feel his eyes lingering, and she liked the warmth of his stare, even if she wasn't exactly minty fresh. Ginny mumbled, "Good morning," trying to redirect her bad breath out of the corner of her mouth.

"Morning." Craig stood up and pulled out a chair. "Have a seat."

"I can't."

"Keep me company." He buttered a piece of toast for her.

"Haven't you heard?"

"What?" he asked. Craig folded the paper neatly and set it down beside his plate. The other people in the dining room were looking at her. She had no choice but to sit down, and she was a little hungry.

"Keith Richards fell out of a coconut tree."

"In Oklahoma?" Craig handed her a strawberry jelly pack.

"No, the Bahamas." Ginny crossed her arms underneath her chest and hiked up her boobs in a lame attempt at a makeshift bra. "The concert's canceled,"

"That explains the mass exodus. Either that or the Stones fans just discovered the hotel won't honor their AARP cards."

"This is serious," said Ginny.

"Oh, I know." He pretended to look concerned.

Damn, he is totally irresistible.

"I like this look on you. Sort of devil-may-care," said Craig.

"This is nothing." Ginny took a bite of the toast, jelly oozing out of the corner of her mouth. "You should see me when I've got the flu." She laughed at her own joke, remembering once again how to be carefree and maybe even a little funny.

He removed the napkin from his lap and dabbed Ginny's face with it. "What's the plan, then?"

"I'm fucked," said Ginny. "Pardon my language, but I'm screwed in a big way."

Craig put his hand on Ginny's. "There'll be other concerts."

"Sure, other concerts. Just at the wrong times." She was somewhere between laughing and crying.

"I'm free for a while," said Craig. "We could hang out."

"See the many sights of Oklahoma?" Ginny finished Craig's piece of toast.

"I hear the bombing memorial's a real hoot."

She laughed. "You shouldn't joke about that."

"I'm kidding. Besides, I'm thinking of someplace more fun."

"Like?" The white-sand beach flashed in her mind as she reached for Craig's uneaten bacon. She surprised herself. Last week she had been scared of her own shadow, but today she was eating food off a stranger's plate.

A loud cheer erupted from the lobby. Ginny could see the Stones fans hugging each other, big smiles spreading across their faces.

"I'll be right back." She ran over to the people gathering around the television set. "What's going on?"

Jonny, the Ronnie Wood look-alike from last night, said, "Keith's gonna make it!"

"The tour's back on?" asked Ginny.

"Quiet," another fan commanded as he turned up the volume.

Ginny moved in closer, pressing up against a bunch of

quirky diehards. Jonny straightened his wig, beaming at the good news. Another man said it would take more than a coconut tree and a Jet Ski to keep Keith down. A woman got all teary-eyed with relief.

Ginny felt right at home.

♪

AFTER BREAKFAST, GINNY WENT BACK TO HER ROOM TO clean up. Riding the emotional roller coaster had left her grungy, to say the least. Dumping in practically the entire bottle of suds supplied by the hotel, she submerged herself in the bath water. There were lots and lots of bubbles, and it reminded her of the pink stuff her mom used to mix in with the steaming hot water. Ginny draped a moist washcloth over her eyes and relaxed, thinking about the safety of her childhood, her mother drawing baths for her while Dad was outside, skimming the leaves off the swimming pool.

The door flung open, and Bree rushed over to the toilet and dropped her pants. "Sorry, I couldn't hold it another sec."

"Help yourself." Ginny kept her eyes covered.

"So?" asked Bree, the stream gushing out. "What happened to *you* last night?"

"I'm not the one who disappeared, remember?"

Bree flushed, put down the lid, and made herself comfortable on top of the toilet seat. "I think I'm in love."

"You just met him." Ginny removed the washcloth and sunk deeper into the water. She wasn't exactly comfortable with Bree seeing her naked.

"He's so funny. He had me in stitches all night!"

"Stitches? Is that what you call it?"

Bree huffed and stomped her foot like a little girl. She was so small, her arms hugging her tiny body. "You're not the first person to think I'm easy."

"I'm just kidding."

"I'll have you know we talked all night. We're practically soul mates." Bree stretched her arms over her head and yawned. "We both refuse to work in an office."

"Wow," said Ginny. "That *is* something."

"Okay," admitted Bree. "Maybe there was a little oral sex involved."

"You gave him a blow job?"

"Hell, no!"

"You mean he went down on you?" Bree hadn't ceased to surprise Ginny yet.

Bree winked in acknowledgment.

"You're my new role model," said Ginny.

"Oh no, not that." Bree went to the mirror and started fussing with her hair. "So, I heard about Keith Richards."

"But everything's good now." Ginny squeezed shampoo into her hand and started massaging her scalp. "The Stones are picking up their tour in Las Vegas."

"Vegas." Bree contemplated the move. "Could be fun," she said, lifting Ginny's clothes from the floor and placing them neatly on the counter. "I've been meaning to talk to you about these."

"My clothes?"

"They're so dull." Ginny turned on the spigot and ducked her head beneath it, rinsing her hair. She didn't like where this conversation was heading. The last thing she needed was another Ray criticizing her appearance. "I dress for comfort."

"Clearly," said Bree. "At first I thought your entire wardrobe consisted of two colors: black and white."

"If you want to be technical," said Ginny, "black and white aren't even colors." She remembered the lesson from her high school art class.

Bree left the room, and Ginny got out of the tub and wrapped a towel around herself. She wiped the steam from the mirror, imagining faint lines forming around her eyes.

Bree barged back into the bathroom. "Until I found these hot numbers in your suitcase." She held up Ginny's two best tops, an eggplant-colored bustier and a pink rhinestone-embellished tank. "Tacky, but I've got to say, I love 'em!"

"I'm saving those for the concerts," said Ginny, a little ticked off that Bree had been rummaging through her stuff.

"I'm sorry, sister, but when you have a hottie like Craig on the line, you bring out the big guns." Bree wiggled the tops in some sort of demonstration of their power.

"He said he likes my 'devil-may-care' look."

"Just trying to help." Bree left the room. "Anyway, I still want to go shopping later." The numbers were adding up. Ginny couldn't justify a shopping spree like the one she imagined Bree had in mind.

"I know what you're thinking," Bree called out. "Would you quit worrying about the money?"

"Easy for you to say. You can afford not to worry." Ginny put the tank on and came out of the bathroom to check her image in the full-length mirror.

"Watch out, Craig!"

"I don't want to blow it," said Ginny. "I like him."

"Are you kidding? Any guy would kill to be with you."

Ginny checked herself out again and liked what she saw. "At first I was a nervous wreck, but the more I got to know him, the better I felt about myself."

"Where is this wonder boy?" asked Bree.

"He wants us to meet him in the lobby. Says it's a surprise."

♪

"FIRST-CLASS TICKETS TO LAS VEGAS!" GINNY WAS SITTING in the lobby, examining the itinerary Craig had printed out.

Ginny had never flown first-class, and she imagined it to be all caviar and champagne dreams. She'd only ever been in coach, crammed between Ray and another hefty person hogging the armrests.

That was probably why she hated to fly. She wasn't scared, like she'd once thought, just uncomfortable. Ray had psyched her into thinking she had a phobia in order to avoid traveling altogether. But these were first-class tickets, and she'd be with Bree and Craig. Two people who knew how to live it up.

"Why not?" said Craig. "I had plenty of miles I was able to cash in, and maybe I'm being a little selfish. Who wouldn't want to see the Stones with a couple of groupies?"

"Shut up." Ginny smacked him on the arm, feeling his muscle flex. Was he showing off? It was a little cheesy but effective, because in a matter of seconds, Ginny was revisiting the fantasy from earlier this morning.

"I ran into Rocky after breakfast this morning," Craig said to Bree. "He's got a couple of gigs in town. Looks like he can't fly with us."

"Rocky who?" asked Bree, burying her face in the itinerary.

"Your soul mate, remember?" said Ginny, shaking her head at Craig.

"I have never used those words in my life." Bree handed the flight schedule to Ginny.

"We're leaving tonight," said Craig. "I booked two suites at the MGM Grand. My treat."

"Perfect." Bree winked at Ginny.

Ginny was nervous and excited at the same time. Did Craig expect her to share *his* suite? Maybe she'd be up for a couple of conjugal visits, but the idea of using his bathroom after the morning coffee kicked in was way too overwhelming.

"But what about my car?" asked Ginny. "These tickets are one-way."

"I saw a dealership around the corner," said Bree. "Sell it."

"Leave behind the Volvo?" A montage of scenes flashed through Ginny's mind. Her mother and father presenting the car to her because it was safe and they were worried. Ray making fun of it, saying it was an old woman's car. It was the car that whisked her away from Ray and brought her to Bree, and it was supposed to be the car that would deliver her to Mick Jagger. She couldn't let it go.

Then Ginny remembered someone telling her that you have to lose everything in order to gain anything.

"Where did you say the dealership was?"

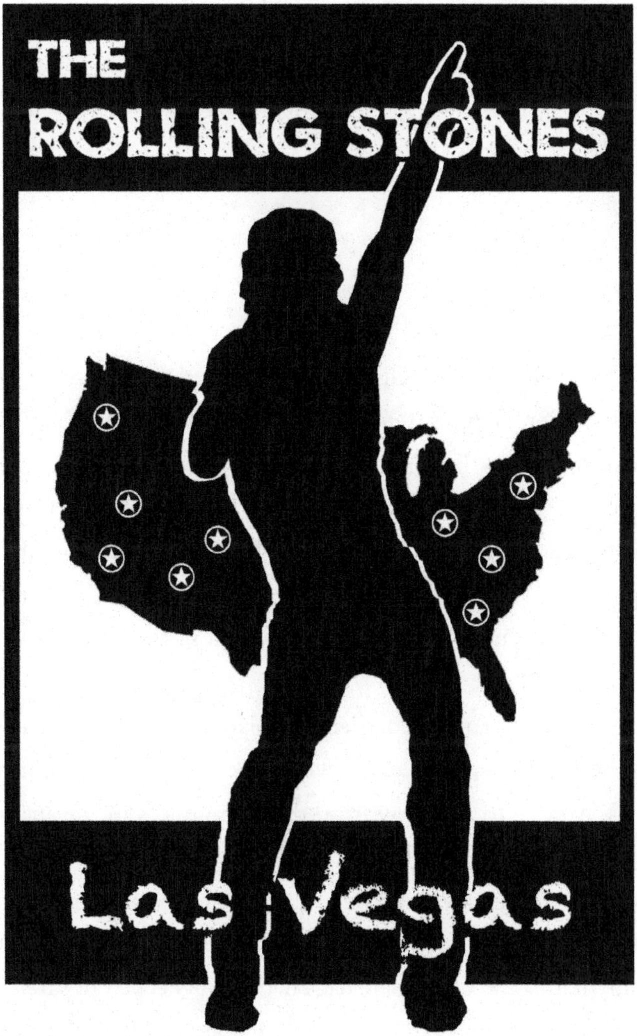
THE
ROLLING STONES
Las Vegas

22

GINNY

It was exactly how Ginny had imagined first class to be—friendlier flight attendants, prettier passengers, and the promise of a better life. She sank into her oversize seat, settled her arms on *both* armrests and closed her eyes. Careful not to fall asleep, she didn't want to miss a moment of the experience. Hopefully it wouldn't be her last time flying first-class, but certainty could not be assumed in the life of a Wild and Spontaneous.

Even before they boarded the plane, Craig took them to the executive club, an exclusive hangout for rich, important types. A place to get away from the commoners in the airport, Ginny assumed. Craig knew everybody in the club, mostly the beautiful women working behind the front desk. They greeted the three travelers with welcoming smiles, and for once, Ginny felt like a VIP. Their bags had been checked in safely by the skycap, and instead of complaining about Ginny's packing way too much, like Ray would have, or making her haul her own bags as some sort of punishment, Craig gladly tipped the man to take care of everything. In fact, Ginny could relax—that seemed to be the theme of the day. Everything had been taken care of, compliments of Craig.

Bree didn't seem to mind the special little extras either. She settled right into the first-class world of Craig Mitchum. But she was a natural, Ginny suspected. It was a place of designer luggage, nonexistent waiting lines, and token security checks. Ginny had never been treated better in her life. The last time she flew, she'd been pushed out of line while checking in, made to walk through the metal detector six times, and patted down by a female security guard who could've played linebacker for the NFL.

While Ginny loved her new life, she secretly felt like a fraud. *What am I doing here?* She was afraid she was going to flub up big-time, especially after she insisted that Orchid come on board with her. But she was well-mannered, said "please" and "thank you," and followed Bree's and Craig's lead. They had no problem being waited on, serviced, and having their whims met. *I'll just have to practice,* she told herself as she summoned the flight attendant.

A pretty young woman came over. "What can I get for you, Ms. Martin?" she asked with a cheery grin. Ginny couldn't believe the woman knew her name.

She tried to think of something to order, recalling an article she had read about celebrities' backstage demands. Britney Spears requested cheeseburgers, figs, and prunes, and Justin Bieber drank only herbal teas. One celebrity even insisted that all toilet seats be replaced in her dressing-room bathrooms.

Pondering the world of choices, she couldn't come up with anything complicated enough. The two women's eyes locked, and Ginny knew the only thing separating them was circumstance. Last week she might have been thrilled to accept a job as a flight attendant, the prospect of traveling the world, a dream.

Before she decided to skip college in favor of cosmetology school, she had worried about her future, like the rest of the kids in her senior class. Taking a test offered by the high school career center, she answered what seemed like hundreds of questions about her interests and skills. It took a few hours, and Ginny struggled to stay focused, working through her tendency to zone out. In the end, she was handed a sheet of career choices and circled "set decorator." The counselor didn't have a clue what set decorator meant; the center didn't have a pamphlet on it, so Ginny was sent home to research it on her own.

The occupation seemed like a perfect fit for her. When she was a kid playing with Barbie dolls, Ginny had grown bored with Barbie's boxy plastic house and always searched for new environments to set up. Clearing out one of the shelves in a bookcase, she created a loft-like atmosphere in the deep, empty space left behind. Arranging Barbie's furniture, she had the doll live there until, like the independent nomad she was, Barbie needed to move on. Ginny covered furniture, chairs, and tables with linen and set up temporary situations for Barbie. Cabinets that stored board games and blankets made cozy nooks and excellent hiding places from big brothers bent on humiliating and destroying Barbie by stripping her naked and pulling off her head. Barbie had been fickle, for sure, but luckily Ginny didn't mind decorating and redecorating her set.

She was excited to tell her mother about her newfound

career choice. It was the first time she'd been enthused about a future and even found a few books on the subject in the library. A set decorator could work in the theater or on movie and television sets to create the environment for the actors, Ginny explained to her mother. Virginia frowned. "You can't just decide to enter a career like that. You're not artistically inclined, and besides, in show business, it's all about who you know."

Left to assume she didn't have the connections or skills to become a set decorator, Ginny returned the books to the library and waited for something else to come along.

"Would you like a mimosa?" asked the flight attendant, nodding her head as if answering her own question.

Ginny was relieved. "I most certainly would."

"I'll have one as well," said Craig. He had taken the window seat next to Ginny, and Bree had grabbed the one across the aisle. Ginny thought about being in the middle once again. Except this time she didn't feel trapped, as she had been between her mother and Ray, the two dominant forces who had bookended her life until then. At that moment, she was free. *What an appropriate way to feel*, she thought, just as the captain made his announcement for takeoff.

The flight attendant returned to retrieve the drink glasses. Ginny clutched hers, the one solid link she had to feeling rich. "I'll hold onto mine," she said.

"Ready?" asked Craig.

"Yup."

"Better than riding across the desert in a Volvo?"

She pictured the station wagon sitting in the dealership lot, a for-sale sign in the window.

At first Ginny thought she would be sad about leaving the car, but surprisingly, once the deal had been made, she felt empowered with a little extra cash on hand. (Bree refused to take any of it as repayment.) That car was never what she would have picked out for herself anyway. After she crashed her little convertible, she'd wanted another one—something a little bigger, but fun and sexy. The Volvo was an old lady's mode of transportation. Practical and boring.

"Way better," said Ginny. "Thank you." She wanted Craig to know how sincere she was. "For everything."

"Thanks for being so open. Most women wouldn't take off at a moment's notice," Craig said. "You're impressive."

"I am?" Ginny sipped the mimosa. It was delicious.

♪

NO MATTER HOW MANY TIMES GINNY WALKED THROUGH the door of their suite at the MGM in Las Vegas, she still couldn't get used to the size of it. A fully stocked bar, a dining table that sat six, and a living room equipped with the works. The best part was the fact that there were two king-size bedrooms, each with its own bathroom. No more barging in while someone was in the bathtub or sharing mirror space when they were getting ready to go out. She liked the gold-and-red color scheme too. It reminded her of something royal, a setting for a princess.

"That was fun," said Bree, dumping her shopping bags on the diamond-patterned sofa.

Ginny opened the refrigerator and took out a soda. "Five thousand bucks isn't going to go far." The salesman at the dealership hadn't budged, and since Ginny didn't have time to negotiate, she took what had been offered.

"Did you see this?" Bree walked over to the giant fruit basket. She opened the card and read aloud, *To my favorite groupies. Viva Las Vegas.*

"From Craig?"

"Of course, dummy."

"I should thank him." Ginny picked up the phone and started dialing.

"Don't call him," said Bree. "Go over to his room."

Ginny hung up. *Well, it would be rude not to thank him face to face.* He was only down the hall, which Ginny thought was a classy move on his part: requesting the same floor but not the suite next door. Being too close would be creepy. He'd be hovering, like Ray would have.

"And wear this." Bree pulled Ginny's new dress out of the bag.

"No way. He'd think I was trying too hard."

"You overestimate men," said Bree. She was settling into the sofa, clearly intent on sending Ginny alone to Craig's room. "They see a pretty woman in a sexy dress and think 'Looks good.'"

"You sound like a caveman."

"'Looks good, me want,'" said Bree, continuing her impersonation. "They don't care how it came to be or even consider whether a woman's *trying* or not. The blood's going to rush to their penises either way."

♪

"Look at you," said Craig, opening the door to his suite.

"Just a little something I picked up." Ginny did a pirouette, showing off her new slinky black dress.

"You look beautiful." He kissed her on the cheek. "I hope you're going to let me take you to dinner. We've got to put that dress to good use."

"Do you mind if Bree comes? I wouldn't feel right ditching her."

Craig walked over to the bar and opened a bottle of white wine. "I've already made reservations for three at one of the restaurants downstairs."

"It's been taken care of," said Ginny.

"What?" Craig offered her a glass.

"Nothing." Ginny accepted the wine. "Check out this view," she said, walking over to the window. The bright lights illuminated the entire Strip. She could see the line of cars below and wondered where they'd end up. They might go to New York, New York across the street, or they could watch the spectacular fountain show in front of the Bellagio. Or they might check out the Roman Forum in Caesar's Palace. The possibilities were unlimited.

"I'm not sure if I can repay you for all of this."

"Oh," Craig said, encircling her waist from behind. "You might think of a way." He pulled her close, turning her around so they could kiss. At first the kisses were small and searching, as if he were trying to get the lay of the land inside her mouth. Once he had her figured out—*she likes it slow and soft*—he lifted her hair and kissed behind her neck. If she let him continue, she'd be in trouble.

Ginny stepped back, her hands still on his chest. "I don't know anything about you."

"What's to know? I'm Craig," he said. "Nice to meet you." Craig stuck out his hand.

Ginny pushed it away. "What about your family? Do you have any siblings?" she asked. "Do you have a girlfriend?"

Craig nodded, as if he'd been waiting for these questions. It was getting awkward, so Ginny poured herself another glass of wine.

"My parents live in South Carolina," said Craig. "I have two younger brothers. What else do you want to know? I'm an open book."

Ginny wasn't about to ask again. She sat down on a barstool, ready to forget the whole thing. *Why do I care, anyway?*

Craig twirled her around to face him. "Come here." He kissed her again. "I don't have a girlfriend."

"It's not my business," said Ginny. *Relax*, she told herself.

"I see a couple of women here and there. Nothing serious." He inserted himself between Ginny's thighs, nudging them apart. "Yet."

"Hey, watch it," she teased. "I'm still a married woman." *At least for a little while longer*, she thought. Divorcing Ray had started to seem like a more realistic goal every day. Before, she'd been overwhelmed by the idea. From separating their finances to their DVD collections, the dissolution had seemed next to impossible, enough to push it right out of her mind.

"I know," said Craig. "And don't think it doesn't turn me on just a little."

"I've heard about guys like you. Commitment phobes

always in search of the most unavailable women." She couldn't count the number of times guys had asked her out, knowing full well she was married. Some of them had even been Ray's so-called friends.

"Blah, blah, blah." He opened and closed his hand like a flapping mouth. "If I'd known Dr. Phil was coming over . . ."

"You're asking for it." Ginny squeezed her thighs.

"I'm suffocating." He freed himself and walked to the other side of the bar.

Ginny loved the way he moved. He didn't have a cocky gait, but it was easy and self-assured. *There's nothing more attractive*, thought Ginny, *than a man with confidence.*

And his clothes were to die for. Beautifully pressed pants and shirts—even the jeans he had worn earlier were probably designer. He didn't overdress, though. It was like he carefully considered his options and always chose the right one.

He is perfect, thought Ginny.

♪

AFTER DINNER, CRAIG WANTED GINNY AND BREE TO PLAY blackjack with him, but Ginny needed to warm up on the slots first. Besides, she could see herself getting carried away, losing all her car money in one evening.

She kept pushing the buttons. The symbols on the slot machine seemed bizarre and confusing. One looked like a fortune-teller's board, and another had a cat face on it. None of the themed slot machines made any sense to her. The way the symbols crisscrossed the screen left her scratching her head. Lining them up on a diagonal meant one thing; horizontally, another. Then there were at least three payout lines, which, combined with a two-times or four-times symbol, would enable her to double or quadruple her money if she could figure it all out.

A win eluded her—she needed to play the old-school slots with the cherries and flaming sevens. All those took was lining up three symbols. *Simple.* She wanted to pull the round ball on the slot's handle and send the reels spinning. There was something more physical about playing a game where she had to work a little. Using her index finger over and over again to press the buttons on the newer machines seemed pointless.

Bree was sinking her quarters into a slot machine around the corner. She hooted and hollered whenever she won, which seemed like all the time. "There's another twenty-five," Bree yelled as the coins clinked into the metal tray. Ginny couldn't seem to hit a jackpot if her life depended on it. She told herself to relax, but it was hard when Bree was always the winner.

Next to Ginny, an old lady was working three machines— all losers. She sat in the middle, slipping three quarters in one and pushing the buttons on the other two. Once in a while, she'd pause to rub her purple rabbit's foot dangling from a set of keys. Even though her face was buried in the blinking, spinning lights of the screen two inches away, she was totally aware of what was going on around her. As soon as Ginny got up from a slot she'd been working for a while, the old woman would swoop in, filling it with coins. Ginny started to feel strangely possessive about her machines.

She might feel better if the cocktail waitress would show up with the drink she ordered thirty minutes ago.

"Let's hit the progressive slots." Bree was carrying a bucket of coins and a cold beer.

"Hey, where'd you get that?"

"You want it?" Bree offered her the bottle. "It's my third."

"Figures." Ginny searched the casino floor. "Have you seen Craig?"

"Don't worry," said Bree. "I'm sure he hasn't gone far."

"I wonder if he's won anything yet." After dinner, they separated without making concrete plans to see each other later. Ginny didn't want to come off as desperate, but she couldn't get the earlier kiss off her mind.

"He's won something, alright."

"How do you know?" Ginny stood on her tippy-toes but couldn't see over the mobs of people.

"I saw the way you were looking at him tonight. You li-i-ike him!"

"You are so immature." Ginny grabbed Bree's beer and downed it. "Let's go find those slots."

♪

"SEE, THIS SHOULD TOTALLY BE A WINNER," GINNY complained. "Look at all of these pictures lined up." She waited for the sweet sound of coinage, but nothing fell from the machine she had been working for the last twenty minutes.

Bree leaned back on her stool and analyzed Ginny's screen. "I can't figure it out."

The first thing she heard was the siren: a faint sort of wailing that grew louder and louder. Then the lights on top of the machine started to swirl and glow, like the ones on a police car. It was making a huge racket, but still, no money.

A crowd of people gathered around. "How much did you win?" they asked.

Ginny stared at the screen but still couldn't discern anything. It was all too confusing. It was taking forever for someone to tell her what was going on. Everybody was closing in on her, and she felt hot and sweaty.

Finally, a worker from the floor arrived with a calculator. He read the machine, uncovering the mysterious combination of numbers and symbols to arrive at a number. He showed her the amount.

"I can't believe it!" Ginny said. "I just won two thousand dollars."

The man tapped Ginny on the shoulder. "You missed the last zero," he said, pointing to the correct amount.

23

BREE

Bree sat on the sofa, leafing through the television guide and watching Ginny take her sweet time getting ready.

"Are you sure you won't come with us?" Ginny pulled a new leather jacket from its garment bag.

She must have hit every boutique in the lobby, thought Bree. "I'm going to hang out here for a while. Maybe watch a little TV and call it an early evening."

"Are you feeling alright?" asked Ginny. She sat down next to Bree and attempted to feel her forehead.

"I'm not sick," said Bree, evading Ginny's touch. "Just a little tired. Can't keep up with you kids."

"Yeah, right." Ginny applied a bright shade of red to her lips. "Too much?"

"Too much is never enough," said Bree. "Isn't that what Mick Jagger says?"

Ginny rubbed her lips together and blew Bree a kiss. "I'm glad you're studying up on your Jaggerisms. But if you change your mind . . ."

"Get out of here already," Bree unmuted the TV. "And I better not see a trace of lipstick on your lips when you come home."

Ginny rolled her eyes and walked out the door.

Bree thought Ginny would never leave. When Craig suggested they see an evening show, it gave Bree the perfect opportunity to resign her position as third wheel. They were too polite to tell her to take a hike, something she might have done in her past life.

More important, the time alone allowed her to work up the nerve it would take to see him. She paced the floor of her suite, back and forth, knowing it was her destiny. Billy Blade, her long-lost love, had managed to claw his way to the bottom. He was playing at an older hotel off the strip. Having followed his career from the almost instantaneous rise to the top to his nightly stint in a Vegas showroom, she knew he'd be there that evening.

She leaned into the mirror and stretched the skin on her jaw so it formed a nice, taut line. Would he recognize her? Had she changed much, she wondered? When she smiled, faint lines formed around her mouth and eyes. *At least these are the marks of someone who's lived,* she told herself—someone who saw opportunities and went for it.

What a load of crap, she thought. The opportunity had been there all along, and she'd always come up with excuses for why she shouldn't confront him, ask him why he'd refused to see her after she left her husband and child behind, traveling clear across the country to be with him. It had been all about *his* pain and sorrow, as he'd sung: "Now how far do I have to go for you to follow me?" She had followed him, and what did she have to show for it? A daughter who hated her and virtually no family to speak of.

What she missed, what she ached for more than anything,

was a person who challenged her, someone complex and full of contradictions. *Is it too much to ask for a man who weeps over Chopin but rocks a pair of leather pants like nobody's business?* Her eyes started to tear up, and she cursed herself for being too sentimental. She had to cut the bullshit and get ready. The show started in a few hours, and as she reexamined herself in the mirror, she realized she had work to do if she was going to look anything like the woman Billy Blade had left behind.

Bree scanned her closet, looking for the perfect outfit. What would say *eat your heart out, but I don't care what you think* at the same time? Whatever it was, it had to go with the lucky red boots. The same pair she wore on their first date almost eight years ago.

When she saw Billy, she would ask him why he had deserted her, pretended she hadn't even existed. She should have learned that *why* was a useless question, but the compulsion, the need to know, was driving her to see him one more time.

♪

NEON-LIT STARS SHOT ALL THE WAY UP THE FRONT OF THE hotel where Billy was playing. As soon as Bree stepped out of the cab, she wanted to make a run for it. This moment, years in the making, terrified her. The entire way over, she replayed what she'd say to him in her head. It had to be something casual, nonchalant, but most of all not full of the desperation or longing she had pretended didn't exist for so long. *Be cool.* That was her mantra.

Billy Blade, practically a stranger to her now, still brought her to her knees. He could turn her into a sniveling, groveling fool if she let him. He was a chink in her armor, but she wasn't about to expose that to someone who had betrayed her. Bree thought about leaving the casino. *It isn't too late*, she told herself. What she needed was a shot of liquid courage to help her face him. She fished out her silver flask and ducked into the bathroom to take a swig.

That was when reality hit her. After she got dressed, she had liked what she saw in the mirror. An attractive woman in a nice pair of tight jeans—the same size she'd worn in high school—and a fun, sexy top. *Not bad*, she'd thought. Perhaps she'd be the best-looking woman in the club. But then she opened the door to the ladies' room and saw a line of women in their thirties and forties smiling at her. They were like clones in their jeans and fun, sexy tops, middle-age contestants in the Ms. America Pageant.

She found a quiet corner in the restroom and took a long pull, the warm liquid burning as it went down. Closing her eyes, Bree thought again about playing the harmonica. After the night at Billy's, she had bought herself one, along with an instructional guide, practicing "Frère Jacques" and "This Old Man," and she'd even memorized "Home on the Range."

Standing alone in the casino bathroom, she sang her favorite lines from that song: *Where seldom is heard a discouraging word, and the skies are not cloudy all day.*

"Hey." The group of women gathered around Bree. "Must be pretty good stuff you've got in there."

"Wanna shot?" Bree offered the flask around.

A woman with dark, flat-ironed hair and a boob job accepted and toasted the rest of the group. "Cheers," she said, passing it to her friend, a bleached-blonde in her fifties sporting an orange spray tan.

♪

WHEN THE MAÎTRE D' STARTED TO WALK BREE TO THE back of the nightclub, she reached into her handbag and pulled out $50. "Can you do any better?" she asked, trying not to dwell on the fact that these days she had to rely more on cold, hard cash than on her looks.

"Right this way." He took her to a small table at the front. Even with the stage lights in his eyes, there was no way Billy was going to miss her.

This is it. The moment she'd been anticipating for years. Her heart was beating fast, and her legs were shaking underneath the table. She was glad Ginny wasn't around to witness this absurdity, her vulnerability exposed.

The announcer introduced Billy Blade, formerly of Cutting Blades. When Billy emerged, Bree was stunned. He wasn't old-looking and fat, like she'd secretly hoped, despite the airbrushed publicity photos in the lobby. Barely any different from the man who left her behind, he was still slim in his black leather pants and embroidered jacket.

The fans, mostly women, were the same type she had shared her flask with in the bathroom, and Bree was relieved she wasn't the oldest member of the audience. It consisted of loyal followers who mouthed all the words to songs like "Rescue," "Waterfall," and "The Way It Goes." Some of them were even crying, Bree wondered what old painful memories were emerging in their minds.

She didn't see Billy even glance in her direction and figured her plan was a bust. Then came the opening chords to "Sarasota." A man approached and handed her a note, which she quickly unfolded. It was from Billy, asking her to meet him in his dressing room after the show. So he had seen her, after all. She tucked the note into her purse and replayed her opening line in her head for the umpteenth time.

♪

BACKSTAGE SEEMED LIKE CATACOMBS. BREE WALKED THE dark hallways, winding around corners until she completely lost her bearings. If she needed to escape, she'd never find her way back, and she envisioned herself trapped in a closet she thought was an exit. Or worse, she'd be buried alive in the walls like some tragic Edgar Allan Poe character.

What would he say to her? Over the years, whenever she found herself pining for the days of Billy Blade, she felt like a fool. Surely she hadn't made the same impact on him. Before she had a chance to practice her line one more time, the door to Billy's dressing room opened.

When she saw him sitting on a stool, strumming his guitar, the well-practiced words went right out of her head.

Billy set the guitar aside and stood up. He had the same weary eyes she remembered.

Bree stepped inside the dressing room. *Hey, stranger. Hello there, long time no see.* Damn it! What was she supposed to say? The keep-it-cool opening line slid from her memory with the rest of her speech.

"Why?" was all she could ask, "Why did you leave me?"

He wrapped his arms around her and pulled her close. She recognized his smell, a mixture of salty perspiration and musky deodorant. "I knew you'd find me."

"But I found you before." Bree freed herself from him. "Remember?"

"I was an idiot. I'm sorry." He ran his fingers through his hair, the same gesture she remembered he did when he was frustrated. "I was hurt because I was willing to do anything for you. To slice open my body and hand you every single part and trust you'd take care of me."

"For God's sake, Billy." The waterworks began, and Bree couldn't believe she was allowing herself to become a blubbering fool. "You always had a flair for the dramatic."

She'd want to know more later, but for now, he kissed her, and Bree forgot all about the *why*s.

24

GINNY

"What are you up to now?" Ginny asked, bumping along in the rented Jeep. When Craig pulled up in front of the hotel, promising her some kind of adventure, she climbed in reluctantly despite the devilish grin on his face.

Gazing out at the wide-open space surrounding Highway 15, she started to regret the decision. The sandy desert looked desolate and lonely, and she couldn't help thinking about movies where mafia guys take care of business by burying their enemies six feet under. At least thirty minutes outside Las Vegas, they were far away from the bustle of the strip and the comfort of her hotel suite.

"You're going to love it." Craig squeezed her knee, and then put both hands back on the steering wheel. He was a cautious driver. She liked that, even as his touch excited her.

His brown, wavy hair flopped over his aviator sunglasses. Ginny pushed it back out of his eyes. "Let's hope so," she said, thinking about how she wouldn't mind pulling over right then and there to get in the backseat.

"I promise." Craig said. "Money-back guarantee."

She fantasized about the private, secluded love shack where he might be taking her. After last night's date, she thought for sure they were going to get close. Instead, Craig had walked her to her room and kissed her goodnight, and she hadn't known what to think. He was driving her crazy, and it was really annoying. Leaving her hanging like a pubescent boy was oddly frustrating *and* enticing. So in control, he teased her. In her limited experience, the men were always the ones who did the initiating.

Even Bree had ditched her. She was nowhere to be found last night, and this morning when Ginny woke up, she could see by the dirty clothes in plastic bags for housekeeping to wash that Bree had already come and gone.

"Jean Sport Aviation Center." Ginny read the sign as they entered a parking lot. They were at a small airport in the middle of Jean, Nevada.

"Ready for a little trip?" Craig said, grinning as he slid the Jeep into a parking spot.

"A trip?" Ginny panicked. The Stones' concert was in a few days, and she wasn't about to dump everything she'd worked so hard for, even if she *was* falling for the guy.

Craig hopped out of the truck and walked over to an odd-looking airplane with a small cockpit and long, narrow wings. "This must be our ride."

Ginny didn't budge. "I'll take a taxi back to the hotel," she called through the open window.

Craig took her hand and helped her out. "I thought you loved to fly," he said. "It's only for half an hour."

Ginny examined the plane. "What is it?" she asked. It

seemed so flimsy, like one of those balsa wood models her brother used to put together.

"It's a glider." Craig was giddy with excitement.

She hated to crush his spirit, but the thought of going up in the air in a plane her brother could have built was more than disturbing. "I don't know."

"It's one of the safest modes of transportation."

"Okay," said Ginny. "Now I know you're lying."

He put his arm around her shoulders. "I thought you were my spontaneous girl."

Ginny felt his warm body pressing against hers. She couldn't believe what was happening, as she heard Mick singing "Under My Thumb" somewhere in the back of her mind.

"Tell me what I gotta do," she said.

"First," said the pilot, walking over to greet them. "Sign this form, releasing us of all liability."

She took the pen and signed, come what may. "Safe, huh?"

♪

GINNY AND CRAIG SAT SIDE BY SIDE IN THE SEAT BEHIND the pilot. He explained that since the glider didn't have an engine, it needed to be towed behind a plane. Once the towplane brought them to a soaring altitude, the towrope would be released and they would be launched.

She didn't like the sound of that word. "So, we're going to be floating back to earth?" Ginny swallowed hard. "Like a giant parachute?"

"Something like it," he said, then warned that they could

experience some turbulence. Ginny figured the pilot must have known about her penchant for puking in front of her dates as he handed her a bag to vomit in, just in case. They started to soar up in the air, and Ginny closed her eyes.

Craig nudged her. "Isn't this great?" he yelled. "You gotta see this."

When she finally worked up the nerve to take a peek, the sky seemed to be swallowing the plane, the terrain below receding as they left solid ground. It was a great big beautiful mosaic of browns and greens. Her hands were hurting, and she realized she was gripping the seat.

"Here comes the fun part," said the pilot, releasing the towrope.

"Yee-haw!" Craig hollered. Ginny panicked, watching their towplane fly off into the distance. They were a mile above ground. The pilot said their goal was to search for air pockets to keep them aloft as long as possible. Soaring, climbing, and dropping, they were maneuvering in ways that should have terrified her. Ginny couldn't believe she was actually starting to enjoy it. *Isn't it something*, she thought, *to be sitting in a tiny capsule, surrounded by nothing but blue sky and puffy white clouds?* She imagined she was a feather, feeling the sensation of being so light and free the wind dictated her direction.

It felt good to finally let go. Micromanaging her life, second-guessing everything she said she wanted. It was tiring, draining, and just plain futile. This seemed like one of the riskiest things she had ever done, and she felt nothing but exhilarated.

♪

"DELICIOUS," SAID GINNY, STUFFING FRENCH FRIES INTO her mouth and eyeing the big juicy steak they'd ordered from room service. Craig had suggested they go back to his suite for lunch, and she was quietly hoping for a little afternoon make out session for dessert.

"Wasn't that cool?" Craig shook the stainless-steel mixer. "Gliding back down to earth like that? Getting so close to the mountains."

"I had a blast!" Ginny held out her martini glass. "I didn't even need the barf bag."

"I hate to admit it," Craig sat down at the table and spread a napkin on his lap. Ginny thought what Ray might have done with the white cloth. *Wipe his ass with it, probably.* She was feeling less guilty and even a little less angry with Ray, and last night, for the first time in a long while, had managed to sleep through the night.

"But I thought for a second I was going to be the one with my insides turning out," Craig continued.

"Thanks for the visual." Ginny cut open her medium-rare filet mignon and took a bite. It was the best thing she'd ever eaten. "I've died and gone to heaven."

"You weren't the least bit queasy when the pilot was turning the plane on its side?"

"Umm, no," said Ginny. "You're kind of a wuss, aren't you?"

"Nice," he said while dipping his fry into some sort of the yummy mayonnaise, ketchup, and chipotle concoction. "Thanks a lot."

"Sorry," said Ginny. "Ray's influence, I guess." She could feel herself blushing, worrying she may have just blown it. "Hey, don't hog the sauce."

"You know," said Craig, "we've been busy running around and haven't had much time to talk about the important stuff."

Ginny's mouth was full, and she pointed to it as she chewed. "And you think right now's a good time for a heart-to-heart?"

"Let's talk about you." Craig handed Ginny a napkin.

"My favorite subject." Ginny hoped she didn't have any food stuck in her teeth. *Nothing worse than laying it all out on the line with a hunk of shiny gristle wedged between my incisors.*

"I mean it," said Craig. "What do you want to do for the rest of your life? Besides, of course, seeing the Rolling Stones in concert?"

His seriousness jarred Ginny. She was twenty-two years old and had been on a path predetermined by her parents, then her husband, for so long that she hardly knew how to respond to such a question. To her husband, and even to her mother, voicing her desire was the equivalent of provoking a fight. Most of the time it had been easier just to go along with everyone else's wishes. It had been all Ray's plan—the house, the future children, the dinners at family-friendly chain restaurants twice a month.

Now she cringed at the thought. But somewhere inside her, she knew it was time to take responsibility. It wasn't like she didn't know what she was in for when she signed the marriage certificate. Blaming Ray had only been a cop-out because she was too afraid to take life by the horns. Fear had been ruling her for a long time, she realized.

While her friends were packing up and heading to college,

Ginny stayed behind. She had been accepted into a state university, and although her parents had never pushed her academically, they were willing to pay for everything. Virginia had been especially forceful, going as far as registering Ginny for classes. But when she saw her fall schedule and visited the dorm room she'd have to share with someone else, she freaked out. The campus seemed too big, the unknown life of a co-ed too intimidating.

Besides, Ginny justified to herself back then, she didn't want to leave her then-new boyfriend Ray behind. Ginny promised to attend classes at the community college, but when the registration deadline came and went, she ended up lazing around the house, sleeping until noon and spending the rest of the day swimming in the pool or hanging out at the mall.

Her parents weren't too thrilled with the direction Ginny's life was taking, and they threatened to kick her out unless she either got a job or went back to school. She didn't have a clue what to do. Nobody had ever told her she was good at anything in particular and she earned average grades her entire high school career, despite her one-percent-below-the-norm label.

But one night while Ginny was in her bedroom painting her nails, she saw a TV commercial pitching a local cosmetology school. "Graduate in fewer than ten months," it promised. Best of all, they guaranteed job placement. It seemed like the best solution.

Ginny put the cover back over her empty plate. She had eaten the entire steak, despite her best efforts to be dainty. "When I left California," she said, "I didn't think about the future beyond the Stones tour."

"No pressure," said Craig. "Just curious."

Ginny thought back to the night she left Ray. She distinctly remembered that her journey was supposed to be an attempt to go back to a time before everything had gotten so complicated. To start over.

"I've always wondered if I had gone to college, what I'd be doing now," she said.

"You never know," said Craig. He took off his jacket and draped it over the back of his chair. "You make a lot of discoveries while you're in school."

"I started a few classes at the local community college." Shortly after her marriage and subsequent miscarriage, Ginny enrolled in the spring semester and went for the first month. Though Ray had made it nearly impossible, calling from work with false emergencies and guilt trips on nights when he knew she had classes. "But I had to drop out."

"That's too bad—who's to say where you'd be now? I went to England for a semester to study literature." Craig uncovered a gooey piece of chocolate cake. "It was a mind-blowing experience." He dug his fork in and offered the cake to Ginny. "Bite?"

He fed her, the dessert melting in her mouth.

"It changed my life. Opened my eyes and showed me there was so much more to see in the world. Vegas is fun, for sure, but London is a whole other experience," said Craig.

Ginny nodded, trying not to make it too obvious that she was checking out the curve of his shoulders through his snugly fitted shirt. She felt a little bad for interrupting his reminiscence with her fantasies, though she'd heard men think of sex every seven seconds and wondered how many times it had crossed Craig's mind.

"Why don't we go sometime?"

"I can't." The knee-jerk response flew out of her mouth before she had time to consider it.

"Why not?" he asked. "It's easy. You just get on a plane."

"I don't know." Ginny washed down the chocolate with water. "I've never done anything like that." Why was she saying this? *Didn't I just leave everything behind to follow the Rolling Stones on tour?*

"I'll show you around. Take you to the theater. We'll shop at the famous stores and spend Christmas Eve in a quaint little pub, drinking pints of Guinness."

"I can't believe I said I couldn't go." She envisioned the two of them curled up by a fireplace in a romantic Tudor house in the English countryside. "Of course I can go!"

He moved his chair closer to hers and gave her a peck on the cheek. She put her hands on his shoulders and held him there for a real kiss on the mouth. He stood up, and Ginny followed him to the bedroom. He continued kissing her and peeled off her clothes, tossing them over the chaise. His movements were slow and deliberate. He unbuttoned her jeans and pulled her blouse over her head, stopping to kiss her exposed flesh. She kicked off her panties while he unlatched her bra.

Once she undressed him, Craig pulled back the covers and they both got into the bed. She inhaled the clean smell of freshly washed sheets. His skin was warm and soft. He was on top of her, and Ginny ran her hands along his body. He was in good shape—toned but not overly muscular. She could tell he worked out, but that he didn't spend all his time in a gym pumping iron, like so many numbskulls she had encountered in her life.

He looked down at her and seemed to like the view. "Let me take a look at you," he said, rolling her on top of him. He moaned as she straddled him.

For the first time ever, Ginny felt sexy and, oddly enough, comfortable. She wasn't thinking about her cellulite or the size of her breasts, only the pure sensation of good, unadulterated sex.

25

BREE

Bree was down two hundred dollars, but it could have been five thousand for all she cared. Playing video poker barside helped pass the time until Ginny arrived. Bree had something huge to share, and she was winning in so many ways that it didn't matter the game was probably rigged or the odds against her. Just last night, she had played the ultimate hand, laid it all out the table, and had hit big-time. The lousy machine at the MGM Grand had nothing on her.

For the first time in years, Bree felt butterflies in her stomach when she thought of a man. It had been difficult getting excited when she'd always kept them at a distance by gaining the upper hand. She had forced herself to see men as predictable creatures. Control the environment—give them just enough attention and a smidgen of hope—and they responded like Pavlov's dogs. Poor Jerry didn't have a chance. Instead, Billy was the one who had Bree panting for more.

Last night, Billy said he'd waited long enough and had to have her right there, and they had the most amazing sex in his dressing room. He practically ripped the straps off her top and they both fell to the floor, making love on the blue-and-gold hotel carpet. It was better than she remembered, and Bree had gotten a little jealous, speculating about how he had become such a great lover. She reached around and rubbed the sore on her lower back. The rug burn was a battle scar she could live with. Glancing at her watch, Bree sipped her sparkling water, hoping Ginny would hurry up. Billy was going onstage again in a few hours.

Strolling over in a black cotton tank, denim jeans rolled up just above the ankles to show off a pair of green suede Mary Jane pumps that Bree would bet her life were brand-spanking new, Ginny sat down at the bar and ordered a Diet Coke.

"Who are you, and what did you do with my dowdy friend?" asked Bree.

Ginny shrugged her shoulders. "I sent her packing."

"Good riddance to her!" Bree raised her glass and took a drink. She was dying to tell Ginny the news but wanted to savor the moment.

"Water?" Ginny asked.

"I've got to run soon." Billy had promised to take her out after his set and show her the *real* Las Vegas.

"But I just got here, and Craig's coming down any minute." Ginny slung her new purse over the back of her chair. "Where have you been, anyway?"

"I've been dying to tell you." Bree inhaled, preparing herself. "It's Billy Blade."

"The singer?" said Ginny. "Your ex-boyfriend?"

"He has an act here in Vegas." Bree took a sip of her water, spilling a little bit on her blouse. "I went to see him."

"What!" Ginny practically jumped out of her seat. "Why

didn't you tell me you were going? You know I'm in love with him too!"

The people at the bar couldn't hear over the loud casino noises, but Bree lowered her voice anyway.

"We've spent every moment together since," she said, replaying their time together over and over in her mind. "I'm going to see him again tonight."

"Oh, Bree," Ginny squealed. "I'm so happy for you. I can't believe it."

"But there's more," she said, anxious to reveal what she'd been waiting all day to tell Ginny.

"More than true love persevering?" asked Ginny.

"You've seen too many soap operas," said Bree.

Ginny whimpered, "Are you gonna tell me or what?"

"When I explained to Billy why we were here: to see the Stones . . . "

"Yeah?" said Ginny, sliding so close to the edge of her barstool that she almost fell off.

"He made a phone call," said Bree.

"And?" Ginny screamed. "You're killing me!"

"Billy scored backstage passes to the concert Saturday night." Bree grabbed hold of Ginny's wrists, as if to brace her for the news. "You're going to finally meet Mick Jagger!"

26

GINNY

Thanks to the heat wave hitting Las Vegas in mid-October, Ginny set up camp at the Producer's Pool, one of the five swimming pools at the MGM. She spread a large beach towel over the full length of the lounge chair and bundled up another to prop up her head. The hotel referred to their pools as "tropical oases in the desert," and this one was indeed paradise, thought Ginny. The water reflected the blue, cloudless sky, and she gazed up at the coconut palms.

The sun was doing its magic, prickling her skin with UV rays. She knew what the dermatologists said about skin cancer, but getting a substantial dose of vitamin D was underrated. Besides, she subscribed to the idea that everything looked better with a tan, especially the coating of fat starting to form around her belly and thighs. She could pinch way more than an inch. Calories did count, even while she was on the road. She vowed to eat better.

Leafing through the latest issue of *InStyle*, Ginny inspected the fall shoes. A to-die-for pair of fancy black designer wedges caught her attention, but at $900 a pop, they were better suited for a wealthy woman. Someone who had more than a wad of twenties and fifties stuffed in a hotel safety-deposit box. It was enough, though, to stay on the road for a while without having to depend on Bree. Finally, Ginny was finding the independence she had been craving all along.

A busty cocktail waitress, wearing nothing more than a triangle bikini top and sarong tied around her waist, brought Ginny the strawberry daiquiri she had ordered before she made her dietary resolution. She sipped the drink and hoped the vitamins from the fruit might justify the rest.

Her mind kept drifting back to Ray and their probable divorce. Would he fight her, take her to court and ask for alimony? He worked so sporadically, sometimes getting paid under the table. It would be easy to say she was supporting him, even on her meager salary. If he knew she'd won twenty thousand dollars, he'd demand half up front. Thinking about it made her miserable. Ray, that little shit, was always lingering in the background and overwhelming her with dread.

He had started calling her three or four times a day, leaving messages she deleted immediately. She didn't want to worry about it anymore, though. The most important night of her life was fast approaching, and she had to start preparing mentally to meet Mick Jagger backstage. Baking her skin to a bronzy shimmer, she was determined to look and feel fabulous. As she imagined what she might wear, it occurred to her that there was probably going to be a whole gang of supermodels and glamorous celebrity types clamoring to make their impression too.

How would she compete? What would she say? "Mick, I'm

your biggest fan." *No, everybody says that.* She could talk about his music. People like their talents acknowledged. She'd march right up to Mick Jagger, take his hand in hers, and, in the sincerest possible way, she'd say, "Your music moves me." He would then look her in the eye and know she meant it; she was the most devoted fan in the room. Surely he'd appreciate her loyalty, even if she couldn't compete with all the super babes surrounding the Stones.

Mick might be so intrigued by her he'd invite her to his hotel room. They'd drink expensive wine and listen to music—the Rolling Stones, of course. He'd ask her to name her favorite song, but Ginny would say it depended on her mood. "Waiting on a Friend" made the top five. He'd say it was one of his favorites too, and then he would talk about his Caribbean getaway on the island of Mustique. He'd say it was his favorite place on earth, and she must come with him.

When he asked to see her again, she'd tell him she couldn't bear to share him with the *other* women. He'd say that compared to her, there were no other women. Then it would be her turn to look him in the eyes and know he meant it.

"*Allo . . . allo, allo, allo.* Beer, a beer. Coca-Cola, beer. Donuts."

The shouting startled Ginny out of one of her most awesome Jagger daydreams yet. Craig was standing over her wearing a tight little pair of swim briefs. They were a cross between tighty whities and board shorts. Even though he had the bod to go with, she couldn't help thinking they were better suited for a professional swimmer than a hotel consultant. But she supposed there was something sort of *international* about them and got over her initial desire to giggle.

"That's what they say in the French Riviera. There are guys who actually go around selling food on the beach."

"Donuts!" Ginny stuck out her tongue in disapproval. "Something about an old-fashioned sprinkled with sand doesn't appeal to me." She tried to yank up her bikini bottoms, thinking half an inch more of fabric might cover the roll of fat.

Craig dragged an empty lounge chair close to Ginny's. "Mind if I open this?" he said, already cranking up the umbrella. "It's hot out here."

"There goes my tan," said Ginny.

"I like you the way you are," said Craig.

His words sounded eerily familiar to Ginny, like something Ray would say to keep her from doing what she wanted. She stood up and pulled her chair back into the sun, rearranged the outdoor bedding, and plopped back down.

"I'll take you there sometime." Craig opened up a bag of pistachios and cracked one open, tossing the nut into his mouth. "You'd love Cannes. And don't worry, your donut won't get sand on it."

"Why's that?" said Ginny. Eating fried dough and exposing her body at the same time seemed almost sacrilegious. She and her girlfriends used to starve themselves before going to the beach. This ensured a flat stomach, they thought ridiculously. On the way home, they'd reward themselves by chowing down on chili-cheese fries.

"Because the shore is covered with stones. People sit on straw mats or rent a cabana from one of the beach clubs. Picture it," he said, "the two of us strolling down the promenade, with fuchsia, yellow, and lilac flower gardens on one side and the azure-blue sea on the other."

Ginny was on her stomach now, looking up at Craig while his head was somewhere in the French Riviera. She untied the strap on her top to avoid any tan lines in case she decided to wear a backless dress to the concert. Asking Craig to rub sunscreen on her back might drive him to give a lecture on the sun and skin cancer. He seemed a little too talkative today.

The night before, she told Craig about the backstage passes. She might have been imagining it, but he'd seemed almost jealous at the idea of Ginny meeting Mick Jagger. It wasn't anything overt. He didn't demand to be by her side or even go with her, but there had been something muted about his reaction. Anxious to tell him the exciting news, she had rushed back to his suite and blurted it out in the hallway, even before Craig had a chance to invite her in.

Without much emotion or enthusiasm, he said, "I'm happy for you." *That was it!* And it was the *for you* part that bothered her the most. It seemed condescending, like he needed to qualify her happiness. As if getting to meet Mick Jagger would only be exciting to someone like her, someone less sophisticated and worldly.

Maybe she was being paranoid, she thought, and tried not to parse out every word he uttered. "That does sound amazing. I'd love to go there someday."

"Let's go," said Craig. "I'll take you."

"First England, now France. I better make sure my passport's not expired." She'd never applied for one in the first place. In her old life, she was certain she wouldn't be going anywhere exciting. Ray wouldn't haul a backpack around Europe to soak in the sights.

Craig slathered sunscreen on his face, making sure to

apply extra on his nose. "Who needs college when you have me to teach you everything you need to know about the world?"

"Some things I want to experience for myself," said Ginny. She felt angry. *Here is another guy standing in my way.* She tried to stay calm, telling herself he was only being generous.

Craig seemed unfazed by Ginny's defensiveness. "What better experience than total immersion in another culture?"

She imagined herself in a Paris café, ordering a croissant with her crappy French accent as the long-suffering waiter tried to correct her pronunciation. "I doubt being a tourist is the same thing as total immersion."

"You're limiting yourself," he said. "What I'm trying to say is, sometimes getting outside the four walls of a state institution is the best thing you can do for your education."

It annoyed Ginny that he assumed she'd be going to a state university instead of the kind of fancy school where she imagined he'd gone. "But I have hardly been inside the walls to begin with."

"Trust me," said Craig. "Someday you'll know what I'm talking about."

"I hope I get the opportunity." She suppressed the urge to tell him to mind his own business.

Her strawberry daiquiri had melted to a sloshy mix of pink water. When she arched up to take a sip, she forgot about the untied bikini. "Oh no." She dropped her drink to clutch the top to her body. "Close call, but look." She pointed to the puddle on the cement. "I guess that's why they serve drinks in plastic cups."

Craig fidgeted with his bag of pistachios. He seemed irritated by the commotion.

She thought it was kind of funny. Of course she'd be ditzy enough to sit up when her straps were undone. It reminded her of the first time she had been drunk. When somebody asked for the time, she checked her watch while forgetting she was holding a beer in the same hand, spilling her drink all over the floor.

"I don't want to get arrested for indecent exposure," said Ginny. She tried to loosen things up. "You'd have to bail me out of jail in time to meet Mick Jagger."

"In France, the women bathe topless."

"Okay," she said, unhappy about his snotty attitude. He was treating her like some sort of backwoods hillbilly. "But we're not in France, are we?"

He shook his head. "That's for sure." Craig lifted his chin in the direction of a nearby family splashing around in the pool.

An overweight mother and her chubby baby girl floated by. She flapped her inflatable pool wings and laughed as her mother smothered her with kisses. Her son yelled, "Marco," awaiting the return call from his father, who was nearby. Ginny saw a happy family, whereas Craig looked on with obvious disdain.

♪

GINNY COVERED HERSELF IN A THIN LAYER OF ALOE VERA gel the guy at the gift shop recommended to soothe sunburns. She only wanted to pretend to fall asleep so Craig would stop talking to her at the pool. Had she known she'd conk out for nearly two hours, she would have covered up or gone back to her room. Except for the white circles around her eyes where the sunglasses had been, her face was burned to a nice shade of strawberry jam. This new look didn't quite fit into the Mick Jagger fantasy she'd had earlier.

When she woke up by the pool, Craig was gone. She guessed he'd thought it was rude of her to nod off in the middle of their conversation and left without saying a word.

He had left a voicemail inviting her to dinner. If she was interested, he'd said, give him a call. Otherwise he'd see her in the morning. *What a cool customer.* From what she could tell, he'd never lose his temper. Craig probably thought it was a sign of weakness to let people see that he could be vulnerable.

Bree was out for the evening, so Ginny thought she might like a night alone in the room anyway. She wanted to paint her fingernails and watch TV. The soft, silky robe was about the only fabric she could tolerate next to her fried skin.

She surfed through the channels in search of the perfect chick flick, relishing this new freedom. Ray said that if he were forced to watch another show on the ladies' network, he'd shoot the TV just like Elvis had. In fact, he said, it was probably Priscilla who drove Elvis to do it by making him watch *Beach Blanket Bingo* or some other air-headed movie a gazillion times. For some reason, Ray felt he had a personal connection with Elvis and could cite a few factoids of his own.

The hotel telephone rang, and Ginny flicked off the set.

"Hello," she said.

"Hey there, sexy mama," said a voice. "Are you being naughty?"

"Who is this?"

"Who's this?" said the voice, embarrassed that he had been

caught trying to play an awkward game of phone sex. He cleared his throat. "Bree?"

"Hey, Rocky." Ginny finally recognized the voice. "Bree's out, but I'll tell her you called." She took down his information and hung up before he pressed her for anything more. Bree would have to deal with her own jilted lovers.

Ginny was relieved it wasn't Craig, but this realization made her uneasy. Wasn't he the perfect man she'd been looking for? He was charming, smart, and fun. He'd been all over the world and was willing to introduce her to new adventures. The perfect man for a Wild and Spontaneous woman, he was the Ken to her Barbie. What had gone wrong?

Ginny feared she was being unreasonable, but when she thought back to the family by the pool, she couldn't ignore Craig's reaction.

Her Aunt Chloe was overweight too, and Ginny could only imagine what Craig would have to say about her mother's sister. Ginny remembered wrapping her arms around a large, loving, and beautiful woman who protected Ginny with her greatness in strength and volume. She realized she wasn't the most noble person, and she sometimes judged people unfairly, but she couldn't tolerate that kind of meanness.

Another thing she couldn't shake was the feeling Craig was just another Ray in a more polished package. What had once started out as a comforting motto—"It's been taken care of, compliments of Craig"—was becoming a warning sign too hard to ignore. Ray wanted to take care of everything as well, even if it was in his own muddled way.

Ginny suspected she might be going backward.

27

BREE

The lovers floated by. Under bridges and beneath wrought-iron balconies inside the hotel, the gondoliers swept the delighted couples, who had just spent more than sixty dollars for the privilege of pretending they were in Venice cruising the real Canal Grande. Dressed in black-and-white-striped shirts with large red sashes tied around their waists, the men paddled as they belted out Italian songs, each trying to outdo the others. When a bride and groom appeared in one of the gondolas, the bystanders broke into applause. Prompted by the cheering, the equivalent of wedding guests tapping their wine glasses, the newlyweds kissed.

Two weeks ago, Bree might have found this performance a cheesy replacement, the poor man's version of world travel. She had been fortunate enough to visit the real Venice a few times in her life, and normally she hated the idea of such a superficial substitute. It was a sorry excuse to stay sheltered and ignorant of other cultures, she had always believed. *What would Billy think of the ride*, she wondered, imagining the two of them gliding past. Somehow, with him, it all seemed so romantic.

Despite herself, she waved at the couples. She felt too good not to share in their joy. For once, she squelched the nagging voice in her head that told her to run away and protect herself and others from inevitable disappointment. Instead she pulled out her phone to see if Billy had called.

He and his band were rehearsing some new songs Billy had written recently. He said he had been afraid to reveal them to his bandmates until he had reunited with Bree. She had been his muse, and her presence inspired him to take the risk and try out the new songs at rehearsal. It had been years since he had produced anything, and Billy worried the fans might boo him off the stage when he tried to incorporate anything unfamiliar into his set of the old standbys.

He was ridiculously talented, she assured him, and even if everybody in the entire place left, she'd still be there standing by his side. She had said she'd follow him to the ends of the earth, and finally she was there to make good on the promise.

A perfect cumulous cloud formation was painted on the ceiling above. Bree suspected it changed as the day progressed, turning to a pinkish glow right around dusk. By then she would be long gone, creating her own idyllic atmosphere.

Hordes of people filed in and out of the shops, and Bree thought she might see Ginny, who seemed to be burning through her winnings at record speed. She searched for her friend but got lost in the sea of heads filling the hotel lobby. Soon enough they'd be face-to-face with the Stones, and she would be there to witness the single most exciting event in another person's life. It was as if she had midwifed the experience for Ginny, and Bree was proud of herself for sticking around.

Everything seemed to be coming together for both of them. Last night Billy had said he loved her. It was absurd—she knew it was impossible to love a person she hadn't seen in years, but it felt good to let go and believe the unbelievable. She was allowing someone to crack open her heart. It was a little scary, feeling vulnerable all over again. A warm and fuzzy Bree seemed to be invading her body, replacing the tough-as-nails chick she tried to be.

She had no choice but to go with it.

"McQueen," said a little boy, holding up a miniature race car and snapping Bree out of her trance. He wheeled the car on her bench, over her knees, and around to the other side.

"Steve McQueen?" she asked, looking around for his parents.

"McQueen." He made a zooming sound as the car launched to the ground. Pulling another toy from his pocket, he handed it to her.

The little boy must have been about four years old and had dark almond eyes and brown hair that Bree thought needed to be trimmed.

"Where are your parents?" Bree took the car and the boy by the hand so he wouldn't run off. His little fingers wiggled in hers. She had forgotten what it was like to hold a child's hand. His skin was so soft and the fingers so small, she had to keep herself from gobbling them up.

"What's your name?" she asked, pushing the fringe from his eyes.

"Felix," he said, holding out his free hand so Bree would give back his car.

"Are you lost?"

"No."

"Where's your mommy?" He shook his little head, and she thought he might have gotten into trouble and was hiding from his mother. She remembered how Tori used to wander off, leaving her mother in hysterics while she notified every salesperson and security guard within two miles.

"Mama," the little boy repeated.

The word startled Bree. It had been Tori's first, much to Dimmit's disappointment. He'd been sure she'd say Dada or Papa first. Even though she hadn't been quite eighteen when Tori was born, Bree thought she'd be a great mom. How could she have known the depression would consume her, and that over time she'd become the living embodiment of everyone's low expectations. Despite the many opportunities she had to make amends, she always failed, even as recently as last year.

At first Bree had been happy to be included in the planning phase of Tori's middle-school graduation party, receiving the emails going back and forth between Tori's paternal grandmother and aunts as they discussed the party theme. Should it be a dance party or a luau? What about a pool party? They even insisted the food have a theme—Mediterranean or Italian? Cuban or barbecue?

Why was it so complicated, she wondered. For Bree's graduation, her own mother had just taken her to lunch. As soon as the rest of the family put Bree in charge of the party favors, she became overwhelmed and blocked their emails.

Living in Seattle at the time, she said she'd pay for Tori's party, praying it would be enough to excuse her from the all-consuming deliberations. She should've known better. Nothing ever satisfied her daughter, especially when her mother was the one doing the offering. Tori called in a huff one afternoon.

"You're embarrassing me," she said. "Aunt Hillary says I shouldn't allow you to do this to me."

"Allow?" Bree wasn't sure what that meant. It seemed that Tori was always allowing herself to resent her mother.

"Every time, I set myself up for this. I think you've changed, and then . . ."

"It's only a party." Once Bree stopped participating, it was only a matter of time before the gossip machine was in full throttle. Dimmit's family made any excuse to remind Victoria that her mother was a flake, a woman too self-involved to be counted on.

"My party, Mom."

How many children had the ability to take an endearing title like Mom and use it like a knife? Bree wondered.

"I've offered to pay for the whole thing," she said, figuring she might as well get out of the party altogether. "Listen, Tori, something's come up and—"

"I don't want your stupid money."

She waited for the click. Tori enjoyed hanging up on her mother, so Bree held on, figuring she owed her daughter that one pleasure. Instead she heard Tori breathing on the other end as she calmed herself down.

"I didn't want the party in the first place. It was Aunt Hillary's idea, and I'm sort of stuck."

"Is it too late to call the whole thing off?"

"That's why I need your help. You only have to stay for a week. I'm sure your bags are already packed for someplace else."

"I'll just get in the way," said Bree, wanting to spare her

daughter the burden of the family feud that was sure to start as soon as she butted in.

"I want my mother."

"You don't," said Bree, believing it at the time.

"Never mind," Tori whispered. She hung up without saying good-bye.

Bree would give anything to take back that moment. It had been an invitation, an olive branch she had been too scared to accept. Instead of booking the next flight to Florida, she'd poured wine at a local vineyard. Tori had needed her mother, had reached out to her and asked her to spend this once-in-a-lifetime moment with her daughter, and Bree had screwed up.

"Oh my goodness," a woman shouted from the entrance of a nearby store. She ran toward little Felix, scooping him up in her arms. "My little stinker. You scared me."

"McQueen," said Felix, holding the car up for his mother to see.

The woman kissed him about a thousand times, crying and thanking Bree for watching over her son.

Tori's graduation party was apparently a huge success. Bree had only seen pictures, tiny digital images sent on her phone. Each month, she promised to visit. Each month, she broke that promise.

28

GINNY

At the entrance of the MGM Grand, Ginny tried to shield herself from the afternoon sun with an advertisement for prostitutes somebody had handed her. She was waiting for Craig, who'd had room service deliver breakfast to her along with a note, asking her to meet him at noon. He had yet another surprise. Figuring she owed him a chance, she agreed and put aside her apprehension about where the relationship was heading. Perhaps she had been too harsh yesterday. After all, Ginny realized she was far from perfect as she adjusted the bra strap that was digging into her burned skin.

With all the traveling and excitement, it was hard to know if her instincts were on track or fried. He paid for their flight and put them up in a gorgeous suite. What more did she need? The bottom line was that he had been taking care of her, treating her like a princess. Wasn't that what she had always wanted?

The funny feeling in her stomach told her otherwise.

She found a shady spot just behind the valet stand. Then Craig pulled up in a large motorhome. The green-and-white monster rumbled to the curb. At least thirty-five feet long, it practically blocked out the daylight.

The spot was tight, but he parked with the skill of an experienced recreational roadster. Who knew Craig was capable of maneuvering a giant motorhome? Fishing or roasting marshmallows didn't seem to suit the guy. It seemed weird, totally out of character for a man who probably equated opening an L. L. Bean catalogue with the great outdoors.

"What is that?" Ginny walked out from behind the valet stand.

Craig honked and waved. "How do you like this baby?"

She didn't quite know what to think. In fact, if someone had told her last month she'd be following the Rolling Stones on tour, hooking up with a new guy, and about to meet Mick Jagger, she'd have given them a one-way ticket to the loony bin.

He cut the motor and disappeared from Ginny's sight. "What we have here," he said, appearing at the side door, "is a 2010 motorhome, Class A. It's slightly used, but she's a beauty, isn't she?" Craig pushed a button, releasing the stairs. He held out his hand to Ginny. "Climb aboard."

She wandered to the back of the RV to examine it, never having seen one up close before. Her mother would have dropped dead before letting the family hit the trail like Davy Crockett or some hokey frontier family. To her, nature was something that grew up between the crevices of her flagstone patio and got sprayed away with Roundup. Virginia had worked too hard to fit in with the upper-class set to roam around the country in a motorhome.

Craig ran outside to a window near the back and cranked

open the awning. "And there's also a great big canopy you attach up to the sides." He paused, perhaps waiting for her full attention. "See?" he asked, pointing to the poles. "This pops up, and you've got yourself a nice, relaxing shady spot. Put a couple of chairs underneath, and you're set."

Ducking underneath the doorway, Ginny stepped inside. She wasn't sure what to expect and was pleasantly surprised by the roominess. Directly in front of her was a full-length sofa, comfy enough to stretch out on and take a long nap. To her left was a kitchen, equipped with a sink, refrigerator, microwave, and oven. She imagined herself at the counter making lunch while Craig transported them to the Hoover Dam or Mount Rushmore. The driver and passenger seats swiveled around to face inward. That's where their friends could sit and swap stories of their adventures. *It wouldn't be so bad*, Ginny thought. When Craig saw her looking in that direction, he opened the closet and pulled out a captain's hat, taking his seat at the helm.

"It's a dream to drive," he said, placing his hands on the steering wheel.

Where did the suave Craig go, and who was this nerd before her? Ginny questioned if she was being shallow and wondered if she had been projecting a fantasy guy onto him all along. "It certainly is different than I imagined it would be."

"It's got satellite and everything." He pulled down a television set. "So you see," said Craig, "our own little piece of traveling paradise. A vacation on wheels."

"Ours?" Ginny opened the door to the bathroom. A little wooden doll sat on the back of the toilet seat with a sign around its neck that read "Home Is Where the Heart Is." "Did you buy this thing?" Ginny wasn't sure if she should sit down or run. She wasn't about to leave one man's home only to wind up in another's.

"No, I rented her. But if we like her, the guy at the dealership said he'd give us a screaming deal." Craig ushered her down the hallway.

Ginny didn't like this whole merging of pronouns all of a sudden. There was *him* and *her*, separate entities. The *us* business, not to mention Craig's constant reference to the motorhome as a woman, was a little freaky. It was getting on her nerves. Nothing was feminine about the massive, loud, and overpowering vehicle, which didn't in any way resemble the Barbie motorhome Ginny had when she was a kid. The sunny yellow and bubblegum pink toy had provided her with hours of entertainment, an opportunity to imagine adventures with Barbie in the driver's seat and Ken along for the ride, if he was lucky.

Suddenly it seemed like the Ken doll was trying to take over. It just didn't work like that in Barbie's world.

"I'm a little confused," said Ginny. "You know I have the concert coming up, and after that, it's Texas."

Craig opened the bedroom door. "And Boston and Philadelphia and Chicago. I know. That's the great thing. You and I can travel across the country in comfort."

"Our home on wheels," she said, knowing the sarcasm would be lost on him. Ginny sat on the bed.

"Comfy, isn't it?"

"It almost feels as good as my hotel bed," she said.

"Probably better. Feel that pillow-top mattress."

Ginny stood up. She didn't want Craig to get any ideas

about putting the bed to use anytime soon. "What about Bree? She's coming too."

"If you can tear her away from her latest soul mate," Craig said, opening the closet to reveal it had already been packed with his clothes.

"She's really in love this time."

Craig shook his head at her as if she were an innocent little girl. "Sweetie," he came at her from behind, massaging her shoulders. "It's only a matter of time before she finds a new project. She doesn't love the Stones like you do. She doesn't have your loyalty."

Ginny thought back to the beginning of their journey. After the Phoenix concert, she had wondered if Bree was in it for the long haul. They had been on their way to New Mexico, Ginny's mind lost in Mick Jagger fantasies, when the steering wheel of the car started to vibrate. The wobbling had alerted Bree to something wrong, and she told Ginny not to slam on her brakes.

"Why not?" Ginny asked but followed her orders anyway. Bree seemed to know what she was talking about.

"Now gradually slow down and pull over to the side of the road."

"What's happening?" Ginny pulled the car over in the middle of nowhere and started to panic. "F-f-f-fudge!" she cried.

Bree laughed. "It's only a flat tire. No need to use the F-word."

She could see Bree was making fun of her. "I'll call Triple A."

"Nah," Bree said, getting out of the car. "I'll fix it."

Ginny unbuckled herself and followed Bree to the back of the car.

"Just gotta get the spare." Bree opened the trunk. "It's in here, right?" She rummaged through their things. "What about the tools? I don't see them."

"Tools?" asked Ginny.

"Tell me you've got a jack, at least."

"I'm not sure," said Ginny. "Ray takes care of all that stuff."

"You can't depend on anyone," she said. "Do you know what this means?"

"We'll wait for a truck driver to come by?"

"I don't know about you, but in the last hour, I've seen exactly one car on the road," said Bree.

"You're just trying to scare me."

"We could be out here all night."

"I'm calling Triple A."

"Go ahead, but it could be weeks before they find us, and I'm getting hungry." Bree gazed out into the horizon. The sun was setting, and it had started to get cold. "Hey, didn't the Donner Party pass through here? We might have to resort to their survival tactics."

Ginny stomped back to the car to get her cell phone. She didn't need the aggravation and was prepared to ditch Bree in Santa Fe.

While they waited for the tow trunk to come help change the tire, Ginny was furious. She hated being teased, especially by someone who was just tagging along. Bree scribbled in her journal and surfed the Internet on her phone while Ginny pouted.

"Done," Bree said, putting down her pen. "I wrote something special for you." She held the opened page underneath the interior car light and began to read:

"Ginny, my 'Lady Jane,' my 'Jiving Sister Fanny.' 'Some Girls' wouldn't be so supportive of each other, but not us. The 'Loving Cup' of our friendship continues to overflow because, as you know, 'Time Is on My Side,' and you can always count on me for an 'Emotional Rescue,' to be here when you're 'Torn and Frayed' and wanna 'Rip This Joint.'"

Bree paused to wait for Ginny's reaction, and probably to make sure she understood that Bree was incorporating Stones songs titles into her apology.

"Don't make a 'Saint of Me' because 'Everybody Needs Somebody to Love,' and you are one awesome 'Honky Tonk Woman,'" said Bree, exaggerating her gestures, moving her eyebrows up and down, winking and smiling at all the appropriate spots to go with what she was reading.

"So 'Take It or Leave It.' You are stuck with me, 'Sister Morphine,' to walk the 'Moonlight Mile' or 'Paint It, Black.' Either way, I'm so proud of you because now you can finally sing 'I'm Free' and mean it."

When she finished, Bree handed the letter to Ginny. "What do you think?"

"I think that's the nicest thing anybody's ever done for me," said Ginny, folding the paper and tucking it into her back pocket so she could put it in her Rolling Stones lunch pail and read it again later.

Ginny removed herself from Craig's embrace. She felt a lump in her throat, the same nagging feeling she got whenever her mother and Ray started up. She didn't have the nerve to tell them both to shut up. Bree was her friend, and by insulting her, Craig was hurting Ginny. It was time to speak up.

"Maybe you're threatened by Bree because she's the kind of

person who doesn't let guys like you tell her what to do."

Craig's face burned red. "Is that what you think I'm doing? I know what I want, and I go for it."

She walked toward the front of the motorhome, wanting to be near the door in case things got weird. "We should slow down a bit."

Craig sat down on the sofa and removed his captain's hat. "Sure," he said. "It's your call."

She felt bad. She was so focused on her own needs, she hadn't considered how she might be hurting others. It wasn't Craig's fault. He hadn't been another obstacle to her freedom. Ginny was the one who had created this idealized relationship with him. It was all an illusion, as authentic as the Eiffel Tower down the street, and because she had wanted Craig to be the perfect companion so badly, she had been willing to turn herself over to a man she hardly knew.

"Yeah, I need to go for what *I* want this time, and I need to do it alone," she said.

Craig offered his hand. "We can still be friends, right?"

A gentleman to the end, she thought, realizing that she might be kicking herself tomorrow for letting this one get away. But she had to go with her gut.

"Is it too late to return it to the dealership?"

Craig sat down in the driver's seat. "The tank's full and the blacktop's ahead of me. You think you're the only one allowed to go on a road trip?"

"I hear Yosemite's a nice place to visit this time of year."

Ginny walked back to the hotel. She tried not to turn around, a cowgirl riding off into the sunset. Surprisingly, she didn't feel sad or let down—for once in her life, she'd actually chosen freedom over security, adventure over another unhealthy relationship.

She heard the motorhome rumble to a start and drive away, and she didn't feel a tinge of regret as she listened to her dreams of London, Paris, and Mount Rushmore drive off down Las Vegas Boulevard. They had never felt true to her, and if she wanted to, she could travel anywhere in the world without Craig Mitchum. Or any other man, for that matter.

29

BREE

Bree hadn't bothered to check her phone messages or do much of anything that connected her with the rest of humanity since reuniting with Billy Blade. It was as if they had shut out the rest of the world, like two junkies getting high on love. They'd spent the past few days in Billy's home, a gorgeous two-bedroom, three-thousand-square-foot condo on Dean Martin Drive with a to-die-for view, leather bedroom walls, and a freshwater fish tank. They'd made love and talked and made love again.

Billy described his Las Vegas fans, who ranged from "*I'm Your Biggest Fan*" to "My *Mother's* Your Biggest Fan." He said they were mostly female, and some of them were "originals." Gigging in Las Vegas hadn't been a resignation to failure or career suicide. He moved there a few years ago and felt fulfilled knowing that thousands of people planned their trips around his performances, buying tickets months in advance. These fans knew all the words to his songs, and he enjoyed reminding them of simpler and better times, perceived or real. Most importantly, he teased, they gazed up at him as if he were the perfect man, one who would never grow old, lose his hair, or get fat.

"You've got great hair." Bree ran her hand through his bleached-blond locks, not caring one bit about the few gray roots peeking through. She didn't want to rehash her own painful past. It was hard to explain her transient lifestyle. Nobody but Ginny seemed to understand or appreciate the desire to escape unhappy circumstances. She had been accused of running away from reality so many times, she had learned not to expose too much of herself. Yet she talked about her daughter, who seemed to be on her mind a lot lately.

Bree started to scrunch her hair, but Billy held her hand in his. "I love the way you play with yourself."

"Stop teasing me."

"Tell me more about Tori," Billy said. "I always regretted not having any children."

"That you know of." She wondered what he had been up to all these years, certain he had been busy dating many gorgeous actresses and supermodels.

"It doesn't matter anymore," he said, pulling her back to his embrace. "You're here now."

♪

ON SATURDAY MORNING, THE DAY OF THE STONES concert, Billy said he wanted Bree to meet his mother and drove her out to Sunset Pointe, an active senior community. "You're going to love her," he promised, parking his sports car in the guest spot.

In the lobby, Bree immediately noticed the rows of

walkers parked outside the dining room. Not the standard-issue numbers, these apparatuses had tires big enough to do some serious off-roading. Streamers and stuffed animals hung from them, and many of their users had attached baskets filled with all sorts of personal items like tubes of lipstick and used hankies. A couple of them had horns, but Bree resisted the urge to honk one just to see who would come hobbling out.

Billy escorted her to the lobby while he fetched his mother, who was finishing breakfast. *A person could get used to this life*, she supposed, noting the comfortable surroundings. Cushy checked-pattern sofas and armchairs were set up around a fireplace, and a grand piano sat in the middle of the room. It reminded her of a luxurious cruise ship, one that never left port, and she wondered if a place like this would be her final destination. Maybe her mind would go first, and every day she'd wake up, thinking she was somewhere new. That might suit her fine.

She sat down, and a man from across the room wheeled toward her, his walker squeaking with every shuffle. He eased into the sofa, creaking and moaning all the way down.

After he folded up his vehicle and leaned it against an end table, he said, "Did the sun come out, or did you just smile at me?"

"You're a sly devil," said Bree. He was a cute old man, and she hoped he had lots of grandchildren who visited on a regular basis.

"The name's Bob."

"Nice to meet you," said Bree.

"Are you moving in?" He tried to scoot a little closer but seemed to be stuck. His legs were betraying him.

"Slow down, Bob. Let's not get ahead of ourselves. I'm a little too young for you, don't you think?" she said.

"We could have lots of fun together. Ever since the medication." He raised his eyebrows as suggestively as he could manage, considering they had grown together.

"Bree," Billy interrupted not a moment too soon. "I'd like to introduce you to my mother, Sylvia."

A tiny woman, maybe ninety pounds, opened her arms for a hug. Afterward, Bree waved good-bye to Bob and followed Billy and his mother to the elevator.

Sylvia had a one-bedroom apartment with a full kitchen—an important luxury, since most senior community apartments came with kitchenettes. She wasn't dead yet, she said, and still baked from time to time, especially around Christmas.

Bree could see Sylvia had a thing for ducks. There were pictures of them everywhere, brown and yellow ones, floating alone and with their babies. Some of the depictions were photographs, while others were paintings. Her end tables were covered with ceramic and wooden ducks of various sizes. On the coffee table sat a mother duck with her five baby ducklings lined up behind.

Bree picked up a wooden one, opened it, and out popped another duck. Inside that was another duck. It was a Russian nesting doll, duck-style.

Sylvia plucked a needlepoint pillow from the sofa and hugged it tight. "Funny little fellow," she said, pointing to the threaded picture of Daffy Duck. "Never lets anything get him down." Sylvia gazed down at the picture and lovingly reset the pillow.

While Billy was checking things off his mother's to-do list

—changing light bulbs, reattaching the shower curtain, moving the hall mirror a little to the left—Bree admired a painting hung above the sofa.

"*Lahaina Starlight*," said Sylvia.

Bree had been to Maui many times and recognized the historical whaling village. She remembered that on Friday nights in Lahaina Town, the art scene buzzed along Front Street. Storefront galleries enticed tourists from the restaurants and shops by offering refreshments and the chance to meet well-known artists. But she had avoided going inside because she hadn't appreciated the high-pressure sales from the employees who acted like used-car dealers, following people around from painting to painting.

Sylvia's painting, depicting a moonlit Lahaina shoreline, was as rich and decadent as a piece of fudge. It radiated color and movement, and she could almost feel the gentle motion of the sea as the waves crashed delicately on the shore and rocked the boats anchored in the harbor. It wasn't Bree's style, but she could see the artist had created the most idealistic picture of Maui.

Before her husband died, Sylvia explained, he surprised her with a five-night vacation to the Hawaiian island. At first, she had refused to go. He had been in and out of the hospital. It was dangerous, ridiculous, she'd said. Sylvia's eyes started to tear up. "We both knew it could be our last vacation together." He bought the painting for Sylvia because he wanted her to have something beautiful to remember, a memento of their time in Maui.

"Now it's just the two of us," Sylvia said. "Isn't that right, sweetheart?"

Billy came out from the bedroom, tub of spackle in hand. "What's that?"

"Come here, and let's show Bree our act."

"Oh, Mom. She doesn't want to see us make fools of ourselves."

"Who are you calling a fool?" said Sylvia, swatting Billy on the leg.

"I'd love to see it," said Bree. After completely failing at family life, she had vowed never be weighted down again, but she felt right at home with these two.

"Sit here." Sylvia tried to move a dining room chair.

"Let me," said Bree, pulling the chair over next to Sylvia's keyboard.

Sylvia took her place at the bench and opened up a songbook. Billy squeezed in next to his mother and played "Twinkle, Twinkle, Little Star."

"Stop fooling around, buddy." Sylvia smacked his hands, and Bree envisioned his years of practicing scales under his mother's direction. Billy had beautiful long fingers. He said he'd played so much during puberty that his fingers had grown around his guitar.

"Buddy?" said Bree. "How cute. I once had a dog named Buddy who licked my toes day in and out. I couldn't get him to stop."

"Ruff, ruff," Billy barked in tune. "I'll be your buddy boy," he sang. Sylvia put her arm around him. "Ready?" she said.

"Ready." Billy played an extended intro.

"Show-off," said Sylvia.

He laughed, and they sang "Moon River."

While they played, Bree thought about her own mother

back in Florida. She wasn't well, according to Victoria, and Bree regretted not calling to check up. Her mother had a tendency to hoard when she was depressed. The last time she had an episode, Bree had gone back to Florida to help clean up her mother's house and get her medical situation straightened out.

The amount of junk was overwhelming. It had seemed as if her mother collected every flyer in town, and on the back of each one had drawn pictures of suns: Aztec-looking suns, suns setting over the ocean, suns with faces that winked, suns wearing sunglasses. There had been rubber rodents and bracelets, miniature cars, and bouncy rubber balls. Like she'd knocked over a row of toy vending machines, scooped up their contents, and strategically positioned each piece around her room. They seemed to be amulets warding off evil spirits. Every once in a while, Bree still woke up from nightmares about her mother, a situation totally out of control.

Maybe it's time I start facing the past, she thought, watching what could only be described as priceless: a sweet elderly lady and her rock-star son singing about drifters setting off to see the world together.

"Isn't he wonderful?" said Sylvia, beaming. "The ladies love him!"

"Is that right?" Bree asked. "Do they fall all over him?"

"Oh, yes. Billy performs once a month at our happy hour, and all the ladies go crazy." Sylvia jumped up from the piano bench as if she just remembered something. The woman had so much energy; it wasn't hard to figure out why she was as skinny as a rail. "Guess what I have?"

She opened up a cabinet underneath the television set and pulled out a video dance game. "Billy bought this for me."

Sylvia held out the controller to Bree. "Take this whatcha-macallit, and hold on to it while you follow the people."

"That's okay," said Bree, pushing away the remote. "I'll watch."

"Nonsense. Now get up here and dance."

Bree hoped Billy would intervene, but he encouraged her to dance, happy to watch her squirm.

"I'm going to kill you," she mouthed to him.

"It's hammer time," Sylvia yelled and pushed Bree to the middle of the floor. She recognized the MC Hammer song but was too embarrassed to move. Both Sylvia and Billy clapped, waiting for Bree to bust a move. The music was infectious. She had no choice but to shake her butt and sing "U Can't Touch This," bopping in front of the TV. Afterward, Bree and Billy sat on his mother's loveseat like a teenage couple being interviewed before the prom. Sylvia served them her famous lemon cake and asked how they'd met. Borrowing Billy's term for his early fans, Bree bragged about being a "pre-original" and described a young Billy back in Florida with dreams of making it big.

"I wish you had come to Hollywood with me," he said. "It was exciting in the beginning."

"In a way, I guess I was with you." Bree hoped her face didn't turn red as the words to "Sarasota" ran through her head: "And you said that you would follow me to the ends of the earth / Now how far do I have to go for you to follow me?"

"She's my inspiration," said Billy. "I owe her everything."

"That's the best story I've heard in a long time." Sylvia patted Bree's knee. "Did Billy tell you he gave up his big Hollywood career for me?"

"Not this again."

"He did." Sylvia ignored his protest. "He was all set to sign with another band, but then his father died. He didn't want to go on tour and leave me all by myself. I said he didn't have to worry about me, but he insisted. We've been here ever since."

"He's an amazing person," said Bree.

"I think you are too." Sylvia winked at Bree. "Don't mess this one up, Billy."

"That's why we're getting married tonight after the Rolling Stones concert."

"Isn't that romantic," said Sylvia, clapping her hands together. "Wait until I tell the ladies at dinner."

Bree's head started to spin. She was all set to change her ways, but it was happening so fast. Before she had a chance to say anything, the front door swung open.

"Fire," a woman screamed. "Poor little Winnie's stuck inside!"

Billy was out the door before she had time to process what was going on.

"I'll call 911." Sylvia turned circles around the tiny dining area. "Where's my phone?"

She picked up piles of paper, tossing them aside. "I just had it."

"Let me run downstairs," said Bree, trying to remember if the staircase was next to the elevator they had ridden up.

She raced past the apartment next door and saw Billy carrying a shivering Chihuahua.

"I'm getting help," said Bree, ignoring Billy's attempt to stop her. He might have been saying something about putting out the fire himself, but she wasn't sure.

A million things were running through her head. *Will the fire consume the entire floor? How do we evacuate a building full of octo- and nonagenarians in a hurry? How many had pets that needed rescuing?*

So when she reached the top of the stairs, she tried to ignore the intense dizzy spell that had made it nearly impossible to see straight. She grabbed the railing for support but fell anyway, tumbling all the way to the bottom landing.

30

GINNY

Ginny gave the cab driver an extra hundred bucks to get her to the hospital as quickly as possible. She knew something wasn't right when she didn't hear from Bree all morning. The Stones concert was in a few hours, and Ginny figured Bree would be around to offer moral support and help psych her up for what might be the biggest moment in her life: the chance to meet Mick Jagger.

"Are we almost there?" she cried. The cab was stuck behind a long line of cars, inching along as they merged into one lane. The last time she was in Las Vegas, when she ran away from her mother and Ray before she was married, the president of the United States was in town. The main boulevard was shut down for hours. She didn't have that kind of time today.

"Hurry up!" she yelled.

The driver turned off the main road to take a back street she'd never seen before. It was depressingly industrial compared to the glitz of the strip. "Hold on," he said and floored it.

Ginny rushed through the emergency room door past all the sick and decrepit people waiting for their name to be called like game-show contestants. She lied and told the woman guarding the entrance that her sister was in the emergency room just in case only family members were allowed. "What happened to her?" Ginny asked.

The woman shrugged and buzzed the door open. "Room 2A."

The nurses glanced up as Ginny entered the ER. Maybe they watched out of habit, but they seemed to follow her frantic movements past them. It was like she represented something alive and vital, an outsider in this room full of sickness and death. She swept past them and squinted her eyes in the brightness. The floors, the nurses' uniforms, the sheets and blankets all radiated a hygienic whiteness. She smelled alcohol and ammonia mixed with infection and vomit. Her own stomach started to burn as she searched for Bree's room.

Sick people in narrow hospital beds lined the corridors, seemingly put out to pasture because the rooms were full. She passed a man who was groaning in Spanish. His hospital gown sagged from his shoulders, revealing his bare chest. Ginny trembled, imagining being at her most vulnerable, sick, and naked in the middle of a cold hallway, surrounded by strangers who couldn't wait until their shift ended and she'd be somebody else's problem.

Bree had her own room. Ginny was happy about that, but wondered if it was because she was in bad shape, and she was prepared for the worst when she walked into room 2A.

Propped up, leg in traction, Bree had the overhead television set on. She was chuckling along with the laugh track and taking bites of macaroni and cheese fed to her by a man at her side. At first Ginny thought he resembled an older version of Billy Blade, then she realized it *was* an older Billy Blade. With his pasty white skin, longish hair, and black clothes, he looked every part the aging rock star. If she hadn't been so worried about Bree, Ginny might have gotten a little tongue-tied. She'd never hung out with a real-life celebrity before; standing in line with Ray all day to get a famous wrestler's autograph didn't count.

Billy stood up when Ginny entered the room and introduced himself and his mother, a little old lady wandering around the room, checking the machines, and reading Bree's vitals. "If you make it to my age, you get a lot of experience with these gadgets," she said.

"Whoops," Bree said. "Looks like I had a little fall."

"Are you okay?" Ginny pulled up a chair. "Billy called and said there had been an accident. Then the call dropped, and the number was blocked. I couldn't call back."

"Sorry about that," said Billy. "There's almost no cell reception here."

"I didn't know if you were alive or dead." She might have been a little annoyed Billy hadn't called her back, but the way he was doting over Bree, Ginny could see he hadn't wanted to leave her side.

Bree muted the TV, reveling in all of the attention. Billy poured her a cup of water while Sylvia patted her hand and told her she was going to be okay. She had her own fan club, and to Ginny, Bree seemed different. The old Bree might not have liked everybody fussing over her. Love complicates things, she once claimed. From the looks of it, Ginny knew Bree was fully immersed.

"Wild horses couldn't drag me away," she said.

Bree couldn't have known that supposedly Marianne Faithfull, Mick Jagger's girlfriend from the 1960s, spoke those words to Mick when she was coming out of a coma. Or that "Wild Horses" was a track from *Sticky Fingers*, one of Ginny's favorite albums. The cover was designed by Andy Warhol and included a real zipper. It was also the first time the band's tongue-and-lips logo, inspired by the Hindu goddess Kali, had been used, symbolizing everlasting energy and free expression. The mouth had undoubtedly been a nod to Mick's famous lips.

Bree probably didn't know these bits of Stones trivia, but she always knew the right thing to say.

"It was awful," said Sylvia. "After she fell down the stairs, the ambulance and paramedics came—not unusual at Sunset Pointe—but poor Bob nearly had a heart attack from all the excitement."

"Bob?" asked Ginny.

"Don't ask," said Bree.

"Worst of all," Sylvia continued. "Billy had already put the fire out. It was just a piece of toast that burned up." Ginny was totally confused. She didn't know whether to back up and start over or try to ignore the sweet old lady who was circling the room like an Energizer rabbit.

Billy must have noticed Ginny's confusion, because he started to guide his mother out of the room. "Let's see what they're serving in the cafeteria." He waved to Bree. "We'll be back in a few minutes."

"You fell down a flight of stairs?" Ginny asked.

"Guilty. I told you I'm a klutz. The doctor said I fractured my femur, and I'll have to stay racked up like this until they can put a regular cast on me."

Ginny thought about the rest of the tour. Tomorrow they were supposed to fly to Texas and rent a car from there to hit the East Coast concerts. "You can't travel like that."

"No kidding, partner. Looks like I'm benched for a while."

"I guess Craig's motorhome would have come in handy after all," said Ginny.

"Motorhome?"

"Yesterday Craig showed up in this giant RV, ready to sweep me off my feet." Ginny sat down on the edge of Bree's bed. "It doesn't matter. He was dragging me down, if you know what I mean."

"Oh, sister, do I ever." Bree straightened out her shoulders as if she couldn't wait to shed the hospital gown and hit the streets to make trouble and break hearts. She still had all the bravado, but the sappy look in her eyes gave her away.

"Don't lie to me! You are so whipped, it's not even funny."

Bree turned down the sides of her mouth, making the same sappy face Ginny used to see on Ray's face whenever he wasn't getting his way. "Is that any way to talk to someone in my condition?"

"You're the toughest chick I know."

"Not exactly. The doctor said my blood sugar was so low, it could have caused me to faint."

"Because you're not eating enough. Look at you, getting skinny on love while I've been stuffing my face at the buffet. I'm never going to fit into the dress I bought for tonight." Ginny hadn't been able to resist nabbing the $2,500 black dress she'd seen hanging in the window of one of the hotel shops.

She might have been able to walk away from it if she hadn't just read an article about how a woman could never have too many LBDs.

"Billy arranged for a backstage pass to be delivered to your room, so be sure to be there around seven."

"I'm not going without you." Ginny panicked. She was way too intimidated to venture into the strange world of rich and glamorous people without her friend along. Bree had absolutely no fear, but Ginny trembled at the notion of being alone backstage.

"Of course you are," said Bree.

"But I can't. What am I going to do, wander around like an idiot? Knock on Mick Jagger's door and say something stupid like . . ." Ginny recalled the silly fantasy she'd had by the pool. "Like . . . 'Your music moves me.'"

"Why not?"

"Because I can't do it without you." Ginny paced the room. "You're the Wild and Spontaneous one, the Hot Tamale to my boring Milk Dud. I need you."

"If I weren't stuck in this bed," said Bree. "I'd give you a good shaking. You were the one who rescued me, remember?" Bree raised her voice. "We went on the road to follow *your* dreams."

"You said it would be fun." Ginny wasn't sure what Bree was getting at. *Am I being blamed for something?*

"What I'm saying is that you did it. You initiated it. Not me. All along, you've been the Wild and Spontaneous woman, the one willing to take the risk of a lifetime."

Ginny hung her head into her hands, unsure what to do next. Her world seemed to be breaking apart again.

Even though Ray had practically forced Ginny out by having an affair, she knew a lot of women who tried to stick out their bad marriages. So afraid of any kind of change, they were paralyzed by fear. She remembered a woman she had once seen vomit all over the gym floor.

The incident had haunted her. At that moment, Ginny had seen her future, as messy and unappetizing as a pile of puke.

The woman at the gym came to symbolize the worst of what Ginny could become. Like her mother, who made up stories about people she didn't know, Ginny imagined the woman's entire life.

She had probably been trying to change for the better. *I don't have to be forty and frumpy*, the woman must have thought. She could be forty and fabulous and would start anew by joining the gym and hiring a trainer. Her family had always come first, Ginny guessed. The woman probably bought her husband designer underwear instead of economy briefs, her kids name brands while she did without. She skimped wherever she could. So what if she didn't have the biggest diamond ring or the newest SUV.

But now it was this woman's turn to shine, Ginny suspected. The woman had hired a trainer just for a month, she'd told herself. So she signed up for three days a week with the most experienced, friendliest-looking trainer. Ginny imagined the woman asked her husband to take the kids to school three days a week, just for now. Hadn't she driven them for years herself? He owed her. She deserved this, she probably argued to her husband.

It was obvious the woman was wearing a brand-new workout outfit. Not wanting to wear her raggedy sweatpants or her husband's T-shirt, she must have gone to the department store to buy yoga pants, shoes, the whole bit. And she also found an official-looking workout shirt, one with breathable mesh. She deserved this, after all—Ginny supposed the woman had sacrificed everything for the family.

She had, no doubt, arrived by 6:00 A.M. to train. Her husband must have thought she was crazy. Ginny imagined he thought it was a waste of time and said it wouldn't last and she might as well not set the alarm and save them both time and money. He loved her the way she was, he probably told her. Wasn't she satisfied, he might have asked? Didn't she love him and the boys? Weren't they enough for her? Why does she have to get all full of herself to be content? Ginny pictured him as being just like Ray.

We have our work cut out for us, the trainer probably thought as he put the woman on the treadmill for twenty minutes. Not too fast to start, just a brisk walk uphill. Her legs must have started to burn, her breath quickening. She probably felt good, though. Twenty minutes went by quickly, and she walked off the treadmill too fast. Her legs probably felt like rubber. *Are they supposed to feel like that?* She must have felt dizzy but didn't say anything to the trainer. He was so nice and sweet that she didn't want to hurt his feelings. She didn't look like she was feeling too well, but the trainer seemed so enthusiastic that the woman didn't say anything. She took a drink of water and the cold liquid must have felt good, but it was too hot in the gym. Ginny imagined she must have been so hot and dizzy. Then, oh no, she felt nauseated and out it came.

The trainer wasn't as smiley and friendly anymore when

he ordered the young girl working at the front desk to clean up the mess. He knew he had lost another client, that her husband had been right: this woman was a loser, and she'd never be anything more . . .

The vomiting was the only part Ginny had seen, but in her heart, she knew the rest was true. She might have only projected misery onto the woman's life, but the path Ginny was on hadn't been too different. The woman at the gym made so many sacrifices that by the time she tried to take her life back, it was too late. Ginny wouldn't let that happen to her, and damn it, Bree was right. Ginny had risked everything, and now wasn't the time to back down.

Ray once told Ginny he knew when she had woken up in the morning because her breathing quieted down. It became more steady, even, and rhythmic. Sometimes at night, he said, she'd toss and yank the covers and gasp for air, inhaling and exhaling erratically. Occasionally she stopped breathing, and he wondered if he should wake her. Imagining what life would be like if she stopped taking in air altogether, he sometimes hesitated. He hadn't wanted her to die, of course, but he said the little glimpse of possibility had made him appreciate her all the more. Ray believed Ginny couldn't go on without him, and his fragile wife would always need him to watch over her.

Bree removed Ginny's hands from her face and looked her in the eyes. "You never needed me," she said. "You don't need anyone."

31

BREE

After the doctor set Bree's leg and put it into a temporary cast, her skin started to itch. She was going crazy trying to figure out a way to get inside to give her busted thigh one good scratch. Once she was back at Billy's place, she'd shove the handle of a long wooden spoon underneath the cast and go to town, unconcerned how ridiculous she'd look or that Billy might tease her about sullying his kitchen utensils. Visualizing it made the skin prickle even worse, and she wanted to tear the plaster from her leg.

Instead she leafed through an issue of *People* Ginny had purchased from the gift shop. None of the celebrities were familiar to Bree anymore. They had all gotten so young and foolish-looking, with their fake body parts and bored expressions. Not impressed with the Hollywood scene, she tossed the magazine onto the chair beside the hospital bed. Luckily she had her own room and didn't have to share the television with a total stranger or make small talk about the latest episode of whatever crappy reality show was on. She searched for an old movie but gave up after flipping past a bunch of commercials.

Billy had taken Sylvia home in time for the five o'clock dinner seating at Sunset Pointe. He said he'd come back to keep Bree company, but she insisted he go to the concert without her. Seeing the Stones play the MGM was the event she was most excited about. The small venue and vibrant energy from the Las Vegas crowd would be a performer's dream come true. The Stones rocked it like no other, she had heard, and being stuck in the hospital with a broken leg seemed like cruel punishment. She'd never get to see Ginny's face the moment she met Mick Jagger. Even Bree wouldn't have minded saying hello to Keith Richards one bit.

But you can't have everything, she told herself.

Picturing Billy wheeling her out of the hospital with a teddy bear on her lap, she couldn't help smiling. By then, Ginny would be off to Texas, and Bree wondered what she'd do without her new friend. Her little baby chick was all grown up and leaving the nest. Bree meant what she'd said earlier. Ginny was the one who had done the rescuing. Still, it was frightening letting someone go like that. She was pushing Ginny into the deep end of the swimming pool, removing her inflatable wings and forcing her to move through the water all on her own.

After Dimmit died, Bree went to live with Tori, who had already learned to swim. Her father had paid for private lessons in their Olympic-size swimming pool, and she had become an expert diver. Bree had missed that moment, along with a dozen other firsts. Thinking about it now sickened her. In the past, she had always depended on the comfortable lie that removing herself from other people's lives was an act of selflessness. It had been a cowardly way to live. Being Wild and Spontaneous, as Ginny had called her, had kept her from experiencing real love, the kind that could be messy and complicated. She had sacrificed so much by avoiding pain, not understanding the entire time that she was causing the grief herself.

She picked up her cell phone from the bedside table and dialed Tori's number. When it started to ring, Bree almost hung up. To free her clammy hands, she pressed the phone to her shoulder and wiped them on the sheets. Her armpits started to perspire, but she forced herself to stay on the phone.

"Mom?" Tori answered. The caller ID had given her away. It was too late to chicken out.

"Hi, honey." Bree tried to sound upbeat, but she expected her daughter to be suspicious right away.

"I'm sorta in the middle of something. Can I call you back?"

"How's Nana?" Bree asked, searching for anything to scratch her leg with. The itch had become unbearable.

"She's back on her meds again. Looks like she'll be okay . . . for a while." Tori sounded tired.

"I'm so relieved." Bree found the pencil she had used for a crossword puzzle and inserted it underneath the cast eraser-end first.

"You're off the hook, then."

"I didn't mean that," said Bree. "I'd like to see her soon." Tori remained silent, probably waiting for the excuse, the cop-out or some other form of letdown to follow.

"She's not going to come to you," she finally said.

"I know."

"That means booking a flight, actually making plans, and following through with them."

Bree stopped herself from blurting out something defensive and said, "Of course." After all these years, Tori had managed to perfect the reversal of roles. Bree felt about six years old.

"I won't hold my breath."

"You won't have to. I'll be there before you can count to ten."

"I should go."

"Wait." Bree couldn't let Tori hang up. It had always been Bree's easy way out, a reason to let things remain status quo.

"Don't you have stuff to do? Tables waiting or whatever?"

"No," said Bree, examining her leg set in traction. "I'm stationary at the moment."

"Are you still in Arizona?"

"Actually, I'm in Las Vegas." Bree tried to make the words sound as exciting and glamorous as the city's image.

"Dad always wanted to go to Las Vegas. Bet you didn't know that." Tori always managed to find a way to insert her father into their limited phone conversations.

"There's no point in going through this again. Your father loved you. That's all that counts."

"He didn't love me enough to keep you from leaving," said Tori.

"I didn't leave *you*."

"No, I was just one of your casualties."

"I think about you every day." Bree's heart beat faster. She needed to let everything out, but Tori wasn't about to make it easy.

"Planes land in Florida every day."

"I don't want to complicate your life."

"Don't you know anything about me? I *want* the complication."

"Not my kind." Bree was sweating up a storm and threw off the sheets.

"What makes you so special? Why is your life more complicated than the rest? I've had my heart broken. I've hurt people."

"Are you kidding? You're perfect."

"You think so?"

"Of course," Bree said. As critical as she was of Tori, she was a great kid. She was at the top of her class and volunteered at the local library, reading to underserved children almost every weekend. "I'm the one always getting into trouble."

"I guess," said Tori

"Sometimes I think I'm the kid and you're the parent. How'd that happen?"

"I'm just lucky," Tori said and laughed a bit. "My friends' parents are pretty boring, but sometimes I wish you were like them."

"I'm sorry." A knot formed in Bree's stomach. *Why doesn't parenting come with some kind of guidebook?* Although if it did, Bree's sure she would have lost it.

"It's not so bad. But it makes it kind of hard to rebel. Isn't that what kids my age do?"

"You're rebelling by playing it straight," said Bree. "It was my plan all along."

"Don't be so sure of yourself. I've been in trouble."

"Not my daughter," said Bree.

"You were there, remember?"

Bree's mind raced. She thought of the worst possible

scenarios. Had it been something she'd done or was responsible for? In the little time she had lived with Tori, Bree had never once left her alone with one of her boyfriends. She'd heard too many horror stories to make that mistake.

"The night of the winter formal two years ago. When you found me crying."

"Yeah."

Here it comes, Bree thought. *Another one of my fuck-ups rehashed.*

"I didn't want to tell you."

"You can tell me anything."

"Some of the older guys brought a bottle of rum, and at dinner, they were pouring it into our drinks. Kyle, my date, kept whispering to me, 'Let's go outside. Let's get out of here.'"

"What did he do to you?" Bree squeezed her hand shut, digging her fingernails into her palm.

"Nothing. I mean, he tried, but nothing happened. He pushed me up against the wall outside of the restaurant and pulled up my dress."

"I'm going to kill him!" One of the nurses poked her head in the room when she heard Bree shout. *I'm fine,* she mouthed to the nurse, who disappeared with her clipboard.

"I spit on him."

"That's my girl."

"He wasn't expecting it and let me go. I ran away. I had to walk four miles home." Tori sounded surprisingly composed, as if she were watching the scene on TV. "Good thing I didn't buy those four-inch heels you suggested." She laughed.

"I still don't understand why you didn't tell me," said Bree.

"I felt guilty. I never told anyone."

"Why on earth would you feel guilty?"

"Because I didn't set boundaries. I knew our drinks were spiked. I willingly went outside with Kyle."

"But you were only thirteen. How could you know what he was going to do?"

"That's why I wanted to move away to boarding school. To get away from him and all the kids at school who would gossip about it the next day. Not because I wanted to leave you."

"I'm so sorry I wasn't there for you." Bree felt deflated, like a complete failure. She wanted to say something comforting but didn't know how. She wished her own mother had consoled her just once, had offered to take her in when she and Tori needed the support. "I'm sorry I set such a terrible example. I only wanted to protect you."

"From what? I needed a mother."

"I wanted to be a good role model for you. I screwed up. I made bad decisions, and I wanted to be strong for the both of us. It just never happened. The more I ran, the weaker I became, until I finally gave up."

"I miss you," said Tori. "I still want you around."

"At first I thought you were better off without me," Bree said, holding back her tears. "You had a stable life, went to a good school. When Dad died, I figured I had another chance to show you I could do it, I could be a good mother. But I managed to mess that up too."

"It wasn't all terrible."

"It's going to be okay. You'll see," said Bree. "As soon as I can, I'm flying back to Florida."

"Thanks for calling," said Tori. "I needed to hear your voice tonight."

"Anytime."

"By the way, what are you doing in Las Vegas?"

Bree thought about the past week with Billy. He adored her, and she loved him so much it made her laugh out loud just to think of his sweet smile, the way he finished every song she sang, no matter how silly it was. His mother called him *buddy*. He was her best buddy too. Only a few hours ago, he had proposed to her, and she had said yes. It was one of the happiest moments of her life.

"Oh," Bree said. "Nothing important."

32

GINNY

Why was it whenever she needed to look perfect, everything went wrong? Ginny tried to blow out her hair, but it resembled a stiff helmet, so she misted it with a wave-enhancing product, only to end up with a sticky, matted mess. She needed a do-over and rewashed her hair, letting it air-dry this time. Maybe the rock and roll goddesses would pity her and let her locks turn out decently for once.

She refused to leave her face to chance and plucked a few stray eyebrow hairs before spreading on a thin layer of foundation. A clean, blemish-free palette was what she needed before painting on the face that would soon be looking into Mick Jagger's. She had considered having her makeup applied professionally but didn't get back from the hospital in time for an appointment at the salon.

This is probably better anyway, she thought, remembering the last time she had her makeup done. It was her wedding day, and she was so nervous that when the makeup artist had darkened her eyebrows to an unnatural reddish-brown, Ginny nearly bit the woman's head off. There had been so many signs the marriage was doomed.

She looked strange in the wedding photo, snapped moments after she and Ray were married at city hall. She was wearing a simple sheath dress and low heels, and her makeup didn't match at all—much too heavy for a low-key daytime wedding. And the fake eyelashes were absurd.

Afterward, there wasn't a wedding reception. Ginny's mom said it would be inappropriate since the bride was pregnant, so Ray thoughtfully surprised her with a small party at their new apartment. Their friends from Hollywood came, and Ginny had so much fun hanging out with Ray's former bandmates. The weather was terrible that day. The storm worsened and the electricity went out, leaving Ginny to scramble for candles to light up the tiny apartment.

At first, nobody knew what to do. The music had gone out along with the electricity, and for a few minutes, everybody just sat and stared at each other. Then someone sparked up a joint, the drummer grabbed a set of bongos, and Ray strapped on his acoustic guitar. They jammed for at least an hour, and when the lights came back on, Ginny switched them off. Everybody cheered. Nothing could ruin their impromptu session. Proud of her musician husband, Ginny imagined that someday she'd be backstage at *his* concert . . .

She jerked back to the present with the realization that all that happened a very long time ago. The moment she'd been waiting for was at hand. The Stones backstage pass had yet to be delivered, and she was getting nervous. It would be so easy for Billy to overlook sending it, seeing as he was wrapped up in taking care of Bree. *Should I call him?* She'd never get this opportunity again, especially with all the talk of this being the Stones' final tour.

She could hear Ray's nagging voice in the back of her head. "How long can those old farts keep rocking?"

Ray's problem was that he didn't have the capacity to appreciate classic beauty. He lacked the aesthetic to understand that with age comes perfection. The Stones might have petty arguments about who said what in the press or felt slighted when certain members of the band embarked on separate projects, but when they walked on stage together, it was the undeniable merging of musical masters. The Rolling Stones were the greatest rock and roll band that ever was and ever would be, and all Ginny wanted to do was to experience their majesty, to meet them face-to-face and glean some of the magic for herself.

When she first became a Stones fan, she went all out, celebrating her fanhood by wearing concert T-shirts, covering her schoolbooks with pictures of Mick Jagger, hanging posters on the inside of her locker, and declaring her allegiance to anyone who would listen. She rambled on about the important contribution the Rolling Stones had made to the history of music, but most of her peers didn't care because, like the rest of her outcast friends, she was out of sync with the popular set. The cheerleaders, the jocks, and the student government types hadn't seen anything retro or cool about loving a band whose members might be as old as their grandfathers. Being unconventional in middle school had been about as comfortable as getting her braces tightened every four to six weeks.

Even her loyal school friends challenged Ginny, arguing The Beatles or The Who were superior to the Stones. She had to become educated in her responses. Her father helped with the wording as she diligently recorded facts and statistics on a lined piece of notebook paper she kept folded in her back pocket. Once she had the information memorized, she tossed it into her lunch pail for future reference.

After carefully unfolding a ragged piece of paper titled *Why the Rolling Stones Are the Greatest Rock and Roll Band Ever,* she reviewed her points.

1. Longevity. Billed at first as the Rollin' Stones, they played their first gig at the Marquee Club in London in 1962. Later the Rolling Stones signed with Decca Records, releasing songs like, "Come On," "I Wanna Be Your Man," and "Not Fade Away." In 1964, shortly after The Beatles arrived in America, the Rolling Stones toured the United States, paving the way for other English bands who would continue what was known as the British Invasion. In 1989, the Rolling Stones were inducted into the Rock and Roll Hall of Fame. Still performing today, they are the longest touring band in history.

2. Biggest-selling. The Rolling Stones' fan base is massive, having bought an estimated two hundred million records worldwide. They are ranked by Rolling Stone *magazine as one of the greatest artists of all time, and they are one of the most successful and longstanding rock-and-roll bands in history. They've recorded more than thirty-five albums and hundreds of songs, and their tours continue to be the highest-grossing in history.*

3. Generational appeal. The Rolling Stones are a pheno-menon. They are the world longest-standing rock stars. They appeal not only to their own generation but also to

their children and their children's children. Because their
appeal is universal, they have fans from all over the world.
Everybody who's anybody knows who the Rolling Stones
are.

4. Talented and diverse. Rolling Stone *magazine listed*
Keith Richards as one of the top ten guitar players of all
time and one of rock and roll's most successful composers,
along with Mick Jagger, who also happens to play a mean
harp. Bill Wyman, an original member of the band, left in
1992 and has been called one of the best bass players ever.
Charlie Watts is an accomplished jazz musician, and in
addition to being one of rock's great guitarists, Ronnie
Wood is a successful artist—his paintings have been exhi-
bited around the world.

5. Mick Is Hot. Period.

Someone knocked at the door, and she was so thankful the
pass had arrived that she almost answered it in her underwear.

"Just a minute," she yelled, putting her lunch pail away and
throwing on a bathrobe.

"Surprise." Ray held out a bouquet of daisies as Virginia
pushed past him and walked inside the suite.

Ginny stiffened, unsuccessfully blocking their entrance.
"What are you guys doing here?"

"Aren't you glad to see me?" Ray stepped back and resur-
rected his dopey, feel-sorry-for- me face.

He hasn't changed a bit.

"Give her some room," Virginia said, embracing her
daughter and giving Ginny a big hug.

The last time she spoke to Ray, she said she never wanted to see his sorry ass again, yet there he was standing in her Las Vegas hotel room, probably ready to make amends.

"Here," Ray handed Ginny the flowers and a card while Virginia flung her coat and purse on the living room sofa.

Ginny opened the envelope to find a cartoon bear holding a red heart and smiling up at her. "All that matters is you," she read aloud.

"Couldn't say it any better myself."

"Mom, I can't believe you did this to me," said Ginny. A few days ago, she had contacted her mother so she wouldn't worry. Virginia had convinced Ginny to reveal her location. She had no idea Virginia had been conspiring with the enemy all along.

"I had no choice, honey. Ray showed up at my house and told me you were pregnant." Virginia practically wept when she said the word. "I can't have my daughter traipsing around the country with a baby on board."

"I'm not pregnant," said Ginny, clutching the neck of her robe so it wouldn't fly open. She felt exposed enough.

"But I found a pregnancy test under the bathroom sink." Ray started to nose around the suite, opening Bree's bedroom door and giving it a good look before slamming it shut.

"I'm *not* pregnant," Ginny repeated.

"It's not my fault. My sperm count's all good."

"Moron," Virginia whispered under her breath as she sat down at the dining room table. "We're doing what's called an intervention." She folded her hands together and looked appropriately solemn, as if she were a paid TV personality digging for the truth. "Are you on drugs?"

"Don't be ridiculous," said Ginny.

"It's the only explanation. It's why she left me," explained Ray, plopping down across from Virginia.

"We don't know that," said Virginia. "For the sake of argument, let's suppose she left you of her own free will."

"If you want to be in denial about it, but I'm telling you—"

"In denial. Me?" Virginia interrupted him, the two of them going at each other as if Ginny weren't in the room.

"We're going through a rough patch," said Ray. He hung his head, probably to avoid Virginia's scrutiny.

"A rough patch is an argument, a small fight. A woman doesn't leave the state unless she's running away from something."

"Not me," said Ray. "I love her." He started to whimper.

Virginia reached across the table and patted his hand, an uncharacteristically nice gesture on her part. Her touch must have startled Ray, because he recoiled as if a snake had bitten him.

"Don't worry, Mom," he said, probably feeling sorry for his reaction. "She'll come back to us."

"She *has* to come back to me. I'm her mother."

"Well, I'm her husband."

"Some relationships are easier to dissolve than others."

"Enough!" Ginny yelled. "I'm sick of the fighting. Can't you see you're *both* the reason I left?" She pushed one of the dining chairs into the table. "I want to live my own life. I can't make a move, I can't even *think*, without the two of you around to dictate my entire life."

Ginny stopped to catch her breath. She needed space and went to the bedroom, locking the door behind her so Ray wouldn't come barging in while she put on her dress. He'd start quizzing her about the cost and asking her why she was getting all dressed up.

It wasn't going to be easy, but Ginny knew she had to do it. She had to finally stand up to her mother and, at the same time, end her marriage.

Ray whistled when Ginny emerged from the bedroom. He and Virginia were still sitting at the table, and Ginny could see Ray eyeing the bar. There was no way she was offering him a drink.

"How long are you gonna keep this up?" said Ray. "I said I was sorry already. Now come home."

"I don't remember a *sorry*. Anyway, what about your girlfriend? Might get kind of crowded with the three of us."

"I dumped her," Ray said. "She's crazy."

What a creep, thought Ginny. Shannon wasn't exactly Ginny's best friend, but it was just like Ray to blame the woman without taking any responsibility for what he had done.

"What, are you having your '19th Nervous Breakdown' or something?"

Figures he'd quote that song from Aftermath *about a spoiled girl*, Ginny thought. She didn't like it and had once read it wasn't Mick's favorite either.

Virginia cracked open a bottle of water. *That stuff is ten bucks a pop*, Ginny thought, wondering how much more their little visit was going to set her back.

It was a quarter after seven, and if the backstage pass didn't arrive soon, she'd have to go without it. It was almost time to leave. She panicked, picturing some dumb groupie gripping Mick Jagger's hand. *That handshake belongs to me!*

"I want you to leave."

"She's right, Ray. You can wait in the car." Virginia leaned back in the chair, a squatter unwilling to vacate the premises.

"I mean both of you," said Ginny.

One of the reasons she had been avoiding Ray and her mother was because she didn't think she'd be strong enough to stand up to them. Most of the time Ginny kept quiet, trying to think of ways to get along and not stir up too much trouble. When she finally spoke up, they made it seem like she was at fault for whatever was wrong. They'd have her believe she was just the spoiled, unsatisfied girl having her "19th Nervous Breakdown."

"But I came all this way to rescue my daughter," said Virginia. "Forget about him."

"Hey," said Ray, puffing out his chest.

"I'll set up your bedroom just the way it used to be," she continued.

"No," said Ginny. "I'm not some silly child who needs to be saved." She directed the comment at Ray, making sure he knew she was talking to him too.

"After everything I've done?" said Virginia, her face turning red. "That's gratitude for you." She stood up and gathered her things.

"I appreciate the money, but it doesn't mean you get to have a say in my life," said Ginny, intercepting her mother, "for the rest of my life."

"I'm only trying to help."

"Don't you want me to be strong?" said Ginny. "Don't you want me to stand up for myself?"

"I'm not the bad guy here," Virginia said in a huff. Ray

seemed to be enjoying the confrontation between mother and daughter, and he unsuccessfully suppressed a smirk.

"You're right," said Ginny. "I allowed you both to control me for too long. You're not the bad guy, Mom. I am, and now I'm asking you to leave. I've got plans tonight."

"I know," said Ray. "Some skinny English dude in tight pants is gonna try to satisfy my wife."

"I don't have to take this," said Virginia. "If anyone cares, I'll be playing blackjack."

Always with a flair for the dramatic, Virginia took her exit. For once, Ginny didn't follow her mother to apologize up and down in an attempt to spare her feelings. She let Virginia go and took the chance that her mother could take care of herself.

"Finally," said Ray. "A chance for us to talk."

Ginny fought the urge to send Ray after her mother. She had to get the breakup over with.

"A lot's changed since you've been gone," said Ray. "Including me." He tilted his head to the side and thought about it. "You complete me," he finally said.

"That's from *Jerry Maguire*."

He knew it was one of Ginny's favorite movies and quoted the line as if it could erase the past.

"Do you even know me? What I want out of life? What my dreams are?" Ginny started for the door. She still had her concert ticket. It would have to be enough for tonight.

Ray followed her. "Why do you always say that? I do know you."

"You don't." Most of all, he should've realized how much tonight's concert meant to her. "You know what you want me to be, but that's it. And to be honest," said Ginny. "I guess I don't know you anymore either."

"What's to know? I'm a simple guy."

Ray stood in front of the door. He wasn't going to give up, and Ginny wasn't sure what to do. Eyeing a vase on a nearby table, she realized she wasn't prepared to hurt the guy physically. It was bad enough that she was breaking his heart. She didn't need to fracture his skull too, although he deserved it.

"Exactly," said Ginny. "You may be simple, but I guess I'm not so easy."

"But I love you. Doesn't that mean anything?"

She didn't want to get into all the reasons why Ray, of all people, had some nerve to try to make her feel responsible. *He* was the one who had done the manipulating and cheating.

"When you made the choice to be with another woman, you broke up our marriage for good," she said. "We don't have to waste years of our lives trying to repair a relationship that wasn't any good to begin with. Let's admit we're not right for each other anymore and move on."

"I don't want to move on."

"You deserve a woman who loves you."

"You don't?"

"No, I'm sorry," said Ginny. "I'm not sure I ever did."

33

GINNY

Las Vegas, Nevada: MGM Grand Arena

As Ginny made her way through the MGM Grand Casino, her senses were inundated. The slot machines were the loudest, with their bells, sirens, and occasional payouts. Coins dropping into metal trays made a sharp *clack*. Here and there, a celebratory cheer cut through the low hum of thousands of people commingling. She would never get used to all the cigarette smoke that clouded the already dim lighting. All week she had lost track of time whenever she was inside a casino, but tonight she knew she was running out of it. If she didn't get inside the arena soon, she'd miss her chance.

She reached inside her purse to make sure the ticket and the backstage pass were still there. After Ray left, the messenger had arrived, apologizing for the delay and wishing Ginny luck. He must have known she needed it.

Even though it was the evening of a Rolling Stones concert, the casino seemed like any other Saturday night in Las Vegas. The card players still crowded the tables, slot players continued sitting at their favorite slot machines, and crap players carried on shooting the dice. Some won money, but most probably lost. Cocktail waitresses and card dealers continued to endure rude customers and cheap tippers, perhaps by mapping out what they'd do on their days off. Most likely something far from the Vegas strip, like going to the zoo or volunteering in their child's third-grade classroom. Everything seemed normal—as normal as possible in a state where gambling and prostitution were legal—but none of them were prepared for the onslaught of Stones fans.

Ginny recognized them because they were unlike the rest of the casino patrons. They had purpose in their eyes; they were on a mission. One might have stopped to play a slot or two along the way, but they were all headed down the same road, following the signs to the MGM Grand Arena, which took them through the casino, past the bars and restaurants, and to the back of the building. The mood was upbeat and excited. People were a little drunk or just plain high on life. Somebody yelled out the opening line to the chorus of "Sympathy for the Devil," and the fans continued with the rest of the lyrics.

Ginny jumped into the stream of people, feeling so nervous and excited that she thought she might need to go to the bathroom. Her stomach ached, but she tried to ignore it and focused on figuring out what to do. She had no idea where to go once she was inside the arena, and even though she kept telling herself she could do it on her own, she wished Bree was with her.

"I love your shoes," said a teen girl walking with her parents.

"Thanks," said Ginny. Her feet were already killing her. "I got them just for tonight."

"This is her first Rolling Stones' concert," said the girl's mother, who didn't look much older than Bree.

"You're going to love it." Ginny felt a tinge of sadness about prolonging the start of motherhood, but it wasn't as if she were dismissing the possibility all together. First she needed to fulfill her dreams, and perhaps along the way, she'd meet the right man. Then maybe one day, she'd be lucky enough to turn her own daughter on to the Stones.

"Jack Sparrow's father is awesome," said the girl, referring to a movie where Keith Richards had a brief but memorable cameo.

"She's a big Keith fan," said her father.

"That explains the hair," said Ginny. Beads and silver charms dangled from her tiny braids, an homage to the man who called himself Keef. She reminded Ginny of Cathy, her old school friend who said she wanted to have Ozzy Osbourne's love child.

Just outside the venue, she parted ways with many of the fans who gathered in a sort of self-imposed purgatory. There were a couple of bars before the entrance to the MGM Grand Ballroom, and some concertgoers probably downed a few beers there rather than going inside to pay twice as much for the same thing. Others might have waited for friends to join them, headed to the bathroom, or taken a few moments to watch people.

If Ginny had any time to spare, she might have stopped in purgatory to gather her thoughts and prepare. The day had been such a whirlwind of madness, she hadn't been able to clear her mind and psych up for what lay ahead. In less than twenty-four hours, she had visited her best friend in the hospital, stood up to her mother, dumped her husband, and faced the prospect of meeting Mick Jagger.

This could have been a cleansing spot, a place to wash away her sins before entering the pearly gates. Instead Ginny rushed past her fellowship and handed the attendant the ticket.

It was packed inside the arena. People were lined up to buy souvenirs, food, and alcohol, and to use the bathrooms. The opening act hadn't started yet, and she relaxed a little. She had at least an hour to find Mick Jagger so she could tell him . . .

She had no idea what to say. Something brilliant, of course, but Ginny worried about what might come tumbling out of her mouth instead. Bree's final piece of advice was, "Act like you belong." *Easier said than done*, Ginny thought and started to wipe her sweaty palms on her clothes but stopped when she remembered the expensive dress she was wearing.

An usher guarding the entrance to the floor seats scrutinized Ginny's backstage pass. If she hadn't felt so clueless, she might have milked this moment and pretended to be a big shot. She might have said something about Jack or Drew expecting her—Jack Nicholson and Drew Barrymore, of course! Instead she smiled and was courteous, which paid off, because the usher called a security guard to escort Ginny.

"First time?" asked the guard.

Ginny ran after him. He was quick, which was not helping the blister forming on her baby toe. He navigated through the crowds, trying to get to their seats in time for the opening act.

"It's that obvious?" Ginny asked.

"You don't look angry."

"Am I supposed to be?" Ginny wondered if she was in

trouble. She showed him the VIP pass but worried he might have thought it was counterfeit.

"A lot of the showbiz types look either busy or annoyed. I think it's in the manual or something."

She laughed. "Clearly I don't have one of those, or else I wouldn't be so worried about making a fool of myself." The guard reminded Ginny a lot of her father. He was distinguished and handsome in a Michael Douglas sort of way.

"Once you're inside, if anybody asks, say you're an assistant to so-and-so or something like that. Don't tell anybody you're just a fan, and for crying out loud, don't ask for a picture or an autograph."

When she made it past the two large men guarding the entrance, she felt like all eyes were on her. She knew she was being paranoid, but she tried to look busy anyway. Bree said to act like she belonged, so Ginny fidgeted with her watch and glanced around like she was expecting somebody. She started to text imaginary friends on her phone but got distracted by the people who kept bumping into her and suspected they were doing it on purpose.

Along the corridor, signs pointed to a greenroom. While she worked up the nerve to infiltrate, she noticed the photographs hanging on the white brick walls. They must have been of the acts that had performed at the MGM, and she studied the pictures of Paul McCartney, Steven Tyler, Bon Jovi, Madonna, and tons of other entertainers she recognized. Several people were standing around the Rolling Stones photograph, commenting on how great the guys still looked.

Most of the people backstage didn't look familiar to Ginny. Not that they should, but she'd imagined banking a celebrity sighting or two. There were a lot of beautiful, cool-looking people wearing torn jeans. Looking so rock 'n' roll with their disheveled hair and laid-back attitude that Ginny felt a little overdressed. She spotted a group of tall women, probably models, hovering around a doorway and was glad for the high heels she was wearing. Straightening her posture and sucking in her tummy, Ginny squeezed past the models and entered the greenroom.

There were about fifty people standing around a large buffet backstage, eating and schmoozing. She didn't see the Stones anywhere. Figuring out how to hang with the band backstage was not as easy as it looked in the movies where they seemed so accessible.

She needed to be cool; she needed a drink.

Fortunately the booze flowed freely, so Ginny knocked back a couple of shots and waited for somebody to talk to her. She assumed what she imagined was a friendly, open expression, but after a while, she felt stupid. Somebody might mistake her for the village idiot. Instead of trying to blend in, Ginny found a corner and waited for courage to take hold.

The time had finally arrived to do something monumental. She took a big breath, petrified of what she might say to Mick when she found him. It was as if her entire life had been designed for this moment. Her reality had been created by dreams and visions put into motion by a series of connecting dots that would lead her to him. He was a bright and shiny star, and Ginny wanted to capture a piece of his splendor, put it in her purse, and save it for later. The meeting would change her life, and she knew it was time to take action.

In the hallway, Ginny followed the signs to the dressing

rooms, and as she ventured deeper down the passageway, she heard a guitar being tuned. A sign on the door identified Keith Richards's room. Ronnie Wood's was right next door. Her head tingled. Her heroes were just a few feet away. It was beautiful and heartbreaking. She loved these men because they knew how to cut through the distress and commotion of everyday life and play music that moved through people's bodies, past their guts, and all the way down to the soles of their feet.

Mick Jagger's name was on the third door, and Ginny stood still, afraid to move. Afraid to breathe. She could hear Mick inside, warming up his voice by doing scales. She was fucking terrified. Her thighs felt like rubber, and her heart was beating so fast she thought she might keel over right in front of the dressing room. Steadying herself, she was about to knock when the door flew open.

A team of people came rushing out. They brushed by Ginny, practically knocking her off her feet. She stood firm and hoped they wouldn't tell her to leave, but nobody seemed to notice her. They were making way for Mick Jagger, who came bouncing out of the room. He seemed to be in full warm-up mode, stretching and breathing as if he were getting ready for the New York City Marathon. Then he took off, booking down the corridor so fast that Ginny could barely keep up. Her feet went numb.

Mick ran toward the stage and beyond her grasp. Ginny could only reach out and feel the draft he'd left behind.

One of the technicians saw her standing around and said, "Hey, you can watch the show from the wings."

He led her to a spot where a bunch of other people stood

gawking out into the crowd. They all looked so smug, like they had beaten the system, probably thinking they were better than the rest of the herd sitting in expensive seats to watch the Stones through binoculars and on giant screens.

Ginny scanned the audience as they screamed, awaiting what they knew would be an unforgettable show. It was meant to be experienced from the audience's perspective, a full plunge into the world of the Rolling Stones. Was she supposed to watch from the side with the rest of the roadies and music executives in their designer jeans and baseball caps? Hell, *no!* She wasn't one of them. She was a fan—always had been, always would be. There was nothing wrong with that. Those were her people out there, and she belonged with them.

♪

GINNY FOUND HER SEAT, ANOTHER GOOD ONE NEAR THE stage. The Vegas crowd was the best so far. Everybody was amped, and when Keith played his signature opening to "Gimme Shelter," they screamed at the top of their lungs. Bree's favorite, Ginny remembered when she heard Mick sing the lyrics.

When the catwalk lit up, she knew it was time. Keith, Ronnie, and Charlie walked to Stage B and took their positions. The music started for their 1970s hit "Miss You." Mick skipped along the walkway, singing about missing his gal so much he'd been practically abstinent. She laughed at the thought. He stopped along the way to touch some of the outreached hands.

Ginny stuck hers out too. She reached so hard, she

thought she might dislocate her shoulder. But it was totally worth it. *Dear God, I'll be a better person if you just let Mick Jagger touch me.* He was so close to her. She could see the beads of sweat along his hairline and believed if she concentrated hard enough, she might hear his heart beating.

"Mick, I love you," she screamed.

Her stomach hurt with a love pain only somebody invested in a one-way, unreciprocated relationship understands. Goosebumps ran up her body, and she tried to keep from passing out. Mick Jagger, the man she'd dreamed of meeting, whose music she had listened to for what seemed like a lifetime, was only a few feet away. Her body electrified, a particle charged by Mick's voltage.

Then it happened. Mick Jagger paused in front of Ginny Martin and grabbed her hand. He made contact, and although it was only for a few seconds, it was as significant as God giving life to Adam. Their eyes met, and she could swear he was saying something to her with his. *Mick Jagger.* His image burned into her retina like a religious vision, holy water for a parched soul. He was the dream fulfilled, the living embodiment of what she could become. By acknowledging her, it was as if he had given her permission to seek out a better future.

When he let go, she slowly pulled her blessed appendage close to her body. It was vibrating and hot, and she felt the need to protect it.

By the end of the song, Mick had made it to Stage B. He walked behind the drum set and pumped a handful of hand sanitizer into his palm. One of the roadies tossed him a towel to wipe off the excess. Mick Jagger, icon and mythical creature, had just decontaminated himself. Ginny stared at her hand again, then out into the audience. She imagined all the germs floating above them. Mick had just touched hands that hadn't been washed after using the bathroom, or had covered sneezes, or were harboring viruses.

He was just a man, vulnerable like the rest of them.

Like Mick's touch, this revelation gripped her. She listened to the band play one of her favorites, "You Can't Always Get What You Want," and in that moment, understood that it had always been simply about the music. It was the one true thing in her life. Capturing moments, concentrations of time, the music articulated everything she had ever felt, wanted to say, or needed to say, but couldn't find the words.

The Rolling Stones were expressing her soul, transporting her to a moment of emotional purity. It was as if the music were capable of reaching down into her guts and pulling out what was authentic and real. Great songs purge the soul, but they also energize with idealism and joy. They fueled her tank and propelled her forward.

The moment was frightening. It was invigorating.

It wasn't only the man himself who had brought out the best in Ginny. She loved the Rolling Stones because of the way their *music* had made her feel: like anything was possible.

34

GINNY

As she waited for class to begin, Ginny flipped open her laptop and pulled up the syllabus the professor had posted online. An American literature survey course wouldn't have been her first choice, but she promised Bree she'd start with an English class. She scrutinized the list of readings and knew she'd be able to keep up, especially since she was only working part-time now. Thanks to her little nest egg, she had enough left over from her Las Vegas jackpot to pay first and last month's rent on an apartment and tuition at the local community college.

When Ginny decided to return to the salon, Shannon quit. She thought it would be awkward after she and Ray had moved in together. Ginny couldn't care less. Weirder things had happened, like attending her five-year high school reunion and actually enjoying it.

The students were filing into the classroom, and they seemed incredibly young to Ginny. Their faces were blank, registering neither fear nor enthusiasm. They acted as if they had all the confidence in the world. A college education was merely a layover on their road to greatness. *You don't know how lucky you are*, thought Ginny.

She was glad she'd arrived early and taken a seat in the third row. If she had been late, the only seats left might have been in the front. Until she got used to the class requirements, her strategy was to blend in.

An older female student hovered in the doorway. She was probably nervous too, gripping way too tightly to her book bag. She was a redhead, just like Bree. Ginny waved her over and pointed to an empty seat nearby.

When the woman settled in, Ginny introduced herself. "Don't worry," she said. "It's my first day back too."

"I hope the professor's cute, at least," said the woman.

Funny, Ginny thought. *That's exactly what Bree would have said.* Ginny missed her friend, the way she scrunched her hair when she was tense. All the times she had said the most absurdly inappropriate things and had gotten away with it. But most of all, she missed Bree's willingness to take chances in life, to move on—or stay put—when she had to.

They had plans to hang out over spring break, and Ginny couldn't wait to drive her sweet little convertible to Las Vegas to check out Bree and Billy's pad.

It seemed like a minor miracle, but Bree was married and had a permanent address in Las Vegas. "What better place to settle down?" she'd said. "I can visit Paris, Venice, and Cairo all in one day." Tori had decided to stay at St. Andrew's so she could get into a choice college, so Bree bought a house near the boarding school and flew back to Florida at least every other month.

After the Vegas concert, Ginny visited Bree in the hospital

before heading back home to Los Angeles. She couldn't to wait to tell Bree about her Mick encounter, even though Bree would probably be disappointed Ginny hadn't slept with him. It had been enough, though. She had touched the hand of Mick Jagger, the man she loved so much it hurt, and the man who, when she'd been willing to take a risk, had changed her life forever.

"What?" Bree had yelled from the hospital bed when Ginny had told her she was finished touring with the Stones. "You can't stop now!"

"I already got what I came for," said Ginny. "Besides, I gave the tickets away."

Ginny explained that toward the end of the concert, she had tried to ignore the couple fighting next to her.

She heard the woman say something about not wanting to go home. The man put on his jacket anyway and picked up the woman's purse, shoving it at her. But she kept her arms crossed and let it fall back onto the seat.

The Stones started to play "Memory Motel," and Ginny redirected her attention to the stage. She loved the song from the album *Black and Blue*. Mick and Keith shared the singing duties equally, an oddity even for the Glimmer Twins. Mick took the lead while Keith joined in for the refrain. Written in Montauk on Long Island and named after the Memory Bar & Motel, it ran longer than seven minutes—one of the longer Stones songs. It was about the waning love for a woman; some speculated it was about Carly Simon.

Rocking back and forth singing, Ginny had closed her eyes but opened them just in time to see the man toss beer in the woman's face. He threw the empty cup to the floor and darted out, which was a good idea, considering Ginny—and probably several others who saw what happened—wanted to kick his ass.

"Are you okay?" Ginny reached into her purse and handed the woman a tissue."Yeah." She blew her nose and started bawling.

"He's not worth it," said Ginny.

"He knows how much the Stones mean to me," she said between sobs. "Why does he have to ruin everything?"

"I don't know," said Ginny. "Some men are just like that."

"And he thinks I'm going to marry him tomorrow. He's seriously delusional."

The Stones started to play "Monkey Man." As Mick sang, Ginny knew what she had to do. She reached into her purse, pulled out the manila envelope with tickets to places like Texas, Philadelphia, Boston, and Chicago, and handed them over.

"These are not pairs," she said.

Bree pushed her hospital-issued lunch aside. "So, you just gave away your tickets?

"Yup." Ginny set the orchid she had lovingly nurtured through their journey next to Bree's bedside. "For you."

"But—"

"Don't forget to fertilize it once a month."

"You're one weird chick," Bree said, adjusting the plant so the direct sun from the nearby window would not burn its fragile blooms.

"And you're the best friend this weird chick has ever had." Ginny wouldn't let herself cry.

"Oh no, this isn't good-bye, is it? I don't do good-byes," said Bree.

"What do you do, then?" asked Ginny.

"I say, 'See you later.'"

"Okay," said Ginny, leaning over to hug her. "See you later."

"I still think you're crazy," said Bree. She always had to get in the last word.

♪

ON THE WAY HOME FROM CLASS, GINNY PLAYED "Satisfaction," a Stones song that had, up until now, been her least favorite. Now she thought about the song in a way she never had before. It's the story of a man who, despite his best efforts, can't find anything to make him happy. Maybe it was human nature to hold on to glimmers of possibility. The man in the song longs for fulfillment even though it eludes him. There is a line about *trying* plugged right into the middle of the refrain. The repetition made it hard to ignore.

GINNY HAD LOST EVERYTHING—HER HUSBAND AND HER dependable life. She knew, though, that she had gained something more valuable.

The right to try. The right to seek satisfaction on her own terms.

ACKNOWLEDGMENTS

This is a story about the strength of friendship. Encouragement for this project has come in many ways, and I'd like to thank the following friends for their support.

The talented and generous writing faculty at UC Riverside, Palm Desert: Tod Goldberg, Deanne Stillman, Mary Otis, and Elizabeth Crane. Special thanks to my mentor, Mark Haskell Smith, for believing in me when I was working on early drafts. Victoria Lea, my agent and tireless champion. A patient and determined woman, your vision and support kept me going. Crystal Patriarche, I am honored and delighted to be part of the BookSparks team. One of my early editors, Jennifer Pooley. You truly are seamstress for the book band.

Dianna Olea, thank you for a lifetime of swapping secrets and sharing dreams. In this world of over seven billion people, you make me feel special. I hope I do the same for you, my soul sister and best friend forever. Debbie Graber and Tiffany Hawk, friends and writing compatriots. You kept me sane through the ups and downs of this long journey. I wouldn't have made it without you.

My big brother Mike, who introduced me to rock 'n' roll. Mom and Dad, thank you for encouraging creativity, expecting excellence, and letting me play my music loud when I was a bourgeoning rock chick.

Loving husband and ardent supporter, Jack Reilly. You've read more drafts and listened to more stories about this book than any person should and never complained. You are my very own rock star.

ABOUT THE AUTHOR

ANDEE REILLY was born and raised in Los Angeles. She received her MFA in Creative Writing from the University of California, Riverside and teaches literature and writing at California State University Channel Islands. As a teenager, she fell in love with the Rolling Stones, and their music has long served as an inspiration to her writing. She currently divides her time between Los Angeles and Maui.